DEATH
AND THE
DOGWALKER

ALSO BY A. J. ORDE

A LITTLE NEIGHBORHOOD MURDER

A. J. ORDE

DEATH AND THE DOGWALKER

DOUBLEDAY

NEW YORK   LONDON   TORONTO   SYDNEY   AUCKLAND

PUBLISHED BY DOUBLEDAY
a division of Bantam Doubleday Dell Publishing Group, Inc.
666 Fifth Avenue, New York, New York 10103

DOUBLEDAY and the portrayal of an anchor with a dolphin
are trademarks of Doubleday, a division of
Bantam Doubleday Dell Publishing Group, Inc.

This novel is a work of fiction. Names, characters, places, and incidents are either the product of the author's imagination or used fictitiously. Any resemblance to actual persons, living or dead, events, or locales is entirely coincidental.

A. J. Orde has lived in or near Denver for decades, and knows many parts of it intimately. Despite this, the author frequently chooses to use fictional locations to avoid giving offense through unflattering references to specific addresses, neighborhoods, or places of work.

Library of Congress Cataloging-in-Publication Data

Orde, A. J.
    Death and the dogwalker / by A. J. Orde. —1st ed.
        p.   cm.
    I. Title.
    PS3565.R36D4 1990
    813'.54—dc20   89-38625
                                                                    CIP

ISBN 0-385-26671-5

DESIGNED BY PATRICE FODERO

Printed in the United States of America
April 1990
FIRST EDITION
BVG

DEATH
AND THE
DOGWALKER

1

Grace Willis, my friend and favorite policewoman, had to go to San Francisco to get her brother Ron out of trouble. No particular trouble specified; the subject mentioned with an attitude of stiff-upper-lip which prevented my pressing for details. She asked me to please take care of her cat until she got back. I had never seen her cat, though I like to think that my fondness for Grace would have made me say yes even if I *had* seen him. I owe Grace a great deal more than a mere cat-sit.

She had, however, neglected to say that the cat was a mature Maine Coon bullcat named Critter who weighed in at roughly twenty-eight, twenty-nine pounds.

"You don't mind if he sleeps on your bed?" she asked doubtfully, cradling the red tabby monster in both arms while he regarded me balefully.

"Where does he sleep at your house?" I asked dubiously. I had spent a few memorable nights in Grace's bed, and this monster had not shared our couch, which, in any case, would not have had room for him. I recalled that on one or two of our more athletic evenings it hadn't even had room for us.

"With me," she admitted, blushing a little. "Except when I have company." Grace was not, she was at some pains to tell me, in love with me. She forgot that, once in a while. Not quite

1

often enough for my taste, but thank God for any loss of memory.

The cat yawned widely, displaying teeth capable of dispatching fairly large herbivores. Then he blinked at me, lazily, deciding I was no threat. His eyes were amber.

"Why is it I've never seen him before?" I asked, still clinging to the idea it might all be a joke.

"Jason, when I first met you Critter was at the vet's for almost a week because he had a hurt leg, and then I had to keep him quiet until the leg healed, so he was in the little back room I haven't finished yet. . . ." Grace was converting her grandmother's Victorian house into four apartments, and the unfinished ground-floor unit was occupied by herself. "And then, later," she went on, "I took him up to my cousin Charlene to breed her two female Coons—that's my cousin in Cheyenne who raises these gorgeous-shaded apricots—and then after that you went on a trip for a while, and . . ."

"What does he eat?"

"I brought a sack of kibble. And I usually give him some of whatever I'm having. Chicken. Or fish. Or whatever."

Since dining with Grace was an exercise in trying to get some for myself before she ate it all, I was surprised that she and Critter shared. "I suppose he uses a what-you-call-it."

"Litter box. It's in the car. And a sack of litter to go in it. I thought you could put it in the hall by the back stairs. And he'll get along with Bela fine, he likes dogs. . . ."

Likes them for breakfast, I thought.

"I wouldn't take him outside for a while, Jason, until he knows you, because he might run off, trying to go home, and there won't be anybody there."

Critter had his own ideas about staying in the house. He regarded staying inside as cruel and unusual punishment, and he let me know it clearly and continuously. He sat on the windowsill and cried, heartrending little cries, like a grief-stricken toddler. If he kept it up, someone was going to turn me in on suspicion of child abuse. After two days of this I gave up and bought him a harness and leash.

Which explains, more or less, what Bela, the hundred-pound Kuvasz dog, Critter, the thirty-pound cat, and Jason Lynx, the hundred-eighty-pound dealer in old furniture and related stuff, were doing entering Cheeseman Park shortly after dawn. We were having our morning constitutional. It had taken Critter about three minutes to figure out the leash, after which his attitude conveyed that Maine Coon cats had invented leashes as a kind of ornamental linkage indicating the relative status of the two creatures involved—the one in front being in charge. Critter paraded, tail lashing. Bela slouched, nose to ground, smelling what was new, his heavy tail making a steady drumbeat against my leg. I strode along, taking deep breaths, trying to convince myself I needed these jaunts because the doctor said exercise the leg, no matter how much it hurt. Which, since I'd had it shot out from under me by a bad guy a few months ago, it did.

Just inside the park there's a grove of big old spruces. The ground beneath them is usually dry and needle-covered and in midsummer and fall it's littered with the chunky white-fruiting bodies of *Agaricus nivicens,* which are great with hamburger or scrambled eggs if Bela and I get there before the mushroom kickers and the squirrels do. Squirrels you can't blame, but mushroom kickers ought to be hung up by their heels. At this season, *nivicens* were not in evidence, their space being occupied by Frederick Foret. He was lying under the spruce farthest from the path, one knee up, one arm draped dramatically over his eyes. This world-weary, emotionally exhausted posture was a frequent accompaniment to what Fred called the "essential surrender of meditation, the passive aftermath of positive motion." Fred was always eager to talk about essential surrender or any other emotion he happened to be feeling. "I have just experienced an insight," he might say, summoning me over with an imperious wave. I need to tell someone. . . ."

I can't recall his ever saying, "How have you been, Jason?" or showing any interest in anyone other than as a potential audience.

The path went directly by him. There was no way to avoid him, but I decided not to see him. If I zoomed by, eyes front, he might meditate right through my passing. If he was still there when we left, I could call a hurried greeting and plead the pressure of business prevented my staying to hear his latest saga of the human spirit.

The latest, as of a few days before, had been ominous hints that Fred might be thinking of getting involved, once again, with World Peace. His youthful interest in the Rosicrucians— about which I had heard much—had been followed by a long-time involvement with est, which had given way to Carlos Castañeda and, more recently, a brief flirtation with Shirley MacLaine's more-things-in-heaven-and-earth cosmobabble. I had refused at least twenty times to attend meetings or get involved in any way, but this had not discouraged Fred, who, since his recent retirement, was totally indefatigable in his own mystic interests. The latest thing seemed to be to "walk for peace" while carrying "the light of peace" (i.e., burning candles) from place to place, or, in Fred's case, to fly about, mostly in Europe and England, getting other people—mostly small children—to carry candles into people's offices and shops, generally making a nuisance and fire hazard of themselves while doing nothing identifiable to reduce international tension. Fred had accompanied the children into some fairly high places, and the name dropping (the Minister of Education, the Secretary of State, the Prime Minister, blah-blah) could go on for several hours.

Critter, Bela, and I speeded up to a gentle lope and went quietly past, though Bela jerked nervously at the leash, making an abortive lunge in Fred's direction. Fred did not move his arm, though I caught the white gleam of half-opened eyes as I went by. So. Biding his time. Or maybe he hadn't recognized me with the cat.

We made the usual circle, about thirty minutes' worth of brisk walking and occasional jogging, slowed this morning by people stopping me to ask about Critter. Most of them were regulars, people I saw every morning when I walked the dog. The gray-haired couple in the purple outfits. The two guys with the soccer ball. The very stout white-haired woman in sweats, dark glasses, and flowered kerchief. The redhead with the serious runner's body. No one could believe the size of the cat, and all I could tell them was that I didn't believe it either.

We made the turn at the flower plots—recently bedded out and still sparsely grown enough so that Critter could find plenty of toilet room between the petunias—and then started back the way we'd come. Fred was still right where he'd been when we came in. This time Bela did not go on past. He stopped, pulled hard on the leash, and howled.

Fred didn't move. Bela stared at the recumbent form and howled once again, a long, lugubrious sound. When he stopped, he gave me a significant look from his dark, mournful eyes. The scars on the back of my neck prickled. If I'd had any hair there, it would have stood up.

"Sit," I said to Bela, realizing all at once, and not for the first time, that he had better sense than I did. Bela sat. "Stay." Bela would stay until hell froze over or until I called him, whichever came first. I still had one animal left over. "Hold it," I said, putting Critter's leash in Bela's mouth. He held it while I skulked into the grove of trees. Fred hadn't moved. His eyes were still half open under the concealing arm. I thought at first he might have fallen asleep or have had some kind of seizure, then I saw he wasn't breathing. I said something obscene or blasphemous, half under my breath. Bela whined. I said again, "Stay. Hold it," as I reached down and moved Fred's arm. His eyes glared up at me, unseeing. My first feeling was one of guilt that I hadn't spoken to him earlier. Then I realized it wouldn't have mattered. I wasn't the only one who'd gone on past without noticing that Fred wasn't his usual, very important self. He'd been dead long enough to get pretty cold.

I stood up to see a Laurel and Hardy duo jogging toward me along the path, guys I'd seen out there most recent mornings. I hailed them, told them what had happened, and asked them to call the police. The skinny one zoomed off down the path toward Thirteenth Avenue; the other one, a stout, fiftyish man already red in the face, stayed with me.

"My neighbor," he said between puffs. "Thinks he's doing a marathon every morning. Makes me feel like a couch potato."

I turned back to Fred as the potato stared down at the body with no visible emotion.

"Think it was a heart attack or something?"

I shook my head. "I don't know. I don't think we should touch him. He's been dead a while."

He nodded. "He was here when we came into the park. We just speeded up a little so he wouldn't catch us."

"You know him?"

"Well, not really, but I know who he is, you know what I mean? The guy's here most mornings, almost always sprawled out under a tree, or on a bench if the ground's wet. Talk your arm off if you let him, makes no sense so far as I can tell, and he's hard to get away from. Lately it's been this walk-for-peace business. My God, there must be a lot of people in the world with nothing to do, you ever think of that? I guess maybe he runs, but I've never seen him running."

I'd never seen Fred running either. "His name is Foret," I said. "Fred Foret. He lives over there in that high rise next to the Twelve Hundred building."

"No kidding? He's a neighbor, then. I moved in there four months ago." He mopped at his face, eyes fixed on Critter. "I been meaning to ask since I saw you yesterday, is that a regular cat?"

We talked about the cat. I sat down on the ground; Critter

climbed onto my lap and washed his face. Bela leaned over one shoulder, his lop ears, black nose, and dark eyes making a sad mime's face against his white fur. We were sitting like that, my companion talking about pets he remembered from when he was a kid and scratching Critter's stomach, when the police arrived, two cops in a white car with the blue logo on the door.

It turned out the fat man's name was Clive Corvallis, of the Corvallis Funeral Home, which explained his lack of emotion on viewing the body. He gave his business and home address to the officers and told them he'd seen Fred lying there earlier. His friend, Ben Maurier, arrived, panting, and told them the same thing. I repeated the information for the third time and added that I knew who he was.

"He got a wife, family?" the officer asked.

"Divorced," I said, trying to recollect what Fred had told me. I had, literally, not listened to him most of the time. He was so full of how he felt about things and what he thought about things, so unaware of there being another human being present who might also have thoughts and feelings, that I had usually just turned him off. "Divorced," I repeated, feeling foolish not to know more. "But I think his ex-wife and kids live here in town."

"How well did you know him?"

"We met at a party at his sister's; her name is Marge Beebe. That was over a year ago. Then I saw him here, one morning a little later, and since then we've chatted about this and that when I've been walking the dog." I decided I didn't have to say I'd avoided him whenever possible.

Marge's husband, Silas, is my broker. I have taken them out to dinner a few times. Also, the Beebes throw occasional mob-scene barbecues at their farm, and I usually drop by briefly to show my face, drink one beer, and sneak off before the burned meats are served. At last summer's, Marge had introduced me to her baby brother Fred; he'd stuck to me like strapping tape, talking about est. Since he was completely impervious to social

signals like "I've got to run," or "I'm meeting a plane," I'd
sneaked away while he was in the bathroom, thinking the
rudeness wouldn't matter because I'd never see him again. The
rudeness didn't matter because he didn't recognize it for what
it was, and I saw him altogether too often. Fred was incapable
of believing he was boring. I gave the officers Marge Beebe's
name and told them she was listed under S. R. Beebe in the
phone book.

"What made you go over to take a look at him?" the officer
asked.

I pointed to Bela. "He howled," I said.

The officer nodded as though this was the usual thing. Then
he asked me, "Say, is that a regular cat?"

When we got back to 1465 Hyde Street, which is both home
and shop, I took the leashes off the animals while admiring the
tulips, daffodils, and grape hyacinths among the evergreens out
front. Mark MacMillan, my assistant, had planted the bulbs
the previous fall, and I had to admit they brightened the rather
dowagerly façade. I took my usual good-luck swipe at the brass
plate by the front door that reads: "Jason Lynx Interiors."
Some people immediately think, "Ah, interior decorator,"
which isn't quite it. Every paint and fabric shop has someone
on staff they call a decorator. I can do that, of course, but I
don't, except as part of a total design for a room or rooms,
furniture and all. Mostly I'm into antique furniture, period
rooms, and occasionally some good reproductions. Before my
name went on the entry, the business was Jacob Buchnam's,
my foster father's, and when he had his stroke, he asked me to
come back from the East Coast and take it over. He got a nice
check from it every month, and I got a business it had taken
him fifty years to build.

Once inside, the three of us went under the latest in a series
of crystal chandeliers, $8,000; over the current Persian rug,
$24,000; past the pair of Edwardian rosewood chairs, $3,400;

and the English oak dresser, $5,200 (but I'd take four-eight), that I'd bought from a suddenly impecunious Londoner who'd found himself stranded in Colorado with all his furniture (which is another story). And up the curving stairs to the private part of the house. Bela galumphed along at my heels and Critter bounded ahead like a huge, furry basketball. We stopped in the kitchen, them for breakfast, me for coffee to drink before, during, and after my shower. By the time I was dressed, Critter was on my bed deeply involved in his morning wash and Bela had gone down the back stairs to the dog door and the back yard. During the fifteen or twenty minutes that had passed since we'd arrived, I'd been trying to decide whether I should go see Marge Beebe.

If the police mentioned my name as the one who discovered Fred's body, she'd be justifiably hurt that I hadn't told her personally. Maybe the police had already informed her, maybe not. I'd told them she was next of kin, but who knew how prompt they'd be. Though Fred had not been a particular friend of mine, he had been Marge's brother, and any debt I owed, I owed to her.

Marge didn't work, so the chances were, this early in the morning, she'd be home. The calendar said nothing on Wednesday A.M. until ten-thirty, so I left a note for Mark and for Eugenia Lowe, the showroom person, saying I had a personal errand to run but would be back by ten-thirty. They both had keys to the shop and would let themselves in.

The Beebes live outside of Littleton, a sprawling suburb that once had been a rather nice small town. The town, or what remains of it, perches like a pimple on a vast suburban carbuncle, and is notable for having had one of the ugliest Main Streets in the urban U.S. Some con artist sold the city fathers an endless line of concrete umbrellas, which, until recently, stood along the curbs like so many upended stumps, offering neither shade nor grace and ruining the facades of the few good buildings in town. The once elegant town library had been remodeled into a restaurant that has changed hands so often no one remembers what it's called. The once authentically Victorian courthouse has suffered from chronic accretionosis. A little south of Main Street is the prison-gray bulk of Arapahoe Junior College, an accidental-looking concrete pile possibly stacked by the same guy who put up the street umbrellas.

I don't have to drive past the courthouse to get to the Beebes', but I always do, just to get my animosity flowing. Betweentimes I can't believe it's as bad as I know it is. The Historic Preservation people call it "remuddling," and there's a lot of it around.

Marge and Silas live west of town on what remains of an old farm property off Bowles Avenue. When I drove in, Marge waved at me gaily from the stables out in the front pasture, so I knew no one had called her yet. She left the horse she'd been grooming and met me near the front door with her usual friendly hug. Marge offered coffee. I accepted. We sat at the kitchen table. I took her hand and said I had some bad news for her. She thought I was kidding, and that didn't make it any easier. When she finally heard what I was saying, she just sat there, her face very still, not crying, not anything. Marge has a plump, jolly face. When she stopped smiling, it looked old and yellowish, like an almost healed bruise.

"Marge?" I said. "Marge."

"I was thinking it happened too late for Shannon," she said in a shrill, empty voice. Then she burst into tears. I put my arms around her and let her cry and wondered what in hell she meant about too late for Shannon. I seemed to recall Fred mentioning a daughter Shannon: Shannon and Keith, the names popped into my mind, daughter and son.

"Do you want me to let her know?" I asked gently when she quieted a little. "His daughter?"

She turned her stricken face on me and said, "God, no. No, Jason. I'll call Lycia, and she'll tell Shannon."

"That's his ex-wife?"

She nodded. "Oh, God, Shannon will feel so guilty."

I must have looked confused, because Marge said, "Only the other day Shannon said she wished he was dead." She went back to crying.

On occasion, I had wished Fred Foret would drop dead, and the desire had not occasioned excesses of guilt. Still, it did seem an extreme emotion for Fred to have evoked in a daughter. I wondered what he'd done to deserve it, confident that the Fred I'd known was fully capable of doing whatever it took.

"Marge, would you like to go to your sister-in-law's? I'll drive you. Maybe it would be better if you told her in person." I wanted to give her something to do, and I didn't want her to be alone. A thought occurred to me. "Unless you don't get along. . . ."

"Me and Lycia? Oh, no. I like Lycia. We were never really close, but we like each other. I think you're right. I should go over there. If you'll take me. . . ."

I took her. We went back into town and ended up at a building not far from my own place, a tall, impersonal apartment house with a phony French name (the Louvre, for God's sake) and bad-fake Louis XIV lobby furniture. Marge asked me to come in with her, so I followed along while she pushed the button and spoke her name into the mike and got buzzed in through the security door. A stout, red-faced man with two toy poodles got out of the elevator, and one of the poodles started to lift his leg, using me for a tree. I jumped back, and the man peered at me apologetically through thick-lensed glasses as the assembly of dogs and man rushed untidily for the door. Poor pups. Probably hadn't been outside since yesterday, and the dumb sod that owned them expected them to hold it forever.

Lycia Foret, a smooth-faced woman with a charming smile and short gray hair, came to the door in a housecoat, obviously bewildered by this early visit. It was half past nine but I felt it should be about noon. Marge didn't even wait for the door to open. She launched herself through the crack, already bursting with tears and explanations, while I stood behind her staring at Ms. Foret with a very strange feeling of . . . what? Recognition? No. Certainly not recognition, but a weird, inexplicable sensation nonetheless. I couldn't stop staring at her. Luckily neither of them noticed as they noisily sorted it out. Then Lycia turned to me and asked, "How did he die?"

I was so intent upon trying to figure out what it was about her that troubled me, it took me a minute to apprehend the question.

"There was no cause of death I could see, Ms. Foret. The police didn't invite me to stick around and wait for the medical examiner. Since I happened to know Marge, I thought it would be appropriate to tell her. . . ." Ms. Foret turned back to Marge, and I resumed my analysis. Her hair was gray. That didn't describe it. It was the color of falling water. And her eyes were water-colored, too, the darkness that lies in deep, slowly moving rivers, almost green, almost brown, and utterly still. Quite honestly, until that moment I hadn't been particularly curious about what killed Fred Foret. I think I had rather assumed a heart attack. He was at the age when that happens, not to oneself but to other people. Meeting Lycia, I was suddenly interested. Seeing her, I wanted to know everything about her, even if that meant getting posthumously involved with Fred.

She shook her head at me sorrowfully. "Come into the kitchen," she said. "The children and Ross and I were just having breakfast."

Marge followed her closely, dabbing at her eyes with a soggy tissue. I went after Marge, wondering how I'd ended up here. I hadn't intended the good deed to become a half-day expedition, though it was turning out to be interesting. As we walked through the apartment, I gave it the professional eye. This was a place where people lived, a place alive with color and life and healthy-looking real plants. We went through the dining room, through a swinging door into a sun-drenched kitchen where two shelties looked lazily up from their baskets under the window and three people sat at a round table over the remnants of a sizable breakfast. The daughter: pale blond with dark brows and lashes, a sweet, slightly pensive expression, and none of her mother's tranquillity. The son: same coloring; lean, hungry face; husky body; pouting, demanding lower lip. Both of them in baby-blue sweats and white headbands. She looked about twenty, twenty-two. He was a little older. There was another guy at the table, fiftyish, bearded.

"Keith," Lycia said to her son. "Shannon honey. I'm afraid your Aunt Marge and this gentleman have brought some bad news." Though there were no tears, there was tension in her voice and she choked, unable to go on.

Shannon threw me a fearful glance, light hair falling across her open, childlike face. There was no guile in it. She stared up at her aunt, at me, lips already trembling. She didn't know what the news was, but she was ready to cry. Her brother furrowed his brow in my direction. Marge was busy wiping her eyes and making swallowing noises. Lycia Foret wasn't saying anything. The room teetered with expectation. One of the dogs whined, and I didn't blame him. I don't tolerate tension well either.

So I pushed us off dead center. "I was running in the park this morning," I told them. "And I found your father's body. He'd evidently come to the park sometime earlier. . . ."

"Dead?" asked the bearded breakfaster in a deep, matter-of-fact voice. "Are you saying he's dead?" He moved his short, compact body out of the chair and I stepped back, almost behind the kitchen door, to give him room. "Fred?"

I nodded. "Body" usually meant dead, to me. Shannon started sobbing. Her brother just looked at me, as though I'd said it was raining outside. "Son of a bitch," he whispered. A dog got out of her basket and came over to him, putting her head on his knee. "Son of a bitch," he said again, stroking the dog gently.

I couldn't tell if he meant the words as an imprecation or an expletive.

"How?" he asked.

"Yes," the older man agreed. "How?"

"Mr. Lynx doesn't know," Lycia told them, laying a hand on my arm as though to forgive me for not knowing. My skin actually quivered where she touched me. "The police will know. Ross, will you call and find out what you can."

The bearded man moved from the table to the wall phone at the other end of the kitchen. He mumbled into it while I answered what questions I could. Where Fred had been lying. The jogging suit he'd been wearing. I fluffed over my first view of him, saying I'd seen him there but figured he was meditating.

"Meditating," his son snorted. "Oh, sure, meditating."

"Keith," his mother said warningly. "Keith!"

"Well, Mother! You know Dad. He was about as far from being able to meditate as you can get. He couldn't forget his audience long enough!"

"Oh, Keith, don't," the girl cried. Her Aunt Marge went over and sat by her, hugging her. "He shouldn't say things like that. . . ."

Lycia shook her head warningly at her son.

"I hate that park," the girl cried. "Melody was in that same park!"

"He was shot," Ross said as he hung up the phone.

"Murdered?" Keith breathed. "Murdered?"

"Melody was shot, too," Shannon cried hysterically. "And I hated her. And I hated Daddy. They'll think I killed them both. After what I said. . . ."

"Shannon. Don't be silly!" Marge shook her, then hugged her again. "You didn't mean what you said. We all know that."

I started to excuse myself, but Lycia was speaking to Shannon in a low, intent voice, so I extricated myself from where I was standing, beside the kitchen door, untangling the dog leashes that had wrapped themselves around my arm and straightening the several framed award certificates I had unsettled. As I went quietly to the front door, I heard Lycia saying, "Shannon, no one will think you had anything to do with it. We've been together, all four of us, since yesterday afternoon. There's no way you could have had anything to do with it at all."

I thought how convenient it was that the whole family could alibi one another. Considering that victims' husbands or wives, even ex-wives, are usually immediately suspected, it was nice to know that Lycia could not be. The thought surprised me. I didn't even know her. Why would I care? I wondered who Ross was. Then I told myself it was none of my business who he was, and anyhow, Lycia was considerably older than I, so forget it. I looked at my watch and realized the day had begun, ready or not, and I had a customer coming in at ten-thirty.

I had parked the car in my garage before I noticed that Marge had left her purse in it. I took the bag upstairs with me and asked Mark to call her at Lycia Foret's place and tell her I'd bring it to her that evening. When I came back from getting a cup of coffee, Mark said Marge needed her purse, so her nephew Keith was driving her over to pick it up. Fine, well and good.

My ten-thirty customers showed up and we spent almost an hour choosing among four carpet samples for their new family room. Normally I don't do jobs which are totally unrelated to the antique business, but he was the son of a client and I had promised his mother I would "help." He was decisive enough, but his wife liked to play cutesy games with him. "On the other hand, Bobsy, this is a lot like the one your sister has. Do you think she'd mind?" Or: "Which one of the others, after we take out the one I don't like, do you really like best?" Since I'd seen the room in question and had picked the samples myself, I knew any of them would do. In this case, "do" meant that the carpet would not detract from the general effect they had managed to achieve on their own. In other words, it wouldn't do any harm. They finally compromised upon my least favorite, and Mark winked at me over their shoulders. He had bet me lunch at Cliff Young's that they'd choose the one I liked least. They and I parted with mutual groans of relief.

"I hear there's been a murder," Mark said in the unenthusiastic voice he'd been using lately. His love life was not going well. "Are we involved up to our ears?"

"We? *We* don't get involved in this one at all."

"Oh, come on, Jason. You like murders."

"I don't like murders. I like solving puzzles, but that's a different matter. Fred Foret's death may not be much of a puzzle. He probably got mugged and shot by some drugged-up kid."

"Not mugged," said Mark.

"What do you mean, not mugged?"

"Not robbed, anyhow. He had a wallet in his pocket with over five hundred dollars in it."

"Who told you that?"

"Some funeral director guy named Corvallis. He called here while you were gone. Said he thought you'd be interested. Evidently he stuck around while the medical examiner took a look. They went through his pockets. The corpse's pockets, that is."

"Maybe somebody shot him, then got scared off before they could go through his pockets."

Mark shrugged at me. "Corvallis said he'd been dead for at least two or three hours."

That gave me pause. I'd passed him at about six o'clock. I'd come back by at six-thirty. The police had arrived ten minutes later, and the medical examiner shortly after that. Say almost seven. So Fred had been shot at four or five in the morning.

"What the hell would he have been doing in the park at that hour?" I wondered. "Very few people up at that time."

"So few a murderer could hide and come back if somebody did come by," he offered.

I visualized the scene. There was dense shrubbery only a few feet from where Fred had been, lilac bushes, fully leafed out, excellent cover, the fading blooms hanging thickly. I'd smelled them at the time without noticing the bushes. Them and something else. Fred had lain in the open, of course. . . .

"He was lying on his back with one arm over his eyes," I said.

"He was shot in the back, according to Corvallis."

In the back? Mark and I stared at each other. If Fred Foret had been shot in the back, he had not fallen gently supine with one knee up and one arm over his eyes in his usual dramatic posture. He had been, one might say, arranged.

Marge and her nephew Keith came by about one. Something had been nagging at me, and when she came upstairs alone (leaving Keith to roam around the main showroom, running his fingers either disdainfully or covetously over the eighteenth- and nineteenth-centuries) I decided to ask her about it.

"Shannon said something about someone else having been in the park," I said. "Melody someone. What did she mean?"

"Melody Steinwale." Marge nodded. "She was killed in the park, but that was some time ago. Shannon was just being hysterical this morning. People get killed in parks all the time. I guess that's true in any big city."

Somehow I do not think of Denver as a big city. It is still the cow town I grew up in, with all a cow town's virtues and faults. Nonetheless, the population makes it "big" enough to stack up a respectable homicide score, that much was true. "Who was Melody Steinwale?" I asked.

"A sort of neighbor of Lycia's. Harriet Steinwale lives up-

stairs from Lycia. In the penthouse. When she's in town. She
has a place in Mexico, and she spends a lot of time there."

"Harriet Steinwale?"

"Barge Steinwale's widow. You know, Jason. Steinwale
Steel? Lycia and Harriet are friends. Harriet's son is Greg
Steinwale, and Melody was married to him. Greg and Melody
lived in the penthouse, too."

"Gregory Steinwale." The name rang a bell. "I should know
that name."

"He's an artist. He was written up in *Time* magazine."

I remembered an article, though I hadn't seen the one in
Time. "In *Art & Antiques* last month," I said. "He signs himself
Grale. Said to be quite the up-and-coming painter just now."

"A rather strange one," she said. "At least, I've always
thought so."

I was remembering what else the article had said. Something
about an emotional or psychological collapse? When his wife
was killed, perhaps? I was sure I remembered something soap-
opera-ish. Well, the back issues of *A & A* were downstairs in
the basement. I'd look it up later.

Marge was shaking her head. "Fred was my brother, Jason,
but he was such a . . . I don't know. It wasn't that he was
stupid. He was very intelligent. He had a high IQ. He was a
physicist, a professor up at CU until he retired a few months
ago."

I nodded, indicating I'd known that.

"Before that, he worked with the Department of Defense,
some kind of science adviser." She sighed. "He made a good
living. It's just that with people . . ."

"He never shut up." The words came out without thought,
and I flushed.

She didn't take offense. "Oh, Jason, that's so true. When he
was a little boy, he used to drive me crazy. He never shut up.
And he got these strange ideas about his relationships with
other people. Like what he did to poor Shannon. . . ."

"What was that?" I asked, curious.

She squeezed her mouth into a prim little line, opening it just enough to say, "I shouldn't have said that. I'm not going to talk about him, Jason. I'm just not. When somebody dies like this, the least said, the soonest mended. Silas says I talk too much, and this is one time I'm not going to."

I didn't press the matter, but despite myself, I was becoming intrigued. I asked her who Ross was. His full name was Dr. Ross Whitfield, Dr. Lycia Foret's significant other. I wished, with a pang, that Grace Willis were back from San Francisco. It was sometimes convenient to have a police detective as the closest thing I had to a significant other. If she were home she could get me a look at the police report.

A funny thing happened when I got back to the office. There was an envelope in the mail with a local postmark and no return address. Any mail addressed to me personally, I open, and I did so. Inside was a plain piece of paper with words and letters pasted on it, words and letters cut out of slick magazine paper.

"If you want to know who you are, get ten thousand together and put an ad in the personals that says, 'J.L. wants to know all.' "

The quote marks were huge, probably from a big ad of some kind. The initials were of two different type styles. The paste-up job was neat, as though done with a ruler. I sat there staring at it for maybe ten minutes.

I was abandoned at a Home when I was three, and my parentage is a complete mystery. Not knowing who I am used to bother me a lot. From the day I'd come under Jacob's tutelage, however, he had insisted that a person's identity is not dependent upon knowing his family name or history. Firmly and repeatedly, he'd told me that Jason Lynx would be who I made myself be. Now, being true to Jacob's tenets, I told myself my identity was my business, and no filthy anonymous letter writer was going to con me out of ten thousand.

I had to repeat it to myself several times. Finally, I put the letter in the bottom drawer with the three almost like it that had come in the mail over the past six months. Somebody was trying to get my attention. I wondered how long I could refuse to notice. I wished Grace was here so I could talk to her about it.

Next-best thing to a look at the police reports on Fred was a look at the newspaper accounts of the Steinwale killing. Not that I had any reason to think they were connected, but Shannon had mentioned Melody Steinwale in the same breath. If you're going to start prying something up, any old corner will do to insert the wrecking bar, or so I often tell myself. I asked Mark to go down to the offices of both daily papers, buy back issues if they were available, or get photostats. It gave Mark something different to do, too. He'd been depressed for the past several weeks since his longtime roommate had left him to move back to California. They'd fought about something, God knows what, and Mark was feeling betrayed and lonely. He didn't get along with his father well enough to make going home a suitable alternative, and with the current health problems among what is called "the gay community," a rebound affair wasn't sensible either. Getting him interested in one of my puzzles might be therapeutic.

Myron Burstein called from New York City around five o'clock. I asked him what he was doing working so late.

"Late," he snarled. "It's barely dinnertime." Myron hated being late for meals. Or maybe it was his wife, Leah, who hated his being late for meals. Since he did commission buying for people in the western U.S., he got caught by the difference in time zones and stayed in the office until seven or eight, but after twenty-five years of being married to him, Leah still put dinner on the table at seven. I'd been a guest in Myron's home often enough to be aware of this particular source of marital dissension.

"So? What can I do for you, Myron?"

"So, you sent me this list of furniture from the treasure trove you uncovered."

"Myron, you've had that list for two months."

"The list I've had; buyers I haven't. Now I maybe have buyers."

Something in me whooped with joy. When the owner of the house next door had died intestate with no relatives anyone could discover, the city had auctioned the house and, separately, the houseful of American antique furniture. They'd put it up as one lot, and I'd come up with the winning bid. The bank and I, that is. The bank with some protest, some glowering, some portentous remarks by senior officials. Then Mark and Eugenia had put together a gorgeous, very expensive brochure, and we'd sent copies everywhere. Since the bank had made it clear it was only in for the very short term, I had to lay off about half the contents of that house immediately at what amounted to little more than dealer prices, and time was getting very, very short. Myron's mention of buyers got my full, enthusiastic attention, and Myron and I talked deals for over an hour. If he could do what he thought he could do, my immediate financial troubles would be over. Then I could take my time with the remaining pieces and end up turning a profit. Jacob Buchnam, my foster father, would approve of that. Since I was making monthly payments to him, buying the business, his income depended on mine. When I'd told him I was borrowing money to swing the deal, he'd been a little worried about it. Jacob had become rather feeble over the past year, and worrying wouldn't help him any. I resolved to go over soon and give him the good news—cross my fingers—about the New York sale.

While I sat there, massaging my aching leg and thinking positive thoughts, Bela nosed me questioningly. I heard Mark shutting the front door as he went out. It was five o'clock. Eugenia had locked the showroom and gone home half an hour ago. Critter came to the door and made a questioning half growl, somewhere deep in his throat. So, all right, why not another walk. The leg often hurt less at night if I walked it twice during the day. I stood up, ready to go get the leashes, and stopped, astonished. Both of them lay on the floor behind Critter. I'd hung them on a hook in the kitchen when we'd come in that morning.

I looked at Bela, who seemed unaware of anything strange, and then back at Critter, who now had the leashes in his mouth and was dragging them closer, as though he thought I hadn't seen them. Somehow, he'd gotten them off the back of the door.

"Critter?" I asked.

He made the growl noise again, leashes dangling from either side of his jaws. A cat to reckon with!

We went downstairs together and out the back door to the parking lot. It had occurred to me that Nellie Arpels, the old lady who lived upstairs across the alley, might like to see Critter. She is a cat fancier who spends most of her waking hours peering out of her upstairs window at anything happening up and down the alley. I waved in her direction, holding up Critter for her delectation. We went down the alley to the cross street, across, half a block over to Hyde, and then down Hyde the two blocks to the park. This time of the evening the traffic was heavy. Both Fourteenth and Thirteenth are one-way streets, though, so we found holes in the traffic and made it into the park.

Something had been itching at me all day. Something I'd seen that morning? Something I'd smelled maybe? When we got to the spruce grove, I stopped, staring. There were no crime-scene tapes, no chalked outlines. The body was long gone and so was any effort to find clues. The dried needles under the spruces had been raked. Little windrows of them stretched here and there across the grove. There was a single dark spot where Fred's body had lain.

Bela sat down and stared with me. Critter prowled to and fro at the end of the leash, three steps one way, turn, tail lash, three steps the other. I put his leash in Bela's mouth as I had that morning. "Hold it," I said. There was something in that grove. I could feel it, like an itch in my head. I stood under the tree, musing, and Bela nosed my leg. I hadn't told him to stay. I patted him; he barked softly, releasing Critter, who went up the tree like a panther, leash dragging.

"Critter, dammit," I said, trying to see where he'd climbed to. I walked around the tree, to the side away from the path. There was a large bush there, screening the path from view. Something white against the trunk of the tree caught my eye, something below the level of my chin. A tuft of something. I pried it out from behind the bit of bark where it had lodged, a dozen or so bits of hair or something that looked like hair, white as Bela's fur. I ran a hand up the trunk and felt a shred of something else. Something black. Was this what I'd subconsciously noted earlier? I had no idea. I might have seen the tuft of white. The more I thought about it, though, the more I thought I'd smelled something. Still, nothing came to mind.

"Critter!" I demanded as I folded the white tuft and the black shred into a clean tissue and stowed it away in a pocket. "You come down here."

He came down out of the tree, trailing the leash Bela had dropped. I got hold of the leash and then waited while Critter groomed his jaw whiskers, looking pleased with himself. In addition to size, Maine Coons have these enormous muttonchop whiskers. He finished his whiskers with a final exhibitionistic lick, then we went on with our walk.

When we got home, I hung the leashes up in the kitchen, paying particular attention as I did it. They were on the back of the kitchen door, on a hook a good five feet above the floor.

Critter could not possibly have brought them down. I must have forgotten to hang them up that morning.

Then I took a look at the tuft of stuff under a magnifying glass. It looked like hair to me. No follicles, but no twisting as thread was twisted either. That didn't rule out some monofilament like nylon. The black stuff was woven. It looked familiar but I couldn't figure out why. I don't have a microscope, so I couldn't look for fine structure. What I really should have done was turn the tuft over to the police, but they'd had their chance. Hell, maybe what I had was a policeman's hair. Maybe some detective had leaned up against the tree while he was supposed to be raking the ground. There was nothing to tell me how long it had been there. I put it away in a sealed, labeled and dated envelope.

When I went into the living room, I found a pile of newspapers neatly stacked on my coffee table with a note from Mark. He'd gone down and picked them up after work and come back to drop them off. Poor guy. He really had nothing to do with himself, and I resolved to invite him to dinner soon. Not tonight, however. I was hungry, and the day had been longer than needful.

We, dog-cat-person, suppered. We retired early. I opened the window and turned on the ceiling fan to let the cold night air into the room. At ten o'clock Grace woke me from a doze, calling from San Francisco to say Ron was in jail and would I mind very much keeping Critter for another few days.

"Grace," I said, "do you want to talk about it?"

"Not really, Jason. No. Not now."

I could visualize her pale face under that tow hair, her eyes looking gray, the way they did when she was sad. When she was joyous, she sparkled. When she was down, she looked like Poor Pitiful Pearl. In the Home, when I was a kid, someone had given one of the girls a Poor Pitiful Pearl doll, and I'd never forgotten that pale, sad, freckled face. "Can I help you?" I asked, longing for her to be closer, where I could hold her.

"Maybe. If you can, I'll call you, all right? I'm not being closemouthed, really, it's just he's so damned dumb! And you hate to tell people your own brother is just stupid, don't you? After being a cop as long as I have, I should be able to be sort of detached about this. I keep telling myself that, but it isn't working. I always took care of Ron when he was little, and I keep thinking I should have taken better care of him lately."

"He's a grown man," I told her.

"I know," she said sadly. "I know. He is, but he isn't. Somehow when he looks at me, all I see is a little boy with a skinned knee."

I made sympathetic noises. To get her mind off it, I told her there'd been a murder, that it was someone I knew, and asked if there was anyone at the station she'd recommend I talk to.

"Don't!" she said. "Not until I get back!"

"Well then, Grace, you'd better hurry back," I said. "They may ask me more questions any day now."

Long silence. Then: "You're not really involved, are you?"

"I found the body," I said. "Maybe I found a clue in the park."

"Damn." Another long silence. Then: "Don't do anything until I get home, Jason. I'll call you again soon, honest. Is my cat all right?"

Critter looked lazily up from my feet, where he had been chewing my big toe through three layers of blanket and bedspread, and purred.

"He's fine," I said. "Don't you worry about him."

She said goodbye and we hung up. I missed her. After all those years without anyone, really, I'd gotten out of the habit of missing anyone except for Agatha, my wife. My wife, who had disappeared, whom I'd searched for and never found. I'd missed her for years, at first in a kind of hopeless agony, then doggedly. Last year I'd found out what had happened to her, found out she was really dead. Now that I knew that, I could miss Grace instead, even though she wasn't in love with me. She said.

2

It was raining when we got up the next morning. Our usual run in the park was canceled by mutual consent. Bela had his breakfast and crawled back into his dog bed. Critter accompanied me into the office—Mark and I have offices next to my living quarters on the second floor—and curled up in a velour-covered wing chair he'd adopted. I made a mental note to trade the wing chair for one of another color. Critter's red tabby fur was garish against the wine upholstery. I had a green chair downstairs he'd look great in. To each of us our own small concerns.

I drank coffee while reading the accounts of the Steinwale murder.

According to the papers, Melody Steinwale had been the thirty-one-year-old wife of "artist Greg Steinwale, better known as Grale, which is how he signs his paintings." As in the Holy, maybe, I told myself, having known a few artists who took themselves very seriously indeed. Melody had managed a small gallery in North Cherry Creek, one of the few interesting parts of town so far as strolling and shopping go. Denver, like most cities, has been malled to death, but Cherry Creek is a nice combination of residential and commercial and arty. The gallery was called Just the Right Touch, which I'd thought a trifle precious each time I'd passed the place—recently taking note of some interesting ceramics in the window: big architectural pieces with unexpected lines and bright glazes. I wondered who ran it now.

In accordance with what Marge had said, the paper reported that Melody and husband had lived at the Louvre in the penthouse apartment of husband's mama, Harriet Steinwale. Melody usually walked or ran in the park in good weather. On this particular October Thursday morning, Melody had left for the park early. At ten in the morning, her body was found on a bench, slumped over a magazine. She had been shot once, at close range, by a small-caliber firearm. Park regulars had passed her without noticing she had been shot. So said the *Post*.

There was an interesting discrepancy between what the *Post* said and what the *News* had to say. According to the latter, Melody's husband had been out of town on a "business trip." On this rather important point the *Post* was mute. I wondered why.

The story was on the front page of both papers on Friday morning, with pictures. Melody looked closer to twenty than thirty, a breathtakingly lovely face with medium light hair piled carelessly above it. I wondered what color it had been. Light brown maybe. Dark ash blond. The eyes were wide and deeply fringed, the nose straight, the lips delicately curved. Pretty, pretty girl. Miss Gorgeous, right down to her collarbones. Gregory, on the other hand, was bony, lumpy-faced, with an odd nose. Of the two, he was more interesting-looking, though he showed every one of his close to forty years.

The Saturday papers carried a joint statement from Greg and from Harriet Steinwale's spokesperson: ". . . confident that the police will do everything possible to bring the perpetrator of this outrage to justice." No rape, said the paper. No robbery. Melody was wearing her wedding ring, a complete circle of diamonds. No indication that the husband was suspected, even though husbands usually are. . . .

"Jason!"

I looked up to find Mark staring at me. "You looked deep into that," he said. "I spoke three times before you heard me." I grunted at him. "Did you read this?"

"Umhm. Yes. Not much to go on, is there?"

There wasn't, yet. A few niggles, but nothing to talk about except for one curious thing. "I think both murders are remarkably similar," I said.

Mark dropped his jaw at me. "Oh, come on, now. They were both shot, sure, but according to the Corvallis guy, Fred had quite a hole in his back. The Steinwale woman was shot with a lady's gun!"

I shook my head at him, telling him I knew that. "What interests me is that both of them were shot but people went by without noticing they were dead. I went right past Fred yesterday. Hurried, as a matter of fact. People went right past Melody. People who knew her."

"Maybe people were avoiding her. Maybe she was a talker, too."

I stared at him with my mouth open. Of such small comments are puzzles further complicated.

I do love a good puzzle. Even as a kid I enjoyed them. Riddles. Conundrums. Word games. Better yet, a real mystery to figure out. The first one I remember was when I was about eleven. Three of us boys from the Home, Jerry Riggles, Prense Brown, and I, used to sneak over to City Park and go fishing. I say sneak because there were certain things we'd been told not to do by one or another of the staff at the Home. Mrs. Opinsky, one of the cooks, had told us not to go to the park because of the "preverts" waiting in the men's bathroom over near the band platform. Better that boys didn't go to the park, she told us, but if we did, we should pee outside, in the bushes.

This was a mystery. What was a "prevert," and why did Mrs. Opinsky warn us against them?

I looked up "prevert" in the dictionary, sounding it out, just the way she'd said it. I couldn't find the whole word, but I found both "pre" and "vert." "Vert" was green cover, like bushes, where deer could hide. "Pre" was before or outside of. Therefore, it seemed to me, these creatures, whatever they were, hid outside in the bushes, and it was bushes we had to watch out for, not toilets. When Mrs. Opinsky told us to go into the bushes, she must actually be setting us up for some monster!

I told Jerry and Prense, and we figured maybe the monster was a relative of hers. Maybe her father or some old guy that ate kids. We stayed out of the bushes, and when we had to go, we used the toilet. Except for one old guy showing off his dick, there was nothing strange there at all. We laughed at him and he put it away. Poor Mrs. Opinsky. If she's still alive, she's probably still wondering why these three brats took such a dislike to her.

I sometimes remind myself of the preverts when I think I've got an answer. Hidden in the bushes of easy certainty, I tell myself, there's probably some prevert waiting!

So, on this fall morning months after the death of Melody Steinwale and one day after the death of Fred Foret, I did not cry "Eureka!" I merely noted, in passing, that Fred's body had been purposefully arranged, and that the newspaper account did not give me sufficient information to know whether Melody's body had been similarly trifled with or had simply slumped where it was shot. The park benches slope sharply back. A body could stay in place without falling over. I confess that I wondered if anyone in authority would take the trouble to check and how, with Grace out of town, I was going to find out.

When Mark finished with the mail, we composed a letter to Harriet Steinwale acknowledging her interest in American antiques (everyone with money *must* be interested in American antiques), referring to our recent "acquisition of exemplary pieces," and enclosing one of the slick brochures.

"You think she'll call?" Mark asked.

I shrugged. I had no idea whether she'd call or not, but at least the signature on the letter would help establish my bona fides if we ran into one another. Which might happen, one way or another, if I started poking around. Meantime, there was Just the Right Touch awaiting. When and if I had time to get around to it.

"You've got to see the Hoopers today," Mark instructed me.

His words were echoed from the door by Eugenia, just arrived. "Yes, Jason, you simply must."

"John and Lucinda Hooper have been talking about buying antiques for over a year now," I growled. "Meantime, they've bought a ranch over at Glenwood Springs, they've been into and out of the classic-car business, they've invested heavily in an AM radio station, and they have still to buy their first piece of antique furniture!"

How did I know all this? Because the Hoopers had told me. People talk to me. Ever since I was a kid, people have talked to me. I come across as the boy next door, I guess. The unthreatening nice guy they can confide in. Other men tell me that when they're alone, say late at night, and they get into an elevator with a lone woman in it, the woman looks frightened. If I get into an elevator late at night and there's a woman in it, she tells me what she had for dinner and about the fight she just had with her boyfriend. I'm not sure that's flattering, and don't ask me what it is, but I've got it, and I know more about some people than I've ever cared to know, believe me.

"It's a waste of time," I said firmly.

"You could charm them," said Eugenia.

"Flirt with her," suggested Mark.

"She looks like a Scotch Highland cow," I told him. "All that hair!" I knew about Highlander cows because Jacob's niece Charlotte raises them on a spread down near Elizabeth, Colorado—which she calls Lizzieville.

"Mrs. Hooper has a thing for you," Eugenia suggested with a well-bred little moue.

"Whatever the thing may be," I remarked with a moue of my own, "she may keep it. Look, Eugenia. I know the type, I really do. They don't buy things because they want them. They buy things to prove they can. We've been going at it all wrong. Tell them the pieces they're looking at are too expensive. Tell them I recently got some new auction catalogues, and after looking at the reserve prices on similar pieces, I've raised the ante. Tell them that highboy they've been wearing the varnish off with their stroking and sniffing has gone up twenty percent. It's now ninety thousand, and it will probably be a hundred by Christmas."

She started to tell me something for my own good, but I scowled at her and she went away. She'd do it, just to prove I was wrong. Which, heaven help me, I might well be.

"All right, Mark," I said. "What else?"

"Willamae Belling wants you to come over today, anytime, she says, and look at that wallpaper in the entryway. Mrs. Belling says it isn't the same color she picked out. She says it's purple."

"Of course it's purple. We agreed on purple."

"She says it's too purple."

I sighed and made a note. "Anything more?"

"On your way to the Bellings', you should stop at that place on South Broadway and look at the Mexican reproductions for George Gorham's office. They came in yesterday."

I grunted. George Gorham, who had bought a very nice and very expensive dining-roomful of furniture from me for his residence, was a collector of Southwestern art. He had asked me to provide a "Southwest" decor for his office and to do it inexpensively. Which meant reproductions of colonial pieces, made in Mexico, usually of wormy pine. They were crude as a drunkard's humor but they did look old. Unfortunately, in some of the pieces, the woodworms were still working. I can remember vividly the first time I moved a genuine eighteenth-century diagonally braced Taos chest in the showroom and found those telltale little piles of sawdust. Actually, the things aren't worms. They're tiny black bugs, no bigger than a pin-head. One solution: put the furniture in an unheated garage in midwinter for a day or two. Or borrow somebody's walk-in freezer. The bugs are perseverant, but they don't adapt well to zero degrees.

With my day neatly laid out for me by other people, I had another cup of coffee and got started on it. If I did Gorham and Belling in the morning, I could stop by the gallery in Cherry Creek at lunchtime.

The colonial furniture looked all right for what George Gorham wanted. There were no piles of sawdust under the legs of the pieces. Of course, the drawers were made authenti-cally—that is, crudely, which meant one couldn't draw them out without their falling on one's feet. No guides, no stops. I made a phone call from the shop to Art Baker, a cabinetmaker who does a lot of work for us, and arranged for him to pick the pieces up: a long table with three drawers, a *trastero* (armoire), and two lamp tables with drawers. Art could salvage the fronts of the drawers while completely rebuilding the backs and sides. He could also insert drawer guides in the frames. None of his work would show, but it would make the pieces func-tional. Since they were only reproductions, authenticity wasn't an issue, and the added cost still fell within Gorham's budget.

I left South Broadway and headed east on Alameda. Wil-lamae Belling lived in the Denver Country Club, a very pleas-ant and expensive area of old, large homes and old, large trees. In Denver every tree has been planted by someone—some-thing I have to remind my eastern acquaintances of when they wonder "why you cut down all your forest." There was no

natural forest before our city was built, only shortgrass prairie
with a few cottonwoods huddled along the creekbeds. Every
bush and tree over eighty years old was lovingly planted by
some verdure-hungry settler who most likely kept it alive with
the weekly bath water.

I'd brought along the Belling file. It had in it, in lightproof
envelopes, a sample of each paint color and each wallpaper we
had selected. When I walked in, poor Willamae greeted me
almost in tears. I saw why. The entry was purple as Cartland
prose. Magenta, really. I spotted the culprit almost immediately, an old pair of rose curtains across the window on the
stair landing. The light coming through was bloody. I told
Willamae to sit down for a minute, then went up and took
down the curtains—being thankful that I'm reasonably tall—
then went back down and collected her.

"Willamae," I said, pouring on the smarm, "we should have
taken those old curtains down before we did anything at all.
Look at it now. *All* the difference!"

She admitted it did look better. I got out the sample, and we
compared. It was purple, rather toward the blue. It looked
nice. She invited me to have coffee, and I said yes. We sat in the
living room and talked. Poor thing. She was lonely. I meet a lot
of lonely old ladies. They call me because they bought something years ago from Jacob and they know I took over his
business. They call me because they got one of my brochures
offering to appraise their furniture. They call me to consult
about refinishing some piece of old furniture for the children
or for a grandchild. They call me because they don't know who
else to call. In Willamae's case, an upstairs bathroom had
flooded and brought the plaster down in the hall. She had a
fixed income which inflation had not treated kindly, and her
insurance did not cover broken pipes. So she had offered to let
me buy her great-great-great-grandmother's silver candlesticks
provided I would see to repairing and redecorating the entry
hall, which I was glad to do because the candlesticks were

beauties! At least in this case, the work was necessary. Often I get calls from old ladies who want to change furniture around just to have something happening. My bread and butter, but I'd give it up if someone could just figure out how to keep old ladies from being so all by themselves. Maybe I only feel for them because I have no old ladies of my own, no grandmas or elderly aunts. And perhaps because I feel for them, I seem to collect them like honey does ants. Old ladies and sad gay guys like Mark and girls who aren't in love with me, like Grace.

Willamae and I decided together that hanging a white sheet over the landing window would do until the new window treatment arrived. "Window treatment." That's decoratese for a pair of filmy, unlined curtains to let the light through plus a pair of heavier, lined drapes to shut the night out. And a fancy pouf at the top for elegance' sake. None of which would solve her real problem with the hall, which was that there was too little traffic in it.

I hung the sheet, then had three cups of coffee and a muffin and saw for the third or fourth time the pictures of her grown-up grandchildren and one great-grandchild who live a thousand miles away. She was lucky if she saw them once a year. I told myself if I had a family, I wouldn't move a thousand miles away from it, but maybe I was only kidding myself. I saw the pictures of her dear departed Flopsy and Mopsy, too, miniature poodles of discouraging mien.

"I keep thinking of getting another dog," she said. "And then I think how selfish that would be, to keep some young puppy from having a home with a whole family just to keep an old lady company. . . ." I nodded and said I understood.

From the Country Club it's only a few blocks east to Cherry Creek. They're building a new shopping center there, so the streets are all torn up and will be for the next several years. Street parking is always difficult. I parked in the garage next to the Tattered Cover Bookstore, one of the largest in the country

and certainly the largest in our town, and walked north a block
and a half to the Right Touch.

There are galleries, and there are galleries. There are those
that try to appeal to everyone with bits and pieces of this and
that, some representational, some kitsch, some way-out. There
are other galleries that appeal to a certain taste. The Right
Touch was of the latter type. The certain taste in this case
would be for the fantastic, the outré, the slightly bizarre. The
huge ceramic pieces were still in the window, organic-looking
planters, like dinosaur innards, gizzardy swellings and intesti-
nal coils. Behind them was a display of skeletal animals made
out of wood and steel rods and wire. The wood had been
burned and then scraped with a wire brush to give a feel of age
and lively decrepitude. Each creature was very much itself, no
fantasy except for the semi-skeletal forms. There were feral
dogs with their teeth showing, deer bugling, fish swimming,
hawks flying, a nightmare menagerie, life-sized. Not weather-
proof, unfortunately, or I could have used two or three pieces
for an outdoor job I had.

Upstairs there were small totem-pole-like sculptures, heavily
decorated with feathers and rough fabric and beads. One of
them I coveted immediately. It reminded me of something
from my childhood, though I couldn't think what. Someone,
perhaps. That straight, upward-peering outline, that feathery
lightness at the shoulders. I have these flashes of recognition
sometimes, outlines of something I think I recognize. Once
these bothered me a lot, but I've gotten used to it. I tell myself.

"Can I help you?" a voice asked. I turned to find a pair of
bright green eyes under a cap of sleek red hair, a light-footed
person of obvious vitality, sparkling at me like a whole cageful
of bright birds.

I got out my card. "I've been noticing the pieces in the window," I said. "Since I had a few minutes to spare, I thought I'd
drop in and see what you have. I don't do a lot of modern
work, but sometimes one needs something a bit out-of-period."

Which was basically hogwash. One can put things of any periods together if one wishes to do so and arranges them properly. There's no law against it. I think Green Eyes knew the hogwash for what it was, though she looked properly awed by my pronouncement. I gave her an apologetic grin, one redhead to another.

We walked through the gallery. She told me about the artists. I told her what I liked, and there were a number of things I really did like. Her name was Nina Hough, pronounced Huff, and she was a graduate in fine arts from a prestigious eastern university. That made me think of my wife, Agatha, and I set the memory aside, ruthlessly. I can't afford to think of Agatha, of what we had or what we might have had. Whole days can get lost that way.

After Nina and I had established rapport, I got around to the real reason for my visit.

"I think I know the family that owns the gallery," I said. "Steinwale, isn't it?"

She got a funny look on her face. "Harriet Steinwale," she agreed.

"Oh," I said, blank-faced. "I thought the daughter-in-law, the one who was killed, owned it."

"Harriet has always owned the gallery," she said firmly. "Her daughter-in-law used to run it." She snipped off the final word as though to prevent other words from following. There had been a peculiar emphasis on the word "run."

I let it pass for a few moments while we talked about a painting I liked. "You were here when Melody was alive?" I asked, returning to my subject.

"I was here," she said. The peculiar emphasis told me that most of the time she had been the only one.

Pique will out. I nodded wisely. "Melody thought it would be fun to play art gallery, did she? Well, that doesn't surprise me."

"You knew her?" A half-suspicious glance.

"Of her." I shrugged. "A friend of mine knew her rather well."

"Male friend, no doubt," she snapped, then became contrite. "I'm sorry. It's just that I'm still trying to undo . . ."

I told her that I understood, suggested that since I was about to have lunch, why didn't she join me and we'd talk about art. She looked doubtful.

"Come on," I begged. "You have to have lunch, too. And I hate to eat alone."

"If you can wait until twelve-thirty," she said. "I have a gal who comes in every day for a few hours. She watches the gallery while I'm out and addresses show announcements, things like that."

I wandered while I waited. The gallery also exhibited one-of-a-kind jewelry, woven wall pieces, several series of paper sculptures, plus a series of exciting ruglike-felt "soft paintings" done in colored wools by an Israeli artist I'd never heard of. When the gallery sitter arrived, Nina and I walked over to Soren's. The sun was out, temporarily, so we asked for a table on the patio. I had artichoke lasagna. Nina had what turned out to be a very authoritative chicken curry, and kept reaching for her wineglass, tears in her eyes.

"They don't fool around," I told her.

Weeping but happy, she agreed, and I ordered her another glass of wine. So far she'd had three. She was beginning to be voluble about a lot of things.

"So tell me about Melody Steinwale," I said when the plates had been taken away and another glass of wine for her and a cup of coffee for me had been delivered.

"I wouldn't want Harriet to think I'd been talking about the family," she said. "Harriet's a perfectly nice woman, but she can be a holy terror if you do something disloyal to the family." She sipped, turning the long-stemmed glass.

"The family being?"

"Her, I guess. And Greg. And maybe a new wife, the way things are going." She sipped again.

"What's she like? The new person? Any similarity between her and Melody?"

She snorted, caught herself, then snorted again. "No, Jason. No similarity at all. In the first place, Trish already has one child—she's a widow—and wants more. Melody didn't."

"You know that for a fact? Melody said so?"

"No. She said just the opposite. She and Greg were desperate to have children, to hear her tell it. She spent half her time going to gynecologists and infertility specialists. They'd put her on pills."

"And?"

"And she'd dump the pills down the john at the Touch. I saw her. She made some lame excuse about it being an old prescription, but it wasn't."

"Well, that's only an isolated incident. Maybe she wasn't feeling well or the pills made her sick."

"The only time she was sick was when the doctor suggested she might best get pregnant. Then she was sick. She had fifty and a half excuses for never making love at the right time."

"You know that for a fact, too?"

"Lord, you couldn't miss it! Greg and she had arguments almost every month. He'd come into the gallery, the compleat angler, bearing little baits of flowers or perfume or cashmere sweaters, ready to catch her for lunch and then take her to bed, and she'd scream at him that she hadn't felt like it last night and still didn't feel like it. I mean, I wasn't eavesdropping; you could hear it down the block!"

Wine had loosened both her tongue and the sill cock on her metaphor tank. I enjoyed the thought of Steinwale as fisherman until I applied the same comparison to myself. What I was doing was also fishing.

"Why didn't she just take the pill?"

"Because then she'd have had to admit she was being dishonest with Greg, that she really didn't want children. So long as she could come up with excuses, she could tell herself it wasn't her fault. You know the kind, Jason. She was good at lying to herself."

"What did she do with the other half of her life?"

"She took art classes, at DU. So she could—and I'm quoting —'share Greg's mental processes, be more attuned to his needs, as well as expressing her own talent.' Christ! At least poor Greg doesn't have that to put up with anymore."

"She wasn't talented?"

"Jason, she did these really painful little paintings. Cramped. Full of fussy detail. No line, no composition, terrible color that always ended up muddy. The instructor was very much on the make—I know him, he always is—so he fed her a bunch of crap about her talent. She used to quote him until I turned blue! The talent he had in mind wasn't on canvas."

"So the new person is not like Melody," I said. "Which is odd, you know. Most of us men tend to go for types."

She considered this. "Well, Trish Watson *is* kind of like Melody, in appearance. Same chestnut hair. Same blue eyes. Same build, even. She's lovely-looking. I admit I was surprised when Harriet brought her in to the gallery. . . ."

"Harriet brought her in?"

"About two months after Melody died. Harriet brought her in, asked if I could use her since I couldn't run the place alone. That was the first I'd known I was going to run it at all. Trish had no art background, particularly. Just what one gets as part of a liberal arts degree. I took one look at her and thought, 'Uh-oh, here's another one.' "

"But you were wrong."

"I was wrong. Trish is just solid, you know? One of those women who had a nice family life, no real hang-ups, pleasant disposition. If I ever really got into trouble, I'd go to Trish for help, she's that kind. And she's got this adorable little girl who looks just like her."

"You know Greg well?"

"Not really. He never looked at any woman but Melody, and he never looks at any woman but Trish now. Greg—well, you'd have to understand about Greg. He never went looking for a woman, you know? He never had time, or let himself have time. And yet, he's a perfectly normal male, so he needs a woman, so he stares around vaguely bellowing mating calls, and then settles on the first reasonably attractive thing that bugles back. That's what he did with Melody, and that's what he did with Trish. After about two weeks with me, Trish left the gallery to manage the studio for him. He gets a lot of visitors, you know, and he's one of those single-minded men who can't cope. He really *needs* a wife, but except for that, people just aren't important to him. His mind is always doing something else. He's perfectly polite, but he's elsewhere."

"He had some kind of mental breakdown, didn't he? When Melody was killed?"

She shook her head. "Before. Months before. It was bad. I thought Harriet would lose her mind, too."

"I wonder what caused that."

She flushed, shaking her head. "It could have been money worries, I suppose."

"I thought Harriet was very well-off."

"Harriet is, but both she and Greg feel very strongly about his being self-supporting. He wants to live on what he makes, not what his mother has, even though he'll probably inherit it someday. Harriet talks a good bit about building character. Then, too, Harriet could have gotten tired of supporting Melody in the style Melody preferred. Melody wanted a home of their own, and not just a plain house, you know? Greg's becoming a very popular artist just now. He will make very good money, but he's got debts and it will take time. Melody wanted a million-dollar house right now, and nothing else would do. I honestly don't know what caused the breakdown. I do know he

spent a while in a private hospital. He was there when Melody
was killed."

"The papers said . . ."

"Oh, I know what the papers said. The Steinwale lawyer
issued a statement, and then Harriet came zooming back from
Acapulco or Yucatán or wherever and issued one of her own.
The paper went along with the 'business trip' because the edi-
tor is Harriet's cousin or nephew twice removed or something.
I guess it's okay. There was no intent to interfere with the
investigation. I mean, Greg was definitely locked up in the
hospital when it happened. It wasn't a case of anyone suspecting him of anything. It was just protecting the family reputation. Harriet is very big on family." She yawned. "Jason,
I've had too much wine. I'm talking too much. Harriet's going
to fire me, sure as summer."

"I'm sure she won't. You're far too knowledgeable to be
fired. My guess would be that the gallery makes a profit."

"Now it does," she agreed, letting me assume what I did,
that in Melody's day it had not.

"Tell me something," I asked her, suddenly remembering
Mark's comment. "Did Melody talk about herself a lot?"

Nina gave me a wink, and a slightly tipsy giggle. "There
were two things Melody could do, Jason, better than anyone
I've ever known. One of them was talk about herself and how
she felt and what she thought and what she was going to buy."

"And the other one?"

She grinned. "She could spend money. God, could she spend
money."

I walked with her back to the gallery, then took myself back
to the parking garage. Clouds had blown in suddenly, and
there were tiny spatters of icy rain on the windshield as I
drove back to 1465 Hyde Street. I hadn't learned much of help
during lunch, except for the answer to the first question that
had come up in the puzzle. Yes, Melody, too, had been a talker.
And so was Nina Hough.

Eugenia greeted me with the news that the police were upstairs waiting for me and that the Hoopers wanted the highboy
if I'd let them have it at the previous price.

I breathed in deeply. "Tell them no. But I will come down
ten thousand, simply because they've been looking at it. However, that price is only good until tomorrow. Tell him we're
going to retag things over the weekend to reflect new values."

"Mr. Hooper wants to know how much of a deposit to hold
it for them."

"I won't hold it for them because I have a possible buyer
coming up from Santa Fe on Sunday," I fantasized out loud.
"A very wealthy man to whom I have sent pictures of various
pieces because he is redoing his three-million-dollar house in
an exclusive suburb. Tell the Hoopers I'm very sorry." Growing up in a Home, particularly playing cards with the janitor,
teaches one how to bluff with a completely poker face.

Eugenia gave me a look: her "I hope you know what you're
doing" look. She has quite a repertoire of looks. There's the
"You have just made a complete ass of yourself" look, and the
"You should have had a mother to teach you manners" look.
None of them has ever been quite insubordinate enough to
make me do anything about it, though each has a definitely
laserlike quality. You can turn your back on Eugenia and still
feel the Look, like a small bonfire between your shoulder
blades.

I found the police in my office, two plainclothes types, glanc-
ing through back issues of *Art & Antiques* and looking bored.
Mark stuck his head in the door and asked if they'd like coffee,
and they both said no in a tone that said yes, so I told Mark to
bring a tray in case they changed their minds.

We went over the same ground I had gone over with the
uniformed men. I had seen Fred on the ground when I went
into the park.

"You didn't say anything to him?" the fatter cop asked me.

"I hoped he wouldn't see me," I confessed. "He was the world's worst bore."

They cast one another significant looks, as though I had just confirmed a private theory.

"Well, he was," I said. "Ask anybody."

"We did," said the fatter cop. "They all say the same thing." Mark came in with the coffee, and the fatter cop poured himself a cupful and sugared it liberally.

Then we covered where the dog, cat, and I had run, who we had seen—I didn't know many names, but I could describe the regulars—and what we had said. Critter wandered into my office about then, lending verisimilitude to what I was telling them about the cat remarks.

"How long have you had him?" the leaner cop asked.

I thought of saying he belonged to Grace Willis, but caught myself. These were her colleagues, and I didn't want to involve her in explanations she might not care to make. I said I hadn't had Critter long.

"So then you came back the same way you went in," the fatter cop prompted.

I agreed. That exit from the park was closest to the shop.

"So you saw him again."

"I saw Fred again, but this time Bela howled. As soon as I saw he was dead, I stepped away from the body and hailed two passersby to fetch the police. I stayed by the body with Mr. Corvallis until they came. Period."

"Okay," said the leaner cop. "Now, how well did you know this guy?"

"Not well. His brother-in-law is my broker, his wife is an acquaintance. I met Fred at their house."

"You have any business or personal dealings with him at all?"

"None whatsoever. He used to talk my ear off in the park, if I gave him a chance. That was my total relationship with the man."

They went over the same ground again, from a slightly different angle, but they weren't pressing. They didn't really think I had anything to do with it.

I decided to try for some information I wanted. "Have there been any other murders like this?" I asked. "In the park?"

The fatter cop responded at once. "There was a woman shot in the park last year. There was an elderly man shot this winter, sort of in the park, on one of the paths leading to his apartment house. That one was a robbery."

"Any similarities?" I persisted. "Between Fred's murder and either of the others?"

Aside from the fact they hadn't caught the perpetrators, either they didn't think there were similarities or they didn't intend to tell me. They were interested in why I asked.

I shrugged. "I go to that park almost every day. I wondered if somebody was wandering around in the park shooting people, that's all. Did you work on the earlier cases?"

They had not. They accepted that I had a legitimate concern. I said a few words more about possible similarities, which should have been enough to make them look at the former case files. Saying anything more than that might get me right into the middle of it, where I decidedly did not want to be!

"What did you find out?" Mark asked me as soon as the police had gone. I gave him an abbreviated version of what Nina had told me while he hmmed and wowed, and said maybe Mark was right after all about Fred and Melody both having been talkers. "Are you trying to solve it?" he asked. "What can I do?"

I'd been thinking up some nice, time-consuming job to get Mark involved. "The people in the park tend to be regulars," I told him. "I've noticed it. Some of them are there every morning. Some two or three times a week. Some of them have been running or walking there for months or even years, certainly since Melody Steinwale's time. What I'd like you to do is take

the picture of Melody from the newspaper and do a little jogging yourself. Ask the regulars if they ever saw her or talked to
her or saw her with anyone."

"You're concentrating an awful lot on her, aren't you?" he
wondered. "Wouldn't Fred's murder be easier. Since it's more
recent?"

I considered it. "What makes them both appetizing is the
family alibis. The woman from the art gallery says that
Melody's husband was in a mental hospital and her mother-in-
law was in Mexico when Melody was killed. That removes the
two nearest family members from suspicion in her case. Also,
it seems Fred's ex-wife and her family alibi one another for the
time Fred was killed. If all husbands and former wives were
verifiably elsewhere at the time of the murders, and if, as I'm
still assuming, the two killings are connected, we're looking
for something outside the usual domestic-violence arena, something unusual. In my limited experience, with unusual things
it doesn't make any difference where one starts, at the beginning or the end, or in the middle so far as that goes." That
sounded very pontifical, though I wasn't sure it meant anything.

"I wish Grace was here," he said. "That way we'd know
what the police are doing."

I agreed with him and told him about her having called me
the previous night. We both said it was tough to have family in
trouble, but when he began to look depressed at that idea, I
quickly changed the subject back to Melody Steinwale.

"When I talk about Melody, what am I looking for?" he
asked.

"Any reason anybody might have to kill her. I know her
husband had a reason, though he might not have known it, but
for the time being we're assuming he didn't do it. So we're
looking for anyone else who knew her. You take the park, and
I'll take the art school."

Before the art school, however, I had the Hoopers. John

Hooper called to say he'd be in within the hour, bearing a cashier's check for eighty thou. He didn't want the highboy to get away from him.

I grinned at Eugenia and she gave me a haughty glare. Score one for Jason, I told myself. Now that the dam was broken, maybe we could sell the Hoopers a few more excellent investments—something that would hold its value better than a shoestring western-slope radio station at any rate.

I got tied up on the phone for the rest of the afternoon. The weather continued lousy, becoming worse along toward evening. I was trying to decide whether to thaw something for supper or go out, when the phone rang. Marge Beebe, asking if I'd come have a meal with her. Silas, she said, was out of town, which was good because she wanted to talk to me privately.

I drove the highway route, taking Bela and Critter along. Marge was an animal person, and I thought she'd like to see them. She told me to bring them on into the brick-floored family room, where they met her two dogs and all settled down among the saddles and tack and dusty boots to concentrate on the meaty beef neckbones I'd brought with me. Marge was broiling lamb chops for us, and we talked about Maine Coon cats for a while. She has quite a library of animal books—dogs, all kinds of livestock, cats. She pulled out one book that said something about Maine Coons, then another book that contradicted the first one. One authority said the cats matured at one year. The other book said at least two, maybe three. The first authority, a West Coast woman, said they weren't any larger than normal cats, ten to twelve pounds. I stared at Critter and wondered what kind of animal she'd been looking at.

Marge sat us down at her kitchen table. "Jason, I know you sometimes get involved with solving things. Betty Garrison told me you did for her."

I'd done a little thing for Betty Garrison, who had been married to a man who had an identical twin, though I was very

surprised that Betty would have mentioned that embarrassing
occurrence to anyone at all.

"Betty didn't tell me *what* you did," Marge went on. I silently sighed with relief. "But you know, Jason, the police
aren't going to get anywhere with this. They as much as told
me so just today. They don't have anything to go on. They say
murder is usually someone the killer knows, or it's during the
course of a robbery or other crime. Well, he wasn't robbed. I've
told the police the names of anyone I knew that he knew. Lycia
and the kids and Lycia's friend Ross—they were all together
from four o'clock on Tuesday until we showed up there
Wednesday morning. No way any of them could have been
involved. . . ."

"All four of them slept together?" I asked.

"Well, no."

"Then they weren't together."

"Wait. Listen. Lycia got burgled two weeks ago. Somebody
got in and she doesn't even know if they took anything, except
she does know they went through her things. I'd dropped by to
return her hot pot I'd borrowed, and I was right there when
she came out of her bedroom, really angry. She didn't say
much, but I could tell how upset she was. Well, wouldn't anybody be? It isn't the first time it's happened either. It happened
last year, and that time she bought herself a little twenty-two,
even though I don't think she's ever fired it, even for practice. I
doubt it's ever been out of her dresser drawer. Ross has a gun, I
know that, but he was in the military for a while and learned
how to use his. Well, anyway, so this time she ordered a new
lock put in, and day before yesterday, Tuesday, was the earliest
the lock man could get there. He put the lock in and gave her
one key, only one. This kind of lock you can only unlock with
the key—no buttons or combinations or anything like that. She
locked up that night, after supper, with the only key. She intended to have keys made for the family, of course, but at that
time, Tuesday evening, she still had only the one. About eight

o'clock Wednesday morning, she took the key out of her jewel box and unlocked the door to get the morning paper, and Ross was with her when she did it. The apartment only has the one entrance. There's no way anyone left that apartment during the night."

"Where was this jewel box?"

"In her bedside table in the room she was sleeping in, her and . . . well, her and Ross. I guess in this day and age nobody has to apologize for sleeping with somebody they aren't married to. It still comes a little strange to me. Particularly since she was my brother's wife."

"Does she plan on getting married?" I don't know why this seemed important to me, but it did.

"Lycia says no. She says once is enough. She isn't going to go through that again." Marge busied herself with her knife and fork, a little pink in the face at the implied criticism of Fred.

"Could either Lycia or Ross have wakened and got up without the other knowing?"

"Ross is a trauma surgeon. Lycia says he sleeps like a cat from having to get up in the middle of the night all the time. And since Lycia's a doctor, she's a light sleeper, too. I don't think either of them could have gotten up and left the apartment without the other knowing. Besides, Ross says he didn't know where the key was. He wasn't in the room when she put it away."

"It sounds to me like there's been a lot of discussion of this." Everything she had told me sounded carefully phrased and rehearsed.

"Well, of course it's been talked over," she said in an exasperated tone. "It was the police, Jason. They asked all the same questions you're asking, and they asked them over and over. Lycia told them, and then Ross told them, and then Keith. Poor Shannon was crying so hard she couldn't even talk. I was there and heard it all two or three times. They even wanted to know where *I* was early yesterday morning. It happened to be one of those mornings when Silas and I had an early ride and breakfast together, so that's all right."

"What do you want me to do, Marge?"

"I want you to look around a little, Jason, please. He was my brother. I feel . . . oh, like I ought to do something."

I didn't tell her I had already involved myself in her puzzle. "I'll look around a little."

"I can pay you, whatever you think . . ."

"No!" I said. "Absolutely not. Buy some good antiques, if you want to, but don't pay me for this. So far as this little hobby of mine goes, I'm an amateur and determined to keep my amateur status." I smiled at her, not letting her know how close to rejection her words had pushed me. Someone had tried to hire me once, to conceal information. As it happened, I'd thought concealment was the best idea, but I would not be hired to do it. That came too close to what Jacob called selling one's soul. I liked solving puzzles, but I would not commit myself to "doing" things about them. Once you take money, you have to impose some sort of ethic or professional standard on what you're doing, and I didn't want to do that.

"Have you got anything to tell me, Marge?" I asked. "Anything about Fred I ought to know?"

"I'm not going to talk about family," she said. "They're out of it. Nobody in the family is involved. I'll tell you anything else you want to know, even though I don't know much. Fred went to school half a dozen different places here and there, fooling around, using up all the money our daddy left him. He came back here for a visit in '58. He'd have been about twenty-two then. Silas knew I worried about my baby brother—well, being ten years older, I'd half raised him—so he told Fred he'd get him a teaching assistantship up at the university if he'd settle down and get his doctorate. Silas could arrange that because his family was very big in the alumni association. Well, Fred took him up on it and stayed. He didn't even go back to collect his things, not that he had much. He got his doctorate, and he got this job and that job in the department and stayed there for ten years. He married Lycia, she was Lycia Meyer, in '60, and the kids were born in '62 and '66, and then in '68 he got a job in Washington with the DOD."

"How did he get that?"

"I don't know, Jason. Politics of one kind or another, I guess. Fred wasn't making much at the university. I used to worry about his family getting along. Though we've never talked about it, I think Silas may have pulled some strings, a political favor, you know. I figured if he'd wanted me to know, he'd have told me. He thinks I talk too much, and I guess I do, so sometimes he doesn't tell me things and I don't ask. Anyhow, Fred went to D.C. in '68, and the family went with him, but about four or five years later, I think it was in '73, Lycia left him and came back here. Some relative of hers had died and left her enough to live on for a while, so she went back to school, to medical school. She'd gone on taking courses all the time she and Fred had been married, so she was well prepared for it."

"She left him in Washington?"

"Left him, yes. She didn't divorce him then, Jason, but I think we all knew it was just a matter of time. Whenever we spoke of him, she got this tight-lipped look. Something happened back then. She never said one word to me against him, give her credit for that. The only hint she ever gave me was she said once that Fred had some problems he should work on. Oh, and once she said he'd let power go to his head. He was something or other on some committee at the DOD, and I guess he did have a little power of some kind. Well, maybe it had gone to his head."

"When did he come back to town?"

"In '78. While he was in Washington, he'd done some favors for people at the university here—seen to it they got some grant money, that kind of thing. He told me he was going to 'call in the IOUs,' and evidently it worked, because he got a job at the university. The funny thing was, he expected Lycia to move in with him as soon as he got back, and he was really surprised when she didn't. She fought with him about that—if you can call it a fight when one person yells and the other one just sits there and looks superior, which is what Fred always did—and then she filed for divorce. Fred talked some about getting custody of the children, but they'd been living separately from him for years, and Silas told him not to make a fool of himself. Fred always listened to Silas. By that time, Lycia was a doctor, making plenty of money to support herself and Keith and Shannon."

"And you're sure they had nothing to do with Fred's death." We had come full circle. I knew a few more unsurprising facts about Fred, but no more about who might have killed him.

"Nothing. Couldn't have. Now, I know Fred made some enemies at the university. He used to talk about that. I know when he was with the DOD, there were people who didn't like him because he reviewed grant proposals. . . ."

"Grant proposals?"

"For money, Jason. Scientists who wanted grants of money to do certain kinds of research. Fred was on this committee, and he turned a lot of them down. He said a lot of them were just half-assed."

"Did you tell the police that?"

"Yes. Of course."

"Did he do anything at the university besides teach? Any committees there?"

"The postgraduate committee, that's all."

"That's the committee that reviews applications for scholarships or fellowships or teaching assistantships for graduate students, some of whom are also half-assed?" I was beginning to see a pattern.

She flushed. "Well, Jason, some of them probably are."

"Still, if graduate students were told so, they might be very angry. Murderous, perhaps?"

She looked away, uncomfortably.

"Did you tell the police that?"

"I didn't think of it."

I didn't press the matter. "If the family's out of it, do you have some other names for me, Marge? People I can talk to?"

"He worked most closely with a Professor Simmons. There were other people, too, but I only remember Professor Simmons. He came out here with Fred a few times, to go riding."

I made a note. She hadn't given Simmons's name to the police because she hadn't thought of him as possibly implicated or involved. We finished our coffee. I gathered up dog and cat and went out to the car. The sleety squall had blown over. Though the city glow paled the northern sky, the country night above me was velvet black, stars everywhere, so many it made me gasp. There's a lot of talk about cities being crowded, polluted, unhealthy, but all in all, I think cities are man's proper milieu. How could we get on with our everyday business if we were confronted, night after night, with stars like these? How could we maintain our necessary sense of self-importance? We probably need that haze of sodium vapor playing on exhaust fumes to conceal what's too magnificent to be lived with. Like frogs need their muck, down in the bottom of the pond, to hide the existence of the uncomfortable stars.

On Friday morning I had an appointment with a plastic surgeon. I've had a mutilated ear and burn scars on the back of the head since I was an infant. I had the injuries when I was abandoned at the Home, and I don't remember how I got them. The records at the Home say they were not fully healed then, so it must have happened when I was three. Kids don't remember much from that early. At any rate, the scars don't bother me too much. I wear my hair a little long to cover them. Agatha used to say they made me mysterious. I'd rather have a nice saber cut, quite frankly. Something a little more traditional and less accidental-looking.

One of my customers happens to be a plastic surgeon, however, and he had mentioned to me that he could do hair im-
plants where the scars are, not one hundred percent guaran-
teed, but worth a shot. He'd said he could take hair from the
back and sides and implant it along the neckline. The first
session was Friday morning.

An hour after entering his office, I walked out. The back of
my head was still numb, but he said it would hurt later. Like
ant bites, he said. He'd given me some painkillers. I felt depressed and sad. Thinking about my origins does that to me
sometimes, but it's a familiar woe that I don't let get to me
much. The doctor had said he could fix the top of my ear, too,
and I was considering that. When I got back in the car, I just
sat for a while. I had no appointments. Mark could take care of
anything that came up. Hooper's check would make the next
bank payment with a little over, so I didn't feel compelled to
go drum up cash business. I decided to drive up to Boulder and
talk with Professor Simmons.

The University of Colorado at Boulder is a flawed extrava-
gance of Italian provincial architecture. The flaws are new ad-
ditions. The dollar is not what it used to be. All that tile and
exterior detailing takes a lot of dollars, and concrete is cheaper,
alas. Ralph Simmons was officed in a science building which
looked like a packing crate and was only marginally better
inside. His office was pleasant enough, if one ignored the dusty
piles of papers.

"Fred's sister called to tell me you'd be in touch," he said in a
prissy voice. He had a face like an unblanched almond, lined
and brown, with a pointy chin above which tiny features
struggled with one another for supremacy. Seemingly the
mechanism that moved his face could only work one feature at
a time. If his mouth was open, his eyes were shut. "I can't tell
you how distressed I was to hear of Fred's death," he said, like
a blind man. His eyes flickered open, closing again when his
mouth cracked to say, "Our society must find ways to protect

itself against this casual crime. Muggers! Thieves!" Eyes and mouth shut, his nostrils flared. He sniffed at me through his closed eyelids, like a blind bloodhound.

"He wasn't mugged," I said. "He wasn't robbed. He was probably killed by someone who knew him."

Eyes opened again. This time they sagged half closed while he hissed, "Surely that's impossible!"

I nodded, conveying certainty. "Which is why I'm here, Professor Simmons. Marge Beebe tells me that you knew Fred as well as anyone."

"We weren't really close," he said with sudden caution. "Not . . . bosom friends." The old-fashioned phrase came out like a cockroach, peeking from a hole, waving its antennae in alarm, as though he were afraid of being accused of friendship. If they hadn't been friends, I wondered what they had been.

"Nonetheless," I continued.

"What do you want to know?"

"I'd like to know who had reason to dislike him. Who had reason to think Fred needed killing."

"That woman," he snorted. "Sally somebody."

"Woman?"

"His neighbor. Where he lived, in his apartment house. She tried to kill him, but he took the gun away from her. Heaven save me from hysterical women!"

"His neighbor, you say?"

"She's not there anymore. Streeter, that was the name! She moved. Too ashamed to face him."

"Can you think of anyone else?" I asked, making a note of the name Sally Streeter.

"There is someone who might have wanted to kill Fred, though it would have been totally without justification," he snapped at me, eyes closed. "Totally without justification. Fred was quite right to deny financial aid to that young ruffian." There was a little foam of spittle at the corner of his mouth. From this, I assumed (rightly, as it turned out) that Simmons was also on the committee and had also been exposed to the ruffian, whoever he was.

I asked him for details and was told of a certain Martin O'Toole, who had only last week been denied the teaching assistantship he needed to continue his work at the university.

"He shows no scholarship!" Simmons pronounced. "Calls himself a physicist. He might as well be doing alchemy!"

I wondered out loud why Fred was still on the committee when he had retired from the faculty.

"He would have stayed on for the rest of his term," Simmons said with an impatient gesture. "He would have received a small stipend. Retirement is not, after all, an incapacitating condition. . . ."

I thanked the professor and slipped away. Since this was the physics building, finding a graduate student who was at war with a couple of physics professors shouldn't be difficult.

I asked here and there. A plump blonde in the office told me, wistfully, that Marty O'Toole was at war with everyone, and further that he hung out at a local tavern. There I found him, ensconced at a rear table, working on a monumental drunk all by himself. In front of him were several empty glasses plus the ones he was working on. From the color of his eyes, I estimated today's bout to be at the tail end of a lengthy series.

I sat down across from him and asked if I could buy him a drink. He glared at me.

"For what reason? To corrupt my soul? To assist my descent into Hades? Or to offer the pleasanter comforts of Lethe?" He was so lean as to be almost skeletal, huge-eyed, like a lemur, his mouth compressed into what looked like a permanent sneer. "Are you astonished that I, a mere scientist, should be aware of such references? I had a mother who read-to-me. . . ." Every few words, his shoulders would jerk, as though something had bitten him.

"Actually," I said, "I wanted to talk about Fred Foret."

He pointed a finger at me, cocked as though he was ready to

fire it. "Dead," he intoned. "Freddy For-it is dead. There is justice. It is slow and incomplete, but there is justice. The mills, as it were, of the gods."

"I take it you didn't like him."

"I hated him. I should've shot him myself! Him, and Simmons, and Graybull. The know-nothing triumvirate!" He circled his half-empty beer glass with several completely empty shot glasses, an alcoholic's solar system. An almost empty bowl of peanuts was Jupiter.

"Tell me about him," I suggested. "I really want to know about Fred."

He sat back, arms above his head, reaching for something I couldn't see and he couldn't find. Finally he came back to earth. "Why?" he asked.

"His sister wants to know why he got killed. I'm trying to find out for her."

He drank, thinking about this. While he thought about it, I went over to the bar and picked up a couple of beers. If I could keep him on beer, maybe he could tell me something.

His glass was empty by the time I got back. I set a full one in front of him.

"I'm going to tell you," he said. "I'm going to make clear what no one understands. I'm going to diagram for you the parameters of the man's stupidity. I'm going to show you what an idiot he was."

"Fine," I said, sipping.

"You know anything about physics?"

"Nothing," I admitted.

He thought about that. "This may be more difficult than I had thought," he said. He drank a few swallows, drumming his fingers and blinking rapidly. "I shall speak in the general rather than the specific."

"Fine," I encouraged him. Anything would do. If I didn't understand it, I could always get someone sober to explain it to me.

"There is a certain method which has been taught in departments of physics for the past thirty or so years. It is a method of making calculations regarding the structure of substances. Are you with me thus far?"

I told him I was.

"This process is assumed, eventually, to have a practical consequence. It is supposed to be predictive. Engineers and metallurgists very much desire some kind of predictive method which will tell them that if they mix element A and element B, the resultant material will behave in such and such a way." He spoke with the precision of someone who has used the same words before—often before. "There would be no reason to engage in these calculations if they had no practical consequence."

I understood him. I was surprised that I understood him, but I did. O'Toole's alcohol content didn't seem to be affecting his tutorial powers.

"For thirty years, maybe forty, physicists have been getting grants from metallurgists to develop a method of prediction. For thirty or forty years the physicists have been promising that any day now they would perfect this process and start predicting things." He nodded at me: great, ponderous nods. "Forty years."

My mind made the intuitive leap. "You've found a new way to do it," I said. It was the only thing that made sense.

His eyebrows went to join his hairline and he smiled, like a sunrise. "Not I." He shook his head at me with the pleased smile still wandering around on his face, trying to find a place to settle. "Not I alone. Several people. Here and there. The man I studied under at MIT. Some people at Oxford. We have found a way to do what these idiots have been promising. . . ."

"Fred Foret?" I suggested, pronouncing it For-ay. "Him?"

"Freddy For-it was one of them. Simmons was one of them. Graybull was one of them. They've been doing the same things over and over for decades. They've been giving all the financial aid to their students, whom they've taught to do the same things over and over. So I come along and say, hey, fellas, here's a way to get somewhere with this, and you know what they do?"

I had a pretty good idea. "What?" I asked.

"They say I'm arrogant. They say I'm wet behind the ears. They say I'm no scientist. They say I make mistakes, which I sometimes do, like they never made a mistake. God. What kind of a scientist does the same calculations over and over again for forty years without figuring out he's not getting anyplace!" He finished his beer, looked startled, as though he'd swallowed something alive, then collapsed face forward into the bowl of peanut shells.

The bartender came over, not hurrying. "Marty passed out, huh?"

"Looks like it," I said. I stood up and put my hands in my pockets, waiting for it. I could see it coming.

Sure enough. "You wanta take him home?" the bartender asked.

I didn't, particularly. "Where does he live?"

He named a street I knew. I told him I'd get my car. When I drove up in front, he hauled Marty across the sidewalk like a sack of grain and dumped him in the back seat of the Mercedes, commenting, "Nice car. I'd get him home right away. Sometimes he whoops after he's been drinking."

I drove as quickly as was consonant with good sense. There were two guys lounging on the front porch amid a litter of empty beer cans when I got O'Toole there. With a minimum of comment, and that jocular, they helped me get him into his place and onto the bed, not much helped by what seemed to be their own customary state of inebriety. When I pulled the pillow over to put Martin's head on it, a gun slid onto the floor.

"What's that doing there?" said one of them, picking it up in a manner that posed imminent danger to himself and me. I took it away from him gently, pointing it in a less dangerous direction. A .38 revolver, fully loaded. Both the gun and the cartridges were filthy. I doubted it had been fired in twenty years, which didn't mean it couldn't do a lot of accidental damage.

"He was going to shoot somebody," the other guy said. "Some professor or other. Don't you remember the other night?"

"Oh, right," he replied, without interest. "Old Freddy For-it. Well, considering what Freddy did to O'Toole, he's got it coming."

Evidently the two of them had not yet heard about Fred's death, or were not sober enough to have taken it in. I didn't enlighten them. I put the revolver away in a drawer under some dirty socks and left without telling them that Freddy no longer had it coming.

On the way back home, the back of my head started feeling as though it had been attacked by a nest of fire ants. I stopped at a service station to get a can of citrus-flavored fizz to chase the painkiller with. After about fifteen minutes, the pain let up enough so that I could get back in the car, wondering whether it was worth it or not to look merely normal. The face looking back at me in the car mirror was the same stranger I always see in the mirror, and he refused to say.

3

Jason Lynx Interiors opens at noon on Mondays. We close at noon on Saturdays, except by appointment. On Saturdays, Eugenia often doesn't come in at all; sometimes Mark's appearance is merely a gesture. This morning he arrived in jogging clothes to report no luck so far on the park circuit. "I'll give it another try tomorrow," he said.

"People run a little later on Sundays," I told him. "Or maybe it's just that I do. I do tend to see the same people on Sundays as on other days, though, so I guess I'm not the only one."

"Are you going to tell the police about O'Toole?" he wanted to know after I'd filled him in on yesterday.

I said no, I wasn't. At least not yet. They could find him the same way I had, and besides, I didn't think he'd done it.

"Why is that?"

"I think he was too drunk to have hidden the fact if he had done it. I think he wanted to do it, sure. Got out his gun from wherever he usually keeps it, loaded it, talked drunkenly to his housemates about shooting the bastard, then fell asleep on top of the gun. When he woke up, he felt like hell and went out to get some more of what ailed him."

"Could have been," Mark agreed. "Is he an alcoholic?"

"He may be merely a genius who drinks," I opined. "If he

gets some help pretty soon, and the establishment doesn't beat
him down. On the other hand . . ."

"What, on the other hand?"

"On the other hand, he could be a very clever killer counter-
feiting drunkenness. He's still on the list, Mark."

Mark gave me a lopsided grin and left. It was the most cheerful expression I had seen on his face for some time. I fervently
hoped he would soon meet someone . . . someone what?
Someone nice. Someone nonpromiscuous. Someone. Well.

I had a quiet morning, doing paperwork, mostly figuring
bills for people. Sometimes I add a little for aggravation. Sometimes I add a lot for aggravation, then have to go back and
refigure it when I cool down. The entry bell rang a couple of
times during the morning. Package delivery. A peerpointer. I
call them peerpointers because that's what they do. Peer, and
point. They seldom buy anything. I locked up at noon, got
some stuff out of the refrigerator for Jacob, took a little box of
chocolates out of the "go visiting" drawer, and started the afternoon by dropping in on Nellie Arpels.

Her daughter, Janice Fetterling, was looking very spruce
and at least five years younger than fifty-five. I complimented
her on her outfit, and she told me she was going shopping with
a friend as soon as Jeannie arrived to sit with Nellie. I told her
I'd stay until Jeannie arrived, and she took off with a smile and
an expression of anticipation. There had been quite a change
in Janice since Jeannie had started coming three times a week
to cat-sit for Nellie, which was actually equivalent to Nellie-
sitting for Janice. Jeannie's salary was a small gift that I gave
Nellie. I hadn't planned it as a present for them both, but it's
nice it worked out that way.

I took the box of chocolates on upstairs. After I'd told Nellie
all about Melody Steinwale, at least the part that I knew, she
licked the sticky chocolate truffle off her fingers, rocked herself
briskly back and forth in her wheelchair, and said, "She reminds me of Hope Dodson. I went to school with Hope, back

in the twenties. Her daddy had run off with another woman when Hope was eight. Hope spent all her time looking for her daddy. I don't mean her real daddy, I mean anybody who'd be her daddy. She had no use for boys. She wanted men. She made up to a doctor for a while, but when his wife ran her off, she got involved with a lawyer about twenty years older than she was."

"I don't see the similarity, Nellie."

"Well, they got married. And she never got pregnant. And her husband was so nice about it, saying it was probably his fault they couldn't. But I knew it was because that doctor had given her some kind of cap—not a diaphragm, something else —to keep from it. That doctor's nurse was my sister-in-law, that's how I knew. We figured out why Hope was that way. Because she was the little girl, don't you see? If she had a baby, she'd have to grow up, and she didn't ever want to."

I had a few fleeting thoughts about a female Peter Pan. "The woman at the gallery says Melody could really spend money," I said.

"More of the same," said Nellie, push-pulling at her chair, back and forth. "Money takes care of you, too. Money and the right kind of shepherd dogs and horses and men, we always used to say. They'll take care of you. Best is a nice older man with money. Sugar daddy is what we used to call somebody like that when I was a girl. I'll bet this artist was her sugar daddy."

Gregory Steinwale was eight or nine years older than Melody, not nearly old enough to be her father. Still, he seemed a lot older, while she'd had a nubile quality. I gave Nellie high marks for perspicacity, as usual. Grale and Melody could have looked almost like father and daughter, and who knows what roles they had played to one another. I had known couples where one of them played the parent most of the time. Still . . . "He didn't have money, Nellie! His mother did."

"Well, you can bet his wife used him to get money out of his mama, then. Bet you anything she spent it faster than he could paint it and his mama kept having to help." She rocked and peeked in the chocolate box, teasing herself, finally giving in and taking another one. "You know, Jason, it's like that old saying. It's a wise child knows his own father. All these little girls looking for their daddies, picking the wrong ones or maybe not knowing them when they show up." She nodded, pleased with herself. Her cat, Perky, came out of the closet and jumped up in Nellie's lap. Perky had been a gift from me, one that suited both cat and old lady.

"I've seen that big cat you've got," Nellie said, scratching under Perky's chin. "Where did you get that monster thing?"

She knew Grace, so we talked Grace and cats until Jeannie Rudolph showed up. Before I left, I promised to bring Critter over so Nellie could get a closer look.

The next stop was at Jacob's place. Francis Fairweather, Jacob's male nurse, opened the door to my knock.

"How is he, Francis?"

"Doing better this week," he told me. Jacob had a stroke a few years back, and he had good and bad days, often perking up with the weather. I handed over my gifts. Jacob likes double cream, soft semi-ripened cheeses, and he's a tiger for caviar, so I'd brought some of each.

I told Jacob the story of my newest puzzle. He subscribed to *Art & Antiques*, and we dug out the article on Grale for him to review.

"I read this when it came out," he said. "I thought at the time we had another Hockney."

The styles were similar. Not derivative, merely similar. A lot of very bright color. A similar use of diagrammatic landscapes, though Grale's were less spontaneous, more controlled, and he eschewed the bright magenta Hockney used a lot of.

"He's good," Jacob said. "He's making a name for himself."

"Now that he's out of the mental hospital," I agreed. "He wouldn't have made much of a name for himself in there."

Jacob sighed. "I've always thought that genius and madness were close kin. I always told myself to be thankful I had neither of them."

He laughed. I laughed. Francis brought in some toast and butter and chopped egg. We had caviar on toast. We had cheese. Jacob really was looking a lot better.

"So what do you do next?" he wanted to know.

I shook my head at him, not sure. "I need to know more about them. Why they were as they were. I thought I'd go down to Grale's studio. It's open to the public. His new girlfriend manages it for him."

"That sounds like a good idea," he said with a satisfied little sigh, his eyes sagging closed. Over his shoulder, Francis grinned at me. Jacob had eaten himself into a nap.

Back at my place, I came in the door just in time to catch the phone: Grace, with her voice full of suppressed emotion. I couldn't tell whether she was trying not to cry or trying not to scream.

"Jason, I've called the personnel office down at the department, and I'm taking all my accumulated leave."

I gulped. "Lord, Gracie, is it that bad?"

"It's that bad. My stupid, stupid brother got himself mixed up with some real rotten people. He's in for drug trafficking, Jason! He's only an accessory, they know that. But they think he can tell them something, and he can't. At least, I don't think he can. If he could, he would have told me. Unless he's dumber than ever before. Oh, God, Jason," she yelled, "I am not being at all professional, and this is such a *mess.*"

I could see her, her eyes squinched shut, tears at the lashes, shouting at me. "Grace, do you want me to come out there."

"Would you? Would you really, Jason? That's so nice. That's really nice. No. I don't want you to. There's nothing you can do, and I'd only feel guilty taking you away from business when there's nothing. I'm just going to stay here until I get Ron sorted out."

"Do you need any money?"

"The rent on Ron's apartment here is paid through the end of the month and it's one of those places that get the last month as a deposit, so next month is paid, too. I'm living there. He had a roommate, but the guy moved out when all this came down. If I need some, I'll call, okay? Will you go by my place just to check? If I'm still here the first of the month, will you or Mark collect from the tenants for me? Will you keep Critter?"

I told her I'd do anything she needed doing. I said I'd keep Critter. I asked her if she was sure this was the right thing to do.

"Jason," she cried, "it's family. When it's one of your own, you have to do everything you can. You know that. You can't just stand around and let people ruin your family."

I had no family anymore except for Jacob, but I agreed with her. When I hung up, I felt alone and sorry for her and sorrier for me. Not that we were an indivisible twosome. We weren't. Grace had let me know in a very gentle way that she didn't think I was ready for that kind of relationship. She hinted that she thought I needed more time to get used to the idea that Agatha was dead, and that was possibly part of her real reason. Though Agatha had disappeared eight years ago, I had only found out last January that she had been murdered by people she and I knew, people who were playing a part, people who sympathized when she disappeared, who acted like ordinary people until the day came when someone killed them both. My son, who had been injured when Agatha disappeared, died soon after we found out about his mother.

Grace was partially right about all that. It had been sad, and I probably had needed some time to adjust to the realities. I'd mourned a lot over both of them, however, and it was time to get on with life. I believe Grace's real reason was that she was afraid I'd compare her with Agatha at some point. Agatha had been beautiful. Grace didn't think she was. Agatha had been a college graduate. Grace hadn't gone to college. Agatha had been an artist. Grace was a cop. Grace saw herself at the short end of any comparison, even though I didn't. I was letting things ride. Either she'd straighten it out for herself or I'd have to figure out some way to let her know there were no comparisons. Not any.

Be that as it might, I didn't want to spend Saturday night worrying over it, or Sunday either. I couldn't very well call Mark for company while he was grieving over his absent lover. Almost everyone I knew was part of a couple. Finally, I called Nina Hough. Nina was, as might be supposed, busy that evening. Discoing, she said, with an artist from out of town. She was free on Sunday, however, and we made a date for lunch and to catch the new exhibit at the Art Museum. Busman's holiday. That still left Saturday night.

The Ogden Theater was having a Kurasawa festival. I went to that, alone. Four hours later, overdosed on pageantry and Round the Corner hamburgers with avocados and barbecue sauce, I made it to bed. Critter curled up in the middle of my back and purred. I thought it was nice of Grace, and the very least she could have done, to have arranged for the substitute.

I was just leaving to pick Nina up at noon on Sunday when Mark came zipping up the stairs, face pink and healthy-looking, eyes shining. I hadn't seen him smiling like that in weeks!

"You found out something," I said unnecessarily. He was only waiting to catch his breath before he told me.

"Found a guy," he said. "About forty-five, forty-eight. Good-looking guy. Has a whole floor in that high-rise condo just past Thirteenth? The new one? The one with the lanais?"

I told him I knew which one.

"His name is Ambler. Neal Ambler. He's something in oil. And he knew Melody. From the way I read him, he knew her pretty well."

"What makes you think so?"

Mark considered this. "The way he talked about her. Very

knowingly. He said things like 'her bitch of a mother-in-law.'
And 'Her husband never understood the kid, of course.' "

"Whoop-de-do," I said.

"Yeah, that's the way I felt."

"Did he express wonder at your interest?"

"Well, Jason, what I did was, I gave him the impression you
were looking into her death for the family. I told him you'd be
in touch with him. I didn't . . . well, I didn't say what business you were in."

I thought about that. I *was* looking into Fred's death for *his*
family. Melody was part of the same puzzle, or so I believed, so
one could say I was looking into Melody's murder for *a* family.
A small change from that to *the* family. Make it the definite
article. "Right," I said. "When I meet Mr. Ambler, I'm not
necessarily an antiques dealer or decorator and I'm looking
into it for the family."

"I wandered around and asked people for a couple of hours.
Several people remember her, used to see her, even spoke to
her, but he's the only one I've found so far who actually knew
her. He says he used to talk to her during their morning dog
walks. He has a Kerry blue. Big thing. It growled at me when I
tried to pet it."

"I've heard Kerries are one-man dogs," I replied absently,
focusing on something else he'd said. "Melody had a dog?"

"Ambler mentioned her collie. Why?"

"The papers didn't say anything about a dog. Was she walking the dog the morning she got killed?"

He shrugged. We stared at each other for a moment, then he
went home and I went to pick up Nina, which soon made me
forget all about the question of Melody's dog.

Nina and I fought about art, not with any rancor but contin-
ually, starting with lunch and without surcease during the museum visit. Her taste and mine were not so much diametrically
opposed as they were antithetical. She liked the kind of thing

she showed at the gallery. Fine. I could take some of it, even like some of it. However, I could also like twelfth-century church art and craft pottery and half a dozen other things Nina cast aside as part of an outmoded canon. With her it was the cutting edge or nothing. Despite the fact that we knew within an hour that we would never be able to share any aspect of our lives except purely social ones, we had fun. I was almost getting used to having fun again.

Our day together was both enjoyable and late: enjoyable enough that we finished up the afternoon at a pizza place, and late enough that when I got home the animals complained about neglect. There's always dog kibble and cat kibble available, so they weren't starving. As is customary, the dog eats the cat kibble and vice versa. They get good stuff in the evening, however, and that's what they were waiting for: people food. Since I'd been with Nina, not Grace, there had been leftover pizza, and I'd brought it home.

Along about nine-thirty the doorbell rang.

Marty O'Toole was on my doorstep, leaning against the door, very pale-faced, his eyes, as Mrs. Opinsky used to say, "like two holes burned in a blanket." He was carrying a crumpled paper sack.

"You're the guy I talked to in Boulder the day before yesterday? The one who took me home?" His eyes were so red, I wondered that he could see me at all.

I said I was the man. I hadn't told him my name at any point. I asked him how he found me.

"Jerome Needleman," he said. "Jerome K. Needleman. He has one of those what-you-call-it memories. He remembered your license number."

Jerome must have been one of the men who helped me carry him upstairs. "You went down to the vehicle license bureau and paid your two dollars?" I suggested. "They told you who I was?"

He nodded and gulped. "Listen, could I come in?"

I led him up the stairs, past the offices to the living room, and suggested we both have some coffee. He nodded with a miserably sick expression on his face, and I told him where the bathroom was before I went to make coffee. I heard the toilet flush, then water running. When I got back from the kitchen, he looked a little better. The front of his hair was wet.

"I am so hung over you wouldn't believe it," he said.

I told him I would believe it.

He drank coffee. I drank coffee. After a while, he said, "From what I remember, you were asking about Freddy For-it. Old Jerome K. says you saw the gun."

"Yes, I saw that you had a gun."

"I didn't kill him, honest."

I told him I'd have called the police if I'd thought he had. Not that I was sure he hadn't, just that I didn't think he had.

"I wanted to," he admitted. "If I hadn't been so drunk, I would have. That bastard. He was such a freaking bastard. You have no idea!"

"Why him, more than the others? Simmons is on the committee, isn't he?"

"Simmons is just ignorant. How he ever got a doctorate, only his keeper knows. But Freddy For-it, damn him, he knows he's destroying people."

"Why him?" I pressed. "Why Fred?"

"Because of what the bastard did," he said. "First, the committee shot me down. He was only one of them, maybe the most important one, but only one. But then afterward, he called me. He wanted to meet with me. Said he thought he could improve my 'standing in the academic community.' I hate guys that talk about the 'academic community' as though it was something real! But I said all right, why not. Maybe the guy has had second thoughts about the reaming he'd given me."

"When was this?"

"I don't know. Last week. Ten days maybe. What's today?

Never mind, it doesn't matter. So, since Freddy For-it is retired from the university, he borrows old Simmons's office and I went there. He sits there with this prissy expression on his face, being kind. He says he believes I am fundamentally an intelligent young man. He thinks he can help me. He thinks I've just been badly taught at MIT. He talks about my professor there, what a nut he is, what a weird reputation he has, how he can't blame me for 'having a crush on someone who seems messianic.' All of which is true. The guy is a nut case, I do admire him, he is messianic, but he's also right! He's eccentric and he's a genius. . . ." He gulped at his coffee, burning his tongue, waving his hand to cool himself before spewing out words again, as though they were bullets.

"Here's Freddy at this puking state university, got on the faculty by bribery, which everyone knows, not even on the faculty anymore, ignorant as a tuna, about as much of a physicist as I am a paperhanger, and he talks in this patronizing way about a guy who's a genius. So anyhow, Freddy For-it goes on about anyone who knows anything in the field knows that the only way to do things is the way they've been doing them for forty years. And he quotes me this guy, and that guy, none of whom have made any progress since the sixties. They're still doing their damned calculations to more and more decimal places, and they still can't tell you what the numbers mean or if they mean anything.

"So, okay, I ask him how he can help me. Well, he says, I should take some of Simmons's courses. He can give me a reading list. I mean, look, Jason—can I call you Jason?—here this guy is, he doesn't know anything about what I do, he hasn't bothered to read up on my field, and he sits there with this fatherly, superior smile and tells me I should go back to being an undergraduate!

"So I tried to tell him. I told him what they're doing at MIT. I told him what they're doing at Oxford. I told him we can predict outcomes. I had a bunch of stuff with me, and I dug out a bibliography for him. I had some reprints, a couple where I'm even one of the authors, you know? And he smiles, and he smiles, and finally, when my batteries run down, he says, 'But, Marty, this can't be more than superficially interesting because it's based on error.'

"What error? I ask him.

"It has to be error, he says, because it wasn't done the right way. Which, as you may have guessed by now, is the way he and his friends do it!"

"He hadn't read any of your material?" I asked.

"Not a word. It was like arguing with some guy who comes to your door and wants to talk about the Bible. No matter what you say, he has some answer from the Bible, and you have to be wrong because what you're saying isn't in his damned book!"

"So then?" I asked.

"So then I told him I'd just have to go to some other university where people cared a little less about how they'd always done things and a little more about reality. And he says . . . he says a bunch of stuff. About men like him with over twenty years' investment in their careers. About giving up kith and kin in order to serve science. About young tomcats rampaging around ruining other people's lives. About he knows exactly how I feel, senses my keen disappointment, how he's an expert in est and could have told me how to deal with my feelings if I'd been halfway respectful. . . ."

"And . . ." Somehow I just knew there was more. What he'd told me so far, no matter how awful, was not enough.

"And, he said, since I'd come across as intransigent and disrespectful—get that, like I was some kid in military school—he says wherever I go, he'll know somebody there and he'll write to them and tell them they shouldn't give me any support, and just in case they do, he'll also write to his old buddies at the DOD and tell the DOD to blacklist whatever school I'm at.

God, do you know how much research money comes from the DOD? Can you imagine what kind of weight they swing?"

I sipped coffee, thinking. "In other words, he promised you a vendetta?"

"Exactly. That's a hell of a good word. He promised me a vendetta. He did it with this expression of kindly concern on his face, and behind it he was so angry he was shaking. I saw his hands, and they were white around the knuckles. I thought the guy was going to hit me, but he didn't. Instead, he talked about the mystical purposes of life and came damned close to saying it was for my own good. That's probably the only cliché he didn't use!"

"Do you think he could have done what he threatened to do?"

"Oh, he'd have tried. What I don't know is whether anybody would have listened to him. I don't know how many old cronies he's got at the DOD. Considering the puking state of science in the U.S. right now, he's probably got some and they're probably running things."

"And you'd like to have killed him."

"Oh, man, would I." He sighed, tears in his eyes. "But I didn't."

I thought about it for a while. "You know, Marty," I said at last, "you're right about one thing. Our university has a reputation, as I understand it, for being a good place to go if you ski, party, play football, or drink a lot of beer. It is not known as a bastion of independent thought, high scholarship, or research achievement. Why did you come here?"

"I grew up here," he said. "I love it here. I was naïve, I guess."

I shook my head at him. "If I were you, I'd go back to MIT."

"Don't I know it," he said, head in his hands. "Or a couple of other places I can think of."

I refilled his coffee cup and asked him if he'd like a sandwich.

He would. I made him one. He ate it, and we chatted, about other things. I told him I wouldn't say anything to the police, not yet, especially if he didn't plan to leave town soon.

"Are you kidding? I've got this term to finish and it's paid for! I can't afford to run out on a whole semester's credits. The credits will be good for something, somewhere. . . ."

"Where'd you get the gun?" I asked him.

"My dad's," he confessed. "After he and Mom died, I put it in a box with some of my stuff. I dug it out after that meeting I told you about. It was already loaded."

So. A fellow orphan. That, in and of itself, was enough to make me feel kindly toward him. "Either put it somewhere safe or learn how to use it," I said sententiously, thinking that drunks and loaded handguns were a very bad combination. "Your friend Needleman almost shot me in the lower torso."

"I brought the gun to you," he said, fishing around on the couch for the paper bag he had carried in. He was sitting on it. "Needleman said you knew how to handle it. I figured you'd keep it for me." He looked sheepish. "I don't manage frustration real well, and maybe I shouldn't have it around."

After Martin O'Toole left me, I put his gun away in the iron safe in the basement. Jacob had the safe installed to keep working capital in, but then Jacob liked the feeling of money in the house. I don't, so I've never used the big box for anything except my own handguns. They've been there for years, and Marty's revolver would be safe enough in their company. I considered firing it into an old mattress, then digging the bullet out and sending it anonymously to the police, but it would be easier to wait until Grace got back. She could credit an "informant," and nobody would push her too hard to know who. Besides, she'd told me not to do anything yet.

As I was dozing off, I tried to remember if I'd ever been as young as Marty O'Toole. Young enough to go get drunk as a response to crisis. Not that only young people do that, just that it's always seemed to me to be a thing kids do. Maybe I'd never really been a kid.

The next day would be Monday. I wasn't in favor of it.

Mrs. Richard Duchesne, whom I did not know, called me at seven-thirty on Monday morning, on my private line, which is unlisted, almost in tears, telling me she had to have her guest suite done over within the next ten days. Finished, completed, within the next ten days.

I demurred. I said I preferred not to do interior decoration except period rooms or as ancillary to the sale of antiques. She cried. Her daughter was getting married. The groom's parents were coming to visit next week and the guest rooms were wrong, all wrong, and she didn't know what was the matter with them. And Mrs. Duchesne's brother had told her to call me. Mrs. Duchesne's brother was Mr. Utterly Powerful, the vice president and loan officer of the very same bank from which I had borrowed a great deal of money at very high interest for a very short time.

I told her I would be over as soon as possible after breakfast.

When I arrived, she took me upstairs, talking incessantly. The suite had been done not long ago. She'd been very happy with it. Now she just knew it was all wrong. Something was wrong. She thought something was wrong, maybe she was mistaken, and it wasn't wrong but it looked . . .

The suite consisted of a small sitting room with fireplace, a sizable bedroom with walk-in closet, and an adjoining bath. I stood there looking at it, trying not to howl.

"You had it decorated a year ago," I said.

She said she had.

I told her who'd done it. "Either him or so-and-so," I said.

She admitted to one of them and wanted to know how I knew.

When she asked, I was standing in the door to the bedroom. From where I stood I could not see one square inch of unencumbered surface except on the floor, and space was at a premium there. There were two bedside tables with floor-length geometric-print cloths on them in various shades of brown, almost brown, and quite brown. Each table supported a tiny lamp with an opaque black shade. In addition, between them they held a pair of marble bookends, three leather-bound books by Dinesen, an ostrich egg in a gilt stand, a turned ebony vase with ostrich plumes in it, two carved ebony animals—lion and giraffe—an ivory(?)-framed tinted etching of someone with his foot on a lion—presumably dead—and a collection of little boxes covered in different kinds of faux animal skins: a zebra box, an alligator box, a tiger box. I went over and turned one of the lamps on. A forty-watt bulb cast a dim, conical glow downward.

The queen-sized bed was a heavy four-poster. Draped oh so casually and artistically over the top of the posts, à la mosquito netting, were a dozen yards of filmy white fabric. The chairs on either side of the bed were an undistinguished rattan upholstered in yet another brown. In the corners of the room were wicker baskets, campaign chests, folding canvas chairs, and more than sufficient other stuff to give the impression the safari hadn't quite unpacked yet. Any space not occupied by this impedimenta was filled by potted palm trees, presumably fake since the rooms faced north and there was insufficient light for real ones. The wall around the Georgian fireplace had been covered with plastic wallpaper in a bamboo texture. More carvings and a few spears on the wall drove the point home. Welcome to the Dark Continent. I sighed.

She heard me. "It *is* wrong, isn't it? What's wrong?" She faltered.

I tried to speak gently. "Mrs. Duchesne, let us suppose that your future in-laws retire for the night. Let us suppose that Mrs. What's-her-name . . ."

"Mifflin."

"Let us suppose that Mrs. Mifflin likes to read in bed before she goes to sleep."

My client nodded doubtfully, as though she could scarcely imagine anyone wanting to read at any time, much less at bedtime.

"She has a book. Let us suppose also that she needs to blow her nose. She has a package of tissues. Let us suppose she needs to take an aspirin. She has a bottle of water and a glass. Where does she put any of these things and how in heaven's name does she see to use any of them?"

She stared at the tiny laden tables and their contents, her face turning an ugly red. "He said little lamps were cozy. He said lots of things carried out the theme and made the room look lived in."

"If you lived in this room, you would have a hundred watts on each side of the bed and you'd have put all that junk on the tables somewhere else by now. You would also have thrown out those tables and replaced them with others with larger surfaces and at least one drawer to hold a box of tissues and a book. You'd have a luggage rack in the corner instead of all that useless junk, because your guests will have suitcases." I gave her my "I am very much annoyed but I understand you were misled" look, the one I'd learned from Eugenia.

I sat on the bed. At least it was all right, comfortably firm. When I stood up, the draped material caught me around the forehead and ears, shedding dust all over my dark jacket.

I snarled, "Also, the first time you got out of bed in the dark, stood up, and wrapped your face in six yards of dusty fabric, you'd get rid of that." The dust was inevitable. No cleaning person of my acquaintance would do anything more than shake a duster at it, or at best a vacuum attachment. It probably wouldn't be taken down, washed, and artfully rearranged any oftener than maybe once a year.

Aside from the African "decor," the whole room was depressingly brown and brown and brown. The carpet was that tan color that looks dirty even when it's brand-new. Aside from everything else the place needed, the touristy African junk should be carted out and buried. I had tallied up the separate jobs in my head. We needed a painter, a wallpaper hanger —unless we got Maggie, who could do both—a carpet layer, a slipcover and drapery seamstress, someone to take the ordinary but well-made rattan chairs down to the spray-paint place, a mover to get rid of the old stuff, plus two or three people at my end to get everything picked out and delivered to the right people in time to get it done in ten days. I could be done. It wasn't a large enough job to make the prospect attractive, but it could be done. I considered briefly whether it might not be possible and preferable to get a loan at some other bank.

I shook off the urge to howl, explained what had to be done, told her the minimum it would cost, and got a budget figure out of her. She wanted everything green. I told her green was out. There was no green, and hadn't been for four years and wouldn't be for four more years. We are between greens. We are at the end of mauve, violet, gray, and thank God for that. My best guess is that we are in for a period of saturated, so-called tropical colors: coral, mustard, and hot pink. She said coral and cream and maybe violet, and we went with that. We agreed on re-covering the love seats and painting the rattan and re-covering the bed. What would replace the tables would depend on what I could find immediately available. "We are not," I told her pontifically, "New York."

She suddenly wanted to argue. She'd seen some tables at a friend's. She really liked them.

"What's the number one priority?" I asked her.

"Getting it done on time," she admitted.

"Then we go with what we can get, not with something we'd need to order months in advance," I said sternly, hoping to heaven she wouldn't make difficulties.

I measured windows, walls, and furniture and told her Mark and I would be out that afternoon with samples, not to leave home under any circumstances. She bridled in a put-upon fashion, and I decided to add fifteen percent over my usual charges for annoyance. I never would have gone into this business except for Jacob, and sometimes I wonder whether it's any way to earn a living. Whenever I visualize myself as something else, however, I have trouble taking it seriously. Jason Lynx, the Used-Car Salesman. Jason Lynx, the Insurance Man. Actually, at one time it had been planned as Jason Lynx, the Art Historian, or Jason Lynx, the Museum Director, but all such roles faded when Jacob had his first stroke and needed me to come home. As close to home as I'd ever had, at any rate.

By three o'clock Mark and I had samples and Polaroid pictures of the tables that were available, including a pair of slightly restored, very nice Portsmouth, New Hampshire, birch end tables, c. 1800, I happened to have at the shop. By four we were back with Mrs. Duchesne, who, forbidden to leave the house, had had frequent recourse to the premixed margaritas.

Margaritas made her happy. She had another one to mark our arrival, offering Mark and me the pitcher. We smiled and refused. She continued cheerful. Indecisive, but cheerful. It took until six to get the necessary decisions out of her and her name on the dotted line. I got a door key as well and told her to forget everything. It would all be taken care of. We went back to the shop. There was still work to do before we collapsed.

Mark was busy with his notebook. "Fabric order tomorrow if you can get Myron to expedite. The one she picked is stocked from New York, and we can fly it in."

"The seamstress needs five days," I said. "Not counting weekends." We talked about timing and getting everything scheduled. I crossed my fingers, hoping we could get people in time.

"Go over the scheme with Eugenia and ask her to find a couple of really nice little things," I said, yawning. "*Only* a couple. Maybe we can use that porcelain clock with the flowers on it. . . ."

"What's her first name?" Mark asked. "Mrs. Duchesne's."

"Gladys," I told him. "Don't forget to arrange for someone to take all that stuff out."

"Pity she didn't do it right the first time."

"She didn't think in terms of anyone staying there," I said. "Just of people looking at it. You know, she says to her visitors, 'Would you like to see the house? This is the guest suite.' And everyone oohs and aahs. She's never actually had anyone stay in it. Well, we'll have it comfortable by the time the Mifflins arrive. The groom's parents are to be suitably impressed."

"This is not our kind of job! Why are we doing this?" he asked with aristocratic distaste. Mark was also in the business because of an interest in fine furniture as art, an interest he could have fully explored with his own resources. He had chosen to work at it instead, and I gave him a good deal of credit for that.

I explained about money and bankers and loans, and Mark made an appropriate face. Annoyance and apprehension, nicely mixed. No awe. Not Mark. His family has too much money for that.

"Shower curtain," he sighed. "There's no shower enclosure in that bathroom."

"We'll find one," I promised. "Or have one made. Or something. Towels, too, but they're the least of our problem."

He said good night. I said good night. Bela whined from the door where he'd been sitting. When I got to the kitchen, Critter was sitting there looking disgustedly at his empty dish. We all went out for Kentucky Fried Chicken—thighs for me, breasts (which I deboned) for my friends. Score for the day: a living earned, if you can call it that, food on the table, but not one damned thing done on the puzzle.

Once Mark and Eugenia had been pointed in the right direction, I left the Duchesne job up to them. It was mostly a case of seeing that things got where they were needed. I called Myron and asked him personally to pick up the fabric and put it on the plane. He said he would. He wouldn't, but one of his assistants (read: brothers-in-law) would, which was good enough. Then I cleared the Tuesday afternoon decks and told everyone I was going to be out.

Mark gave me a questioning look.

"Grale's studio," I said.

He went discontentedly back to his cajoling conversation with the upholsterer.

Grale's studio was on the top floor of an old warehouse down on Lawrence Street, part of a row of remodeled turn-of-the-century buildings given a new lease on life by private entrepreneurs who found they could buy cheaply, renovate inexpensively, rent at fairly low rates, and still make a frugal buck. Of course, seeing them do it led later and greedier owners to assume they could charge an arm and a leg for the buildings and someone would still buy them. Wrong assumption. Renovation in the area has pretty well stopped as a result. There are lots of For Sale signs and not much traffic.

I walked up two flights. The door was open. Inside was a room with a couch and chair. It had a tiny kitchen along one side wall next to a door leading into a bathroom and another one leading into a tiny bedroom. A glass wall separated this living area from the studio below: lofty space with a skylight and a row of tall north windows. Pictures hung on the walls in both areas. Gregory Steinwale was down in the studio with his back to me, working on a picture of two women, a wicker chaise, and a potted palm. The chaise and the palm and one of the women were in front of him. Trish was his model. I recognized her from Nina's description. She saw me, said something to Grale, then got up and came up the stairs and through the glass door, a slight, graceful figure with a mind-melting smile.

"May I help you?"

I told her I knew Nina. I told her Nina had told me to introduce myself to Trish and had also told me what a truly fine artist Gregory Steinwale was. I gave her my card.

She warmed up immediately, glad to meet me because I knew Nina, wasn't Nina a wonderful person, so full of life, so knowledgeable! She offered me coffee or a soft drink (I accepted coffee), got out a sheaf of exhibition information on Grale's works, directed my attention to the walls and to a fat notebook on the table, and then sat down across from me, happily waiting to see what I'd do next.

What I did was look down into the studio. Greg hadn't turned, even when she left. His eyes had remained fixed on the canvas. No, not his eyes. His whole body. Hands, feet, legs, arms, head, even torso seemed somehow bent and focused on the painting. When his hand moved, it moved as though directed by his whole self, like an attachment moved by a huge robot. He was working on the face of one of the women, almost an abstract shape against the background. "He doesn't do portraits, does he?" I asked, noting the lack of detail.

"He can," she said. "Actually, he can do fine portraits. But what he's interested in right now is the sculptural qualities of human figures."

"A nose is a nose is a nose," I offered.

She giggled. It was a nice giggle. "I think that's sort of it. People as compositions, not people as individuals."

"I'm glad to see he's working so well," I said. "Nina told me he'd had a rough time, been hospitalized for a while. We have too few good artists to be able to spare any."

She nodded, soberly, not offering any comment.

"Did you know him then?" I probed in my kindliest voice.

"No," she said. "I met him after that."

I let the silence alone.

"We're getting married. I suppose Nina mentioned that?"

"She did say something like that." I gave her my best boyish grin, the one that makes Willamae and Nellie open up. "Nina said he'd had a hard time with his wife. His first wife."

"I guess she . . . his first wife. Melody." She stopped, giving me a slightly suspicious glance. "Did you know her, Mr. Lynx?"

"No," I said, surprised, letting it show. "And please call me Jason. We're both Nina's friends, so we're friends of each other, right?"

She flushed. "That would be nice, and I didn't mean to be . . . It's just that I hear about Melody knowing so many . . ."

"Men," I said in a sympathetic tone. "Nina told me about that."

The comment overcame her reticence and she leapt to Greg's defense. "But it wasn't that she slept around. Even Greg says that. She didn't sleep around that much. It was just that she kept . . . collecting them. Older men, mostly."

I nodded thoughtfully. "Why do you suppose she did that?" I asked.

"Looking for her father, I guess," Trish said. "According to Greg, that's what she was doing. He's explained to me very carefully that he was never jealous because he understood what she was doing. Evidently her father deserted her when Melody was an infant and Melody kept trying to find him, or a substitute." She bit her lip. "Why am I telling you this? This isn't why you came."

I smiled noncommittally, taking my mental hat off to Nellie Arpels. Bull's-eye! "In a way it *is* why I came," I said, sitting back and sipping. "I won't repeat what you say to me. I'm not a gossip, but I am sincerely interested in puzzles and mysteries, and Melody is—or was—both. Nina told me about her. She died mysteriously, and I'm trying to figure out why."

"You don't think Greg . . ."

"No," I assured her. "I don't think Greg. I don't think her death had anything to do with Greg. It's just a mystery. Call it an intellectual exercise. Did Melody think her real father was here in Denver?"

With the caveat that I wasn't going to involve Greg, she seemed to regard my interest as acceptable, if not totally legitimate. "From what Nina said, Melody's mother died when she was born. She lived with her aunt, and the aunt said Melody's father came from Englewood, Colorado."

"What was Melody's maiden name?"

Trish thought for a while. "I'm not sure either Nina or Greg ever . . . No. I remember. Harriet said it. She was talking about Melody once, and she said, 'Greg should never have married Melody Maudlin.' But then, Harriet believes Melody drove Greg into that hospital."

"What do you think?"

She flushed again. "I think she probably did. Well, she drove him to the point of a breakdown." She stood up, stared through the window intently, sat back down. "You see how he works, so intent, so very concentrated? He needs quiet to do that. According to Harriet, she was always at him. About everything. Harriet used to buy him clothes, and Melody didn't like them, so she fussed at him all the time about what he wore. They lived with Harriet, and Melody didn't like that. She was always complaining about the way Harriet had decorated the place, or about something Harriet said."

"Mothers-in-law," I said sympathetically. Not that I'd ever had one. Agatha's mother had died long before we were married.

"No," she said. "It wasn't that. Harriet's an old bat, she says so herself, but she's a nice old bat. She's opinionated, and she has a right to be. She's over sixty years old. She has a right to have her own property the way she wants it. She even bought the gallery so Melody would have something to do, but Nina says all Melody did was pout or have a tantrum whenever Harriet tried to teach her anything about business, or threaten to fire Nina when Nina did." She turned back to me, her face pink, her mouth angry. "That's not fair. Nina's a good person, and she breaks her neck working in that place. When I was there, I saw how hard she works. I guess Melody couldn't deal with just being a grown-up workaday person. Everything had to be personal with her. Instead of getting to work and doing the job, she kept getting her feelings hurt."

"Doesn't sound like a good bet to manage a business."

She shook her head. "I'm extrapolating. I could be wrong. I get so . . . so *mad* sometimes when I hear things about her because I know what she did to Greg, even though he always makes excuses for her. He doesn't talk that much about her, so I'm putting things together that he's said and that his mother has said and things that Nina tells me. The way I understand it, Harriet finally gave up trying to teach her anything, backed off, and just left the gallery alone. It's a pity, too, because Harriet would have been good for Melody if she could have just accepted there being someone else in Greg's life. She was good for me. If it hadn't been for Harriet, I wouldn't have met Greg."

"She hired you to work at the gallery?"

She refilled my coffee cup. "That was really funny. I hadn't worked since I graduated from college. I got married. I had a baby. My husband and I, jointly, decided I'd stay home until our child . . . or children . . . were in school. Then the accident happened, and suddenly I was a widow with a baby girl. Burt, my husband, was very responsible about insurance and there were benefits from his job, so I had enough to get by on for quite a few years if I went to work and if I was careful, but I did need to get a job. So, as soon as I felt I could, when Frosty was a little older, I started looking. Right away I saw this ad."

"Harriet ran an ad?"

"Right. It said she wanted a working mother between the ages of twenty-five and thirty with a college education who knew something about business. And it said to enclose a photo. How about that?" She got up and stood at the glass wall, looking down at the man hunched before the canvas.

"Did you know something about business?"

"My family had a paint business, back in Chicago. I worked there as a kid, and during summer vacations. I knew about inventory and invoices, and how you keep books. Things like that. So I sent in my picture and my résumé, and she called me up. Took me to lunch." She spoke to the glass, not to me. Our reflections swam dimly in it, like ghosts.

"And hired you."

"And hired me. Took me over to the gallery that afternoon and told Nina I was her new help."

"Nina said she was surprised."

"Nina was mad, to tell you the truth. It was two days before she simmered down enough to get to know me. We got along fine, though, once she found out I really meant to work."

"And then . . ."

"And then Harriet visited me at home. That was kind of a shock, but she and Frosty hit it off—Frosty's three years old. Martha Frost. Frost was my mother's maiden name. Then Harriet invited me to dinner, and I met Greg, and a week or so later, here I was helping him instead of working at the gallery. And a month or so later, he asked me to marry him. Sort of diffidently, between brushstrokes." She turned from the window.

I was staring at her. She caught the look, returned it, then looked away, reading my mind.

"Do you get the feeling . . . ?" I started to ask.

"That I was handpicked? Oh, yes, I sure do. I'd have had to be blind not to see what she was doing. The first time I saw a picture of Melody, I knew exactly what Harriet was doing. She was being a meddling mother. You'd have to know Greg to understand, but I don't blame her for it one bit." She turned back to the studio, peering at the concentrated stance, the wild hair of her fiancé. Her feelings were plain in her face.

"You love him, hmm?"

After a moment she said, almost in a whisper, "Oh, yeah. Yeah, I really do."

"Does he ever go out? To a movie? To dinner?"

"Sometimes."

"If you'd like, you and Nina could get your heads together and see if you're free this weekend," I suggested. "Let's all go to dinner on me. I'd very much like to meet him."

I left, wishing I knew exactly what tap I'd turned to let all that gush out. As I've said, people often talk to me, people I've just met. Women. Men. Even children. Here in the West, people talk more anyhow. About themselves, their jobs, what they think or believe. When I've been back East I've noticed that people aren't as open or friendly. They're more suspicious, more held in, and yet, even there people talk to me. Sometimes I think people need to talk, and any halfway attentive, sympathetic face will loosen the floodgates. But maybe, and I keep coming back to this thought, it's because of the lack of families. The conversation Trish had just had with me was one she might have had with a sister or her mother if they'd been near enough to talk to. Chances are, her sister or mother is a thousand miles or more away. Which reminded me of Willamae Belling. Which reminded me of Nellie Arpels.

Which reminded me that since I had no mother of my own to fret over, or cuss at, I could possibly do a little something for those ladies. I got out my pocket notebook and made a suggestion to myself.

Since the afternoon was yet young, I decided to see if I could locate the woman Simmons had mentioned, Fred's neighbor, Streeter.

The ground-floor apartment was the manager's. I rang several times before she came to the door. She had just washed her hair. The whole place smelled of shampoo and steam with a faint stench of something I recognized, after a while, as home perm, though I could not imagine where I had smelled it before. Agatha had had naturally curly hair. The manager had bare white arms and a great expanse of pillowy chest above a scoop-necked blouse. She had plump cheeks. She had worms of hair dangling on her forehead, like wet springs. She looked like an old-style Campbell's Soup kid, head wrapped in a towel. I told her I was looking for anyone who had known Fred Foret, like Ms. Streeter. Did she by any chance know Ms. Streeter?

"Sure I know Sally Streeter," she said. "She lived here for over five years. She'd still live here if it wasn't for that prick Foret."

"You didn't like him," I said with great perceptivity.

"You're Sherlock Holmes!" she crowed.

I blushed.

"No, I didn't like him," she said. "I liked Sally. We were friends, her and me. She was ordinary people, just like me, except her husband left her fairly well-off when he died, but she was lonesome, and we used to go to bingo together, and we'd bake stuff for sales at the church. Fred Foret lived across the hall from her, and she used to go over to his place sometimes with a plate of cookies or something. Hell, there's nothing wrong with that."

"I didn't say there was."

"You said you were looking for anybody that knew him. Somebody must've told you she didn't like him."

I took the bull by his figurative horns. "Somebody told me she tried to kill him."

The manager turned her attention to her head, toweling furiously. "Oh, hell, she didn't really mean to kill him. She was mad, though. Hell, I'd've been mad."

"Why was she mad?"

She blushed. "Because he . . . he misled her, that's why. And then, afterward, when she tries to tell him how nice it is to be close to somebody, he tells her not to think she's close to him, because she's not up to his standard."

So Fred had been into seduction. Somehow I could imagine Fred saying that to a woman. It was the kind of thing he said.

"Being frank," he called it. "He said that?" I asked, trying to look doubtful.

She tried to convince me. "He said that and some other stuff. About her not being his intellectual equal, plus some junk about his just trying to be nice to women of 'her age.' So she grabbed her little gun and waved it at him and told him to get out and stay out. Hell, it probably wasn't even loaded."

"She told you this."

"She told me why she had to move out; she was so embarrassed, she didn't want to run into him again. He grabbed the gun and took it away from her and called her a silly bitch. She moved out the end of the month and over to the other side of town, halfway to Lookout Mountain. That was six, eight months ago, now."

"She told you all about the incident?"

"She had to tell somebody. She cried and her face got all puffy and she said she wished she'd killed him, because then when they arrested her, the trial would've at least given her something to do."

"Well, somebody shot him," I said.

"I know somebody did, and good riddance," she said. "But you don't think Sally? Oh, my Lord, no. She wouldn't ever have looked that man in the face again."

"Do you have her address?"

She started to tell me, then shut her mouth, firmly, shaking her head. She told me her lips were sealed and to please leave so she could get her curlers in. I didn't press her. If Sally Streeter hadn't changed her name, I could find her one way or another.

Since I was in the neighborhood, I walked a block down the street to the building Neal Ambler lived in and rang his bell from the lobby. No answer. I jotted a message and dropped it into his box. It had been a day for disclosures. Maybe there was another one who wanted to talk.

There was, but it wasn't Neal Ambler.

Mark was just closing up as I got home, and he asked if I'd mind talking to him for a while. What does one say? No, I didn't mind, I said. But yes, I did mind. I didn't want to share his troubles, but I owed him that much.

We went back upstairs to the living room. I pulled the curtains against the evening gray, telling myself, as I had many times, that I wanted a real home, one that didn't look north, into offices. Not that Agatha hadn't made it look like a real home. The curtains were deep wine. The rug was a Pakistan remake of a Persian pattern, burnt orange and deep blue and wine and cream. Jacob's choice, originally, but Agatha had left it there after we moved in.

I poured us both a drink, and Mark said, "I got a letter from Rudy."

"What did Rudy have to say?"

"He said he's going to get married."

"I didn't know Rudy was bisexual," I blurted, in complete surprise.

"He's not," Mark said. "I don't know who he thinks he's kidding. He says he wants a family." He got up and stalked across the room, one hand working at the back of his neck. Mark is extremely good-looking, and emotion had colored his face. I thought, not for the first time, that he really should be an actor.

I didn't know what to say, so I didn't say anything.

"I told him he should find some lesbian who wants children," he said. "She could have them by AI, he could be a daddy, and neither of them would be disappointed in one another. He says no. He wants a straight woman. He says most lesbians are too angry." He turned back toward me, tears in his eyes. "Jason, what am I going to do?"

How the blazing hell did I know?

Apply common sense, someone said in my head. Some female voice. Agatha maybe. Maybe Grace. Maybe Nellie Arpels. Common sense.

I thought it out as I went. "Mark, I think you'll have to accept that Rudy's desire for a family is natural, that it has nothing to do with you or his feelings for you, and that you can't solve his problems."

"They're my problems, too."

"Not really," I said. "The way you feel is your problem, but Rudy's desire for a family isn't. There's no way you can be involved in that. You can't provide him with children. I suppose it's a little like before there was AI, a woman who wanted babies might leave a man who was sterile. If babies were more important than the man, she would. If the man was more important, she wouldn't."

"I thought I was important," he said brokenly.

"Rudy was raised in an Italian Catholic family," I said. "What is he, about forty?"

"Thirty-nine."

My age. I sat and drank. "This isn't the first time he's left. Six months ago you went through this with him."

"He just went home for a visit is all. He was only gone a few weeks."

"He just went home and realized what home meant," I said. "He measured home against his sexual inclinations and decided which was most important to him. Five years ago, he felt differently. Five years ago, he wasn't pushing forty." I knew how that felt. "I've been thinking a lot about this lately," I said. "Families, I mean. People aren't meant to live alone. People aren't meant to grow old alone. The nuclear family is all well and good, but it means a lot of people are left over."

"I can't even manage a nuclear," he said, trying to laugh.

"I don't know what gays do about families," I said. "I don't know how you plan to grow old. I've always wanted to do it with wife and children and grandchildren. If I had a mother, I'd want her around, and maybe an aunt or a cousin or two. Except for Jacob, I've been alone most of my life, but it wasn't my own choice. To me, family is a very powerful concept. I wouldn't let anyone deprive me of that."

"What if one of your kids turned out to be gay? What if there weren't any grandchildren?"

"Maybe that's what Rudy came up against," I suggested.

"I was thinking of my father," he said. Mark's father hadn't really accepted Mark since he'd found out his son was disinclined to marry and produce an heir.

"Rudy has a father, too, remember. An Italian Catholic father, probably sixty-five or so, and Rudy's the only son. Think about that and you'll know what he's been up against."

"Damn," he said. "Jason, I wanted sympathy, not logic."

"I'm sympathetic. Have another drink."

Since he was so alone, I suggested we have dinner together. We fed the animals, then went down to Cliff Young's and pigged out on pasta and two bottles of wine. He told me all about Rudy, in exhaustive detail; I told him what Trish had said about Melody Steinwale and about needing to find Sally Streeter.

When I got home, there was a message from Neal Ambler, Melody's park friend, on the answering machine.

4

Neal Ambler suggested breakfast. I rose at the crack of dawn
to meet him at Le Peep. He was a broad, friendly-looking man
with steely eyes. If you listened to his mouth, you liked him at
once. If you looked at his eyes, you were careful. I knew those
eyes from somewhere, so I played it close to my chest.

"I don't understand what your authority is in all this," he
said.

"None at all," I confessed cheerfully, taking a large chunk of
omelet to give me something to keep my mouth occupied. I'd
discovered a long time ago that it's hard to read a man while
he's chewing. "I'm looking into the case for family members
who want to augment the police investigation. I'm a complete
amateur. I have no status."

"That's what I mean," he said with a little smile belied by an
ice-cold glance. "She had no family who would want to look
into it. I was probably as close to her as anyone."

"You?" I cocked my head at him, making a question. "She
was a friend of yours?"

He thought about this. "Yeah. I was her friend. About the
only one she had."

"Her husband was deeply grieved at her death," I said.

"Her husband was a nut case who couldn't take care of her,"

he replied. "Grief from somebody like that is about as useful as tits on a bull."

"We might suspect her husband of killing her, of course, except for the fact he was hospitalized at the time."

"Yeah, and his mother was out of the country. That doesn't mean they couldn't have hired someone. Or she could have, the mother, by herself."

"Why would Harriet Steinwale have done that?"

"The Steinwale woman hated Melody."

"Why?"

"Because Melody was young. Because she was beautiful. Because Melody was talented in her painting, and the old woman wasn't willing to have her son share the spotlight."

"You gathered this from things Melody said?"

"Gathered, hell. She right out told me. She said, 'My mother-in-law hates me because I'm young and pretty and her son loves me and I can paint as well as he can.' That's about as clear as you can be."

I remembered Nina's assessment of Melody's talent. "I thought she only took art lessons so she and her husband would talk the same language."

"Maybe that's the way it started. Her teacher told her right off she had a very great talent."

"You saw her work."

"I bought some of her things. I'll take you back to the apartment and show you. Very—uh—mystical." For a moment his eyes were clear and unsuspicious, like a child's. Most people he watched like a dog with a bone, but he had evidently felt differently about Melody. He waved for more coffee, which gave me a minute or two to chew and think.

"Had you known her long?" I asked.

He leaned back, coffee cup cradled in both hands.

"Ten years, more or less. I met her before she ever married that guy. I met her when she started living with Rich."

"Rich?"

"He's an oil buddy of mine. Rich in name and rich in fact, he says. I guess he's right about that. There's guys that make it and lose it, and there's guys that make it and make it. He's one of those. Anyhow, Melody came out here in about, oh, '76? That'd be about right. Nineteen, twenty years old maybe. No money. Not trained to do diddly, you know? She had enough money to last her about two weeks if she'd been smart, and it would have lasted her about three days because she picked the most expensive hotel in town to stay in. Rich picked her up in the bar. She told him she'd come out here to look for her daddy. Rich felt sorry for her, took her home with him, gave her a room, a little salary, told her she could keep books for him. Shit, Rich's got six accountants on full time and needs a little girl bookkeeper like he needs an extra ball. Anyhow, she settled in, and pretty soon he had her playing hostess for him. That's when I met her. Her and me used to talk, about her looking for her daddy and so forth.

"Well, a couple of years went by and I guess she got a little bored. Rich was good to her, but he's been around. He didn't hang around her much, you know what I mean? He expected her to be there when he wanted her and kind of disappear when he didn't. I told Rich that wasn't fair to her—hell, she was just a kid—but he just laughed. You'd have to know him. She asked Rich to pay for her to take some courses, maybe get her college degree. So Rich said sure, honey, go to school if that'll keep you quiet. She started taking these art courses. That's where she met the crazy artist."

"Greg Steinwale."

"Him, yeah. Well, she started sneaking off to spend time with this Steinwale, and after a few months she told Rich she was going to leave him and marry the artist. I told her she was making a mistake, and so did Rich. Hell, anybody could see what she needed was somebody to take care of her, somebody that didn't take her too serious, and anybody short of a hundred percent blind could see the artist couldn't do it! Talk about babes in the woods!"

"So she married Greg."

"That was about '81. She married Greg. He was living in some studio place he had, and Melody wouldn't move in there, so they had to move in with his mama."

"I understood that Mrs. Steinwale offered to buy them a place of their own."

"Well, sure, his mama offered to get them a place, but hell, Melody'd been living pretty good with Rich. Rich has one hell of a nice place. Melody wanted something at least that nice, and the artist couldn't provide it and Mama wouldn't pay for it. Mellie was used to nice things. Clothes. A fur coat. Everything cream and clover. Rich used to kid her about how much she'd spend on clothes Anyhow, so the two of them moved in with the artist's mama, right near the park here, and my place is close by, so we used to talk when we'd run into each other, me with Blue Boy and her with that fat collie dog she had."

"You're telling me she wasn't happy." The waitress put a full pot of coffee on the table, and I reached for it.

"First couple of years weren't bad, but no, she wasn't happy. I know for a fact she was always pretty happy with Rich. I don't know what gets into women! Rich would've taken care of her as long as she lived, one way or another, or somebody else with plenty would have, and here she had to leave him for this guy. She didn't really want to eat beans in some dirty studio. Melody got herself in over her head."

"Maybe she just wanted to be married."

"Why? She didn't want kids. Rich must have asked her a dozen times if she wanted a family, and she said no every time. Rich was married twice, and he won't do it again, but he's not one to keep a woman tied to him if she wants kids either. He likes his comfort, but he isn't really a user, you know what I mean? He's got a conscience."

I thought about Rich's conscience for a minute, chewing slowly. "Most women want children," I offered.

"Well, Melody wasn't most women. She didn't want to stretch herself out of shape, for one thing. She used to laugh and tell me she wanted to be beautiful when she found her father, so he'd be ashamed of having walked off and left her."

"Tell me about that," I suggested, sipping at the hot cup. "Had she had any luck finding her father?"

"She knew his name. Rick Maudlin. She knew he was supposed to live out in Englewood. Rich hired some guy to search the city records for her. Nobody of that name had ever lived there, according to the city directories and the phone books. No Maudlins at all."

"Is that all she knew about him? That isn't much."

"Her mother died when she was born, in Baltimore. Her mother's aunt brought her up. All the aunt knew was that her niece had been married to a man named Rick Maudlin from Englewood, Colorado."

"I suppose the search extended past Englewood. Out to Littleton and around to the other suburbs?"

"Rich spent a few thousand looking. I don't think the Maudlin guy ever lived here. I think he lied about it."

"So who do you think killed Melody?"

"Who the hell knows. Rich didn't do it. He'd picked up with somebody else by then, and besides, he was in Texas when it happened. He was really knocked off his perch when I told him about it. Maybe that old guy she used to talk to in the park shot her for her wristwatch. She didn't have it on when they found her."

"What old guy?"

"Some guy she used to talk to. Some friend of the family. I used to see them sitting on a bench, over by the walk."

Ambler couldn't remember what the man looked like. Thin, he thought. Fifty-five or sixty.

Ambler insisted both on paying the tab and on taking me

back to his apartment, where he showed me Melody's works of art hanging on the very expensive grass-cloth walls of his very expensively decorated apartment. I smiled and commented and escaped, wondering what his friends thought of the paintings. When it came to estimating Melody's talent, Nina had hit it on the nose. No line. No color. No composition. No technique. Muddy little daubs of no charm, and yet Ambler's face, when he looked at them, was open and enchanted, like a child looking at a circus. He himself had no aesthetic sense, so much was obvious from the few personal touches he had added to the place. I wondered what he saw in the paintings. I wondered if, perhaps, he hadn't been in love with Melody himself.

There was a message from Trish when I got back to the office. She'd left the studio number, so I called it, waiting while it rang and rang. I could visualize her having to stop her pose and come up into the living area to answer it.

"Grale's," she said at last, breathlessly.

"Jason Lynx, Trish," I said, realizing I didn't remember her last name.

"Hi there," she said. "You asked about this weekend? Friday night there's a family party and you're invited to join. Harriet and Greg and me, and Lycia and Ross, and Shannon and Keith with their dates. You bring Nina."

"I wouldn't want to intrude," I demurred.

"It's not an intrusion. You wanted to meet Greg, and Harriet already had this thing planned—it's Greg's birthday that weekend, but we're not taking much notice, since he's forty—and Harriet is very fond of Nina. So."

I accepted, provisionally, then called Nina. Yes, she'd heard about it. Yes, she'd love to have me as an escort. So. I would meet the whole cast of characters.

I suddenly recalled that I'd already met some of them when I'd been in Lycia's apartment with Marge. Well, my presence would have to be terribly coincidental, that's all. Unless they, like me, did not believe in coincidence.

I had noted the name Rich, Neal Ambler's friend "in oil." I had some friends "in oil," and it took only about half an hour to identify him as Richard Beacon of Beacon Exploration and Leasing. Mike Lessing, one of my informants, even remembered Richard's former live-in wife-surrogate.

"We used to go over there every now and then for dinner," he told me. "Melody was a bit more than a mistress but a good bit less than a wife. Sort of a cross between bedmate and daughter, I'd say." Which fit right in with everything Ambler had to say. "Beacon kept a cook, a houseman, and some other help, so she had it pretty easy. Several of us were rather surprised when she left him, though Vicki, that's my wife, said Melody left because Rich didn't pay much attention to her. My wife said Melody was cute but boring, I guess that's why."

"Boring how, Mike?"

"Vicki said she was the only person she'd ever met who could talk for a whole hour about choosing the dress she was wearing. Vicki said Melody could talk about picking out shoes the way some women talk about picking colleges for their kids. She was real full of herself, even though she'd never done anything or been anywhere. She didn't even read anything. At least, that's what Vicki said."

I thanked Mike and hung up. Puzzle, puzzle, and so far I was getting absolutely nowhere. Wednesday was Mark's day to fix lunch, so I filled him in as we ate. Chicken enchiladas with sour cream, guacamole salad, and flan. Mark makes great flan, only he calls it *crème brûlée*.

"Why did she leave Beacon?" Mark wanted to know.

Why had she? Love? Boredom? Disinclination to be Rich's bedmate any longer? Desire to be with someone who would pay more attention to her? Or from whom she could demand more attention, which was perhaps more likely. She had probably had very little luck whipsawing Rich, or teasing him, or getting him to do anything he wasn't already willing to do.

Greg, on the other hand, could have been an open season, without defenses. She might have thought Greg could tap the Steinwale money at will. She might not have realized he wanted to make it on his own, and her consistent attempts to access Mama Steinwale's money through him might have pushed Grale over the brink. Mark and I talked about possibilities. Mark did not discount love as a reason for her leaving her snug nest; I did not discount boredom or pique. No way to know, for sure, unless she had told someone. Ambler had his opinion; I had mine. She might have told Greg, but I couldn't very well ask him. Maybe I could ask Rich if it became necessary. If he knew. I made a mental note.

And there was the other man she talked to. The fiftyish guy on the bench. The family friend. I'd have to find out who that could be.

"I have another job for you," I told Mark. "The people you talked to on Sunday, the ones who recognized Melody?"

He nodded.

"According to Ambler, Melody used to talk to someone else in the park. A fiftyish man, probably thin." I paused, trying to remember what else he'd said. "He said the bench by the walk. That would probably be the walk nearest to his apartment building. . . ."

"The bench he was talking about would probably be one of those just off Twelfth."

"What we need is to identify the man she talked to on the bench. See if anyone saw her talking to him, and see if you can get a description."

"Are you getting anywhere with Freddy?" Mark asked.

I laughed, shaking my head at him. "I've got a woman who may have tried to kill him, a student who talked about killing him, and several people who probably thought he ought to be killed. Which is to say, nothing so far."

And I got nothing else for several days. The rest of Wednesday went on by in a clutter of little jobs. Eugenia Lowe had a problem with a client charging misrepresentation. The first I knew of it was when a large angry man invaded my office yelling and using words I didn't find particularly coherent. After I asked him for the third time to explain what his problem was, he calmed down enough to thrust an invoice at me and shout, "You rotten liar, you told my wife this was an antique chair, and it says on the bottom it was made by this company in Michigan . . ." and more words to that effect. Even when I pointed to the invoice where the words "Colonial reproduction" appeared in large letters, he still wanted to yell about it. I told him I'd be glad to take the piece back for exactly what his wife paid for it, and he got suddenly quiet.

"She told me it was an antique," he grumbled.

"It's a reproduction," I told him. "Normally I don't handle reproductions, but this one came with a roomful of furniture I bought from an estate. A real chair of that period would cost at least three or four thousand dollars, and it would look very little different from the one you have." I didn't mention that to those who care about such things, that little difference is supremely important. The chair she'd bought was well made and worth every cent she'd paid for it. "As I recall, your wife thought she was buying you something nice for your birthday. So she fibbed a little and said it was antique. You don't like it, I'll take it back."

He grumbled again, then left, saying he'd bring the chair back that afternoon.

"Honestly!" Eugenia was steaming. "That bastard!"

"Don't sweat it," I told her. "You get one like that every now and then. I can see the scenario. He asks her what she paid. She tells him. He rages. To justify the price, which needs no justification if you know good furniture, she says it was an antique. He sees the invoice, maybe he yells at her about it, so she screams misrepresentation, and everything degenerates from there. Put their names in your no-no file and forget it." Jacob had always kept a no-no file. People he would not, under any circumstances, do business with again. Funny how some people will threaten to sue you one day, then come back a week later thinking you'll be glad to see them.

That night Grace called, collect.

"How are you?" I asked her, suddenly missing her more than I'd thought I possibly could. "How are you, Grace!" It wasn't a question. It was a demand. I needed to know.

"I'm lousy," she said in a depressed voice. "I'm terrible. I'm so down, Jason. I've finally found Ron a lawyer, but the man wants the mortgage on the homestead as a retainer. God, I hate to do that. I've put everything into that house."

"Grace, do not, I repeat, do not give him anything but a cash retainer which I will send you in the morning." I caught myself yelling at her. It was usually the other way around. Usually she yelled at me.

"Jason, I can't let you do that."

"Grace, you can owe it to me, interest-free. Put it down to passing on a kindness, okay? Jacob was good to me, I'll be good to you, you be good to Ron. Maybe someday Ron'll be good to someone. . . ."

"He doesn't have sense enough to be good to himself even. Can you spare five thousand, Jason?"

I gulped deeply and lied. "I can spare it, Grace. Is that what the guy wants as a retainer?"

She fussed about paying me back. I told her if it got tough, I'd take her grandmother's Eastlake bed as security. It was the one piece of Grace's grandma's furniture I hadn't sold for her, the one piece still in her garage. Grace hadn't wanted to use any of her grandmother's furniture—too many memories, she said.

"Grace, while Ron's in jail, while all this is being sorted out, you don't need to be there, do you?"

"If I come back, I could have trouble getting away again, Jason. They weren't real thrilled about giving me this leave."

"Do they have to know you're back?" I asked. "I mean, just a

quick flight home. For a day or two. You could stay here, with
me?"

We talked about that. She said yes, she said no, she said
maybe. We left it she'd think about it and let me know. She
gave me the lawyer's name, and I told her I would call him in
the morning and arrange payment. I told myself I'd also arrange a cap on legal fees. "How long will you stay?" I asked
her, wondering how long I could do without her.

"Until he gets arraigned or not. Or they let him go. Or
something. So far they've just been playing games, trying to
get information out of him. He doesn't know anything, that's
his trouble. He's never known anything." She laughed weakly,
and I made comforting sounds. She asked about Critter. Critter
was pressed tightly against my side in a furry ball, fast asleep,
making little chirpy noises from time to time. I told her I
missed her. She said likewise.

I hung up resolved to go to San Francisco and get her if she
didn't get things straightened out soon. Or at least be there
with her while she did. She was not sensible about Ron, any
more than I had been sensible about Agatha. Cutting the cord
between her and her baby brother was being very hard for her.

Thursday was a replay of Wednesday, minus the aggravation. I called the San Francisco lawyer and had a heart-to-heart
talk about what Grace could afford. He told me he'd hold the
expenses down and refund anything not used in the case at
hand. I wired him the money.

Along about three, things loosened up and I decided to see
what Melody's art instructor might tell me. Nina had mentioned his name, and I'd already found out that he had a
Wednesday afternoon class which would end about the time I
reached the University of Denver campus out on South University Boulevard.

His name was Conklin. Stan Conklin. He was feverish-look-
ing, dark-haired, eyes glittery from contact lenses, about five
foot ten, give or take an inch, with something predatory in his

stance. I moved into the classroom when the students moved out, standing by while he said a few dictatorial things to a flirtatious female student whom he patted absently and familiarly on the bottom while he spoke. When she left, I asked him if he could spare a few minutes. He asked what about, and I told him. He gave me a looking-over.

"Are you related to her?" he asked.

I told him no, that my interest was really ancillary to another matter. He suggested a beer. I acquiesced. We went to the bar across the street.

"Melody was cute," he said, after dipping his nose into the foam and wiping it off on his sleeve. "She was cute as a button. I would have loved to do a nude study of her. Like a fairy, a sprite, one of those little ones."

"I've never met one, personally."

"Some famous illustrator used to do bodies like that for fairy tales," he said.

"Rackham?" I suggested.

He waved his hands. He didn't know. "So thin she looked breakable, but with proper little plumpness in all the right places." He sighed. "And no more talent than a cockroach."

"I thought you encouraged her," I said in an innocent tone.

He blushed, grinning at the same time. "I'm rotten to the core," he said. "Mother always told me so. I lie."

The wry grin betrayed a rudimentary conscience. I decided he wasn't so much predatory as just opportunistic. "She told people that her instructor told her she painted as well as her husband," I said.

"She may well have." He laughed. "Who was her husband?"

"Gregory Steinwale. Grale."

"Oh, my God!" He turned pale. "You're kidding. Oh, God, why don't I learn to keep my libido zipped? She was married to Grale?" He leaned forward and knocked his head on the table a few times with a dull, thunking sound. "Oh, shit."

"Those who heard her quoting you may have wondered about your eyesight."

"All she ever said to me was that her husband didn't want to talk about his painting. She never said who he was. And she didn't register as Steinwale either. That would have rung a bell with me. She was Melody Maudlin."

"That was her maiden name. She met her husband here," I said. "Some years ago."

"I've only been here three years."

"What can you tell me about her?"

"She talked like a magpie, mostly about herself or her next shopping expedition. She had no talent for painting, but talked about it anyhow. She had the neatest little body I've ever seen. She thought her mother-in-law had no taste and hated living there but had to because the old lady was crippled and needed her son."

"The old lady is not noticeably crippled," I said. "The consensus seems to be that Melody lived there because it was more luxurious than any of her other choices."

His eyebrows rose. "Oh. Well. Whatever. I am guilty of telling her she had talent. I lied. She sometimes started out with color and form, but by the time she was finished with it, everything was gray and itsy-bitsy. She had no confidence, no eye. I probably should have told her the truth for all the good lying did me. I never got anywhere with her. She said I was 'too young and callow,' laughing like crazy the whole time."

"Did she have any friends? Close associates?"

"She talked to Bess Trumble sometimes. Poor Bess. Oh, and Shannon somebody."

"Shannon Foret?" I think my mouth dropped open. Since Shannon had first mentioned Melody, I'd been looking for some connection between them, but this was the last one I would have expected.

"Shannon . . . Foret is right, isn't it? She audited a class. Last year, I think. The summer term, July, August, something like that. Melody seemed to know her pretty well, maybe better than Shannon liked."

"How do you mean?"

He puzzled, remembering. "I seem to recall Melody introduced Shannon as a relative. No. No, she said she knew they were soul sisters because they looked so much alike. Shannon said she wasn't Melody's sister and they didn't look anything alike. They didn't, of course, except that they were both pretty girls. Melody wasn't too serious about it, kind of kidding, but Shannon was really annoyed."

I thought about that, but it took me nowhere. Melody hadn't resembled Shannon at all, so far as I could remember from the pictures or even the way Conklin described her. "Did Melody ever mention her father?"

"Not that I remember."

"What about Shannon? Did she have any talent?"

"She was taking an art history course, no talent required. I don't remember much about her, to tell you the truth. She'd graduated the year before. She was thinking about graduate school. That happens a lot. Particularly with girls like her."

"What happens? And girls like what?"

"Fragile ones with reasonably good minds but no . . . no gristle. They get through school assuming that they'll have some kind of career later, but they aren't really equipped to do anything, and they aren't suited to the brutalities of the marketplace, so they think about graduate school. It's a way of forestalling decision. A way to put off getting involved with real life. Usually they end up getting married. It's about the only thing they're even modestly equipped for, and I'm not being sexist." He leaned forward and gave me a sincere look.

I knew he wasn't being sexist, at least not in this case, though I wouldn't have given a dime for his not being sexist in all other connections. His words had brought back my own impressions of Shannon, very tremulous, very, as he said, "fragile."

We had another beer and parted. I made a mental note that Conklin might be interesting to know better. He was about my age, presumably unmarried. Pity he was into girls. Mark would have liked him.

Nina told me that Greg Steinwale's birthday dinner was being held out at the Wilshire, a restaurant I like more for the ambience than for the food, which is often quite good, though sometimes pedestrian. Nina didn't know whether gifts were to be proffered or not—Trish had said they were "not taking much notice," but that could mean simply a much appreciated absence of cardboard birthday cake and singing waiters—so I pocketed a little something just in case, a sterling silver snuff box, dated about 1760, useful for stamps or pins or even pills. I wouldn't give it to him unless the atmosphere was right for it. Gifts from virtual strangers can be embarrassing. Hell, gifts from friends can be embarrassing.

The eleven of us were given an alcove and no menus. Harriet had evidently ordered the meal in advance. I was seated between Nina and Trish, with Ross across from me, Greg at the foot of the table, and Lycia between Ross and Greg. Harriet was at the head of the table with Keith's date, Stephanie, on one side of her and a dark, spectacularly handsome young man on the other, next to Shannon.

"Ancel Ancini," Nina whispered to me. "Shannon's escort."

From the glowing look on Shannon's face, he was a good deal more than an escort. "New boyfriend?" I asked.

"Old boyfriend," she whispered. "Something or other happened and they broke up, but they got back together just recently."

"Isn't there an Ancini who's running for the Senate?" I asked.

"That's Ancel's father."

I recalled pictures of the father. Stephan. He wasn't and had never been as good-looking as his son. The son was Prince

Charming, Superman, and the guy in the white hat, all rolled
into one. Eyes that glittered. Dark, velvety skin. Hair that
looked as though it might reach out and grab you, it was so
alive. The contrast between his dark good looks and Shannon's
pale beauty was striking. As a couple they were breathtaking,
an illustration for a romance. I know this sounds gushy, but
Conklin had set me thinking about fairy-tale illustrations and
they could easily have been Cinderella and the Prince.

I remarked, "Good-looking couple."

Nina agreed. An arm came across her shoulder delivering a
hot lobster appetizer, and I turned to talk with my neighbors
across the table. Or tried to. Lycia was charming, remarking
on having met me before under difficult circumstances and
being happy to see me under better ones. Ross, however,
seemed to have a chip on his shoulder about something. He
was almost abrupt. To escape his inexplicable belligerence, I
found my conversational gambits directed more and more at
Lycia Foret.

Her face was not as pretty as her daughter's. Still, of all the
faces around the table, hers was the most attractive. It radiated
with a kind of tranquil strength. Not quiet, for she was very
animated. Still, her expression displayed an inner peace or sat-
isfaction, a kind of ageless tranquillity. I found myself wondering how old she was, counting years, realizing that though she
might be considerably more, she could be as little as five or six
years older than I. Not too old, I told myself, then stopped the
thought, wondering what in hell I was up to. Not too old for
what?

For yourself, buddy, I told myself.

Don't be idiotic. She's spoken for, I replied. There was no
doubt of that. The way she and Ross looked at one another was
enough to make their relationship clear. Close, and loving, and
apparently honest, though why she loved the touchy bastard
was more than I could figure out.

So what *is* it about her?

I passed the salt and smiled and replied to Trish's comments and Nina's gibes and let my eyes slide gently over Lycia's face. Something about her. Something I almost recognized.

Appetizers were succeeded by Caesar salad, by cold curried chicken soup, by breast of duckling in apricot sauce with wild rice. There were several bottles of wine. No one was in a hurry. I had plenty of time to indulge myself in my little obsession. After the third glass of wine, Greg became almost voluble —that is, he actually used sentences of seven or eight words, some of them in series. Trish and Nina talked across me about the gallery. I talked across the table to Lycia. Unlike many doctors I had met, both she and Ross seemed to know and care about other things than medicine or hospitals or medical society politics. When Lycia spoke about her profession, which she did, passionately, in response to something Nina asked her, she mentioned the enormous responsibilities it entailed and was very clear about the value she placed on life. She spoke of a beloved older sister who had died needlessly, and of her desire to prevent others from dying in similar fashion. Everything about her impressed me, and I found myself wondering if this evening might be the start of a friendship between her . . . between the two of them and me. If it happened at all, it would have to be with the two of them. So much was obvious.

Raised voices from the other end of the table drew our attention. Harriet was holding forth to Stephanie about someone abusing a child. With her gray-white hair and virtually unlined face, she looked like a prophetess laying down the law. I raised an eyebrow, and Lycia explained.

"Harriet and I work for the Lighthouse," she said. "It's a home for battered women and their children. I got interested in it when I was in medical school. That's how I met Harriet. She was—still is—on the board."

"She was talking about child abuse just now?"

Lycia's face was concentrated, a little angry, though not at Harriet. "The women who come to the Lighthouse are battered, and frequently the children are abused, too. She's trying to talk Stephanie into volunteering. I think Steph's about ten years too young to care."

"Harriet seems very dedicated."

Nina snorted. "If you want a three-hour lecture, get Harriet started on children and their rights and how they ought to be protected. She's a fanatic!" She said it fondly, which was a good thing, because Lycia picked up on it.

"I agree with Harriet, and I don't think that one can be too fanatical," she said, the little anger hot in her tone. "There just can't be any limits where children are concerned. Children have all their lives ahead of them. If you ruin a child, you ruin a whole life. Harriet feels we should feel about every child the way we feel about our own, and most of us mothers have pretty unlimited feelings toward our own."

Her voice had risen slightly, tight with feeling, and Keith cast a slightly ironic look down the table toward her. "Soapbox, Mother," he said.

Lycia looked down, embarrassed. Ross chuckled. Harriet looked up, caught several sets of eyes on her, and said, "What?"

"We've been caught on our usual lecture platform, Harriet," Lycia commented. "Keith told me to get off the soapbox."

"Oh, we really should stay off it tonight," Harriet said. She was a big, tall woman, with a deep, almost mannish voice, and square, expressive hands that moved in accompaniment to it. Every statement was accompanied by gestures, pointing, prying, fist folding. "Oh," she said, lifting open hands on either side of her face, "we really should," laying them palm down on the table, disposing of the subject. Then one hand flew to her eye. "Damn," she said.

Concerned, Trish turned to her. "Did you lose a contact, Harriet?"

"Just blinked the silly thing out," Harriet said. "Piffle." She found it, put her napkin down, and pushed her chair back. "If you'll excuse me, I'll retire to the ladies' room." She rose to her full height, slightly over six feet; Lycia followed her. After a moment's pause, so did Shannon and Stephanie, Nina and Trish, in couples. The men were left at the table while a busboy trudged around it, readying it for dessert and coffee.

"Not many women your mother's age wear contacts," I remarked to Greg.

"She has trouble keeping glasses on," he replied. "She says contacts are a godsend. I hate glasses, too. I tried them, and I couldn't paint at all. I can't see in them. All I'm aware of is the frame."

"You wear contacts?" I asked.

He nodded, widening his eyes at me to make them shine. Keith leaned across the table and said something to Ancel Ancini. The two of them rose, excused themselves, and went across the room to speak to someone at another table. Ross, Greg, and I were left alone.

"I gathered from what you said the other morning that you knew Lycia's former husband," Ross said to me, apropos of nothing.

"Not well," I said. "I met him at his sister's. I used to run into him occasionally in the park."

Ross frowned, staring at his hands, which were manipulating a dessert fork, turning it over and over. "Now Marge tells Lycia you're looking into his death." The tone was unmistakably annoyed.

Aha, I thought, so that's it. "She asked me to," I said in a noncommittal tone.

"We met Fred once," said Greg, almost volubly. "Melody and I, at that swimming party Lycia gave for Shannon's twenty-first birthday. Shannon said her father wasn't invited. He just showed up. And he had webbed feet." He smiled into his wineglass, privately amused by some image only he could see.

"Webbed feet?" I didn't think I'd heard him correctly.

"Webbed toes," Ross corrected, his voice still angry. "Fred

had webbed toes. He insisted on joining the swimming party, and I remember Keith was kidding him about his feet."

"Is that rare?" I asked.

Ross pursed his lips. "I suppose. It's not really a deformity, more of an anomaly. Any good surgeon could have removed them in five minutes."

"Melody said it ran in families," Greg said.

"It's true that Shannon had webs like it," Ross said. "Between her big toes and second toes. I removed Shannon's webs a few years ago. She wanted to wear thongs and couldn't."

"Webbed feet and sticky fingers," Greg said solemnly. He was nodding over his fourth or fifth glass of wine.

"Sticky fingers?" I asked, keeping my voice carefully neutral, hoping he wasn't talking about Shannon.

"I mean Fred Foret. Melody told me. After she met him at the birthday party, she used to run into him all the time in the park. She said he had sticky fingers."

For a moment I didn't realize that he had just told me who Melody's park companion had been. Though Fred might not have said much to a woman he had just met at his daughter's birthday party, he wouldn't have hesitated to build on that acquaintance. So Fred must have been the man Ambler had seen Melody with. I noted this second connection between Fred and Melody. One that Conklin had mentioned between Melody and Fred's daughter. One that Greg had mentioned between Melody and Fred himself.

"That's what I mean about him," Ross snorted, with a hard look at me. "I think the police should be let alone to do their own thing without some . . . well, some amateur messing in. Fred wasn't worth the effort. Nothing about that guy would surprise me. I know damned well he stole Shannon's house keys out of her purse and had a copy made. Then he'd pick times he knew we were all going to be gone and sneak into Lycia's apartment."

"Why?" I asked, genuinely curious. "Why would he do

that?" I had placed the anger now. It wasn't at me but at the former husband. I was only catching the reflection.

"After some private stuff of Lycia's came up missing, she realized what was going on. I should have realized before. Shannon told us one time she'd been over at Fred's, she'd lost her key. He called her a day or two later to tell her he'd found it. We didn't think anything of it at the time, but then when Lycia missed her stuff and Shannon told us the kind of things he'd been saying to her, it was obvious what he'd done. He was sneaking in and reading private letters, looking through Shannon's diary—she's kept a diary since she was about ten—then he'd be able to come over all omniscient with Shannon. You can imagine the kind of thing. 'I know something's troubling you, dear. It's a man, isn't it? He's said something that's upset you. Let me see if I can figure out what it might be.' Stuff like that." Ross's nostrils flared with frustrated fury. "Poor kid. He had her buffaloed. Like some kind of evil spirit. The Great All-Knowing Father. Know all, see all, tell all. He damn near broke up her relationship with Ancel, too."

The Ancinis were another family "in oil," and they'd managed to hold on to their money when the collapse wiped out the economy of several western states. "How did Fred do that?" I asked.

Ross turned the fork over and over. I could tell he was thinking he had already said too much to me, but his anger and annoyance at Fred got the better of his reticence. "Ancel invited Shannon home to meet his family. She was jittery as a cricket, scared, happy, half out of her head. She was sure he was going to propose. For the last six months it had been Ancel this and Ancel that. Lycia and I kept trying to calm her down. . . .

"Then, along the middle of that week, Fred called Shannon and told her he needed her to come to his apartment that weekend, that he had something very important to talk to her about and it couldn't wait. You'd have to know Fred and his 'talks' for this to make sense. You'd also have to know Fred to realize that the only reason he'd picked that weekend was that he knew she was going to the Ancinis'. A kind of test of his power over Shannon. He did that a lot. I'm pretty sure it's one of the reasons Lycia left him in the first place." He closed his mouth into a tight, straight line for a second, as though he'd almost said something he shouldn't.

I did indeed know Fred and his talks. "What did Shannon do?"

"She said she had an engagement, she told him with whom." Ross shook his head. "No guile in that girl at all, even though she should have known better. Fred already knew, of course. You know what that damned Fred did?" He waited, poised, lips compressed. He had to tell me. He had to tell someone.

I tried to think of the most outrageous thing I could. "He called the Ancinis and said she couldn't come."

"Worse!" Ross slammed his hand down on the table, making the coffee cups rattle. "He called Mrs. Ancini and invited himself along as chaperone. Poor Mrs. Ancini didn't know what to say. Here was this *father* on the line, and he wouldn't shut up. Well, Shannon went out there Saturday afternoon—they've got a huge, expensive showplace out in Cherry Hills—and who was the first person she saw but her daddy. Ancel brought her home early Sunday morning, his face like a thundercloud. Shannon was in tears. She couldn't talk to us for hours. Ancel's father had been insulted somehow. According to Shannon, everything was over."

"Good Lord. What had Fred done?"

Ross shook his head, like a dog with a rat, as though he would shake the words to death. "Who knows what he did! Shannon told us almost nothing except that Fred had invited himself along on her weekend. Aside from that, she wouldn't talk about it, not then and not since. It was all I could do to keep Lycia from going straight out and . . ." He realized what he was saying and bit off the words. "Well, Lycia cried on

Harriet's shoulder instead. None of us knows what Fred actually did, though we can imagine. Ancel hasn't said anything to us. At any rate, the upshot of the whole thing was that Shannon and Ancel broke up. They only got back together after Fred was killed."

I could see it all in living color, full of anger and embarrassment. "Maybe Ancel killed him," I said, without thinking.

Ross's jaw dropped.

"No, no, Ross," I said, embarrassed. "I didn't mean it. My mind works that way, trying to solve things. Looking for motives. Looking for possibilities. That's why Marge asked me to look into Fred's death. You said he wasn't worth the effort, but she cares. She wants to know why he died."

He scowled at me. "Well, if anyone had a motive, I did. When Shannon told Lycia and me that Fred had showed up at the Ancinis', I was ready to kill him myself. I wouldn't have shot him, though. I'd have slit his throat. For sheer, unmitigated gall, Fred Foret took the silver buckle. Shannon didn't eat for a week. She didn't sleep either. All she did was cry. And to top everything off, Fred had the nerve to call her and tell her she was better off!"

"When did this happen? The Ancini thing."

"Oh, I don't know. Six or eight weeks ago. Long enough for Ancel to think it over and make up with her. Thank God. You know the word 'distraught'? I've never seen it anywhere except in old romances, but that was Shannon." He sighed, his dammed-up anger talked out and gone. "Sorry about seeming unpleasant. It's just . . . the bastard was always causing trouble. Now that he's dead, I'd hoped it would be over."

Quietly grateful for whatever emotion had made him so talkative, I added Ross's name to my list of suspects. What he had told me should have strengthened Lycia's motive, too, though I could not imagine her killing anyone. As I pondered this, I saw her across the room, stooping to speak to someone on her way back to the table, her face calm and glowing. Ross shook his

head at me, finger on lips. I wasn't to say anything to Lycia. I
nodded agreement and took a firm grip on my suspicious self.
Both Lycia and Ross had alibis. As did Shannon, who probably
couldn't kill a mouse, and Keith, who looked as though he
could kill something considerably larger if he cared to.

We stood up as the women returned. Keith and Ancel came
back from their visit across the room. The waiters returned
with an elegant dessert without even a hint of birthday cake or
singing waiters. Several people presented small gifts. Since
Greg seemed to be in a mellow mood, I gave him the snuff box.
He asked the right questions about it and seemed pleased. He
was a man improved by wine, made less self-conscious and less
blunt. When I saw him like this, his face quite open and shining with interest, I thought it quite possible that love had made
Melody leave her secure nest with the oilman.

I turned slightly and caught a glimpse of Harriet. She was
looking down the table, seeing no one but her son. The way
she looked at him, with a kind of brooding passion, left me in
no doubt about her feelings for him. Strange man. Both Trish
and Harriet loved him, and he basked in their affection while
remaining almost unaware of it.

After I dropped Nina off, I drove directly home, put the car
in the garage, and went in through the back door. Whenever I
get home, Bela comes to greet me, barking in muted tones,
semaphoring his heavy tail in a message of greeting, sometimes
almost knocking me over. I stood inside in the darkness, half
aware that something was wrong before I realized what it was.
No Bela.

I decided not to turn on the lights, and instead took the large
flashlight from the laundry-room drawer and flashed it around
the laundry and then the old kitchen we use as a showroom for
country furniture—pie cabinets, spice racks, what Jacob calls
kitchen clutter. The place looked as usual. No mess. No sign
anyone had been there.

The kitchen has two doors into the house, one opening into the old dining room, one opening into the back hall, across from the back stairs. Back hall and front hall are separated by another door, one we never use because Eugenia's desk sits almost directly in front of it. I had the choice of the back stairs or the dining room. Flipping a mental coin, I picked the dining room.

Shining tables, shining chairs, sideboards, serving tables. Swagged drapes over sheer curtains with the streetlight showing through. Nothing. Another mental coin, upstairs or the other showrooms. Upstairs.

The stairs did not creak. They would not have dared. Jacob had always said that nothing undermines confidence in a piece of construction more than hearing it squeak. Eugenia and I always pushed and tugged at things like bedsteads and highboys to be sure there was no give. I went up silently. Into the front guest room, nothing; the offices, nothing; my living room and kitchen, nothing. Which left the bedroom. An ideal place for an ambush, really. A man comes in, probably with one arm half out of his suit coat, unsuspecting, a perfect target. Though who might be lying in wait and for what reason, my frantic brain didn't tell me.

My sensible self said go back downstairs and call the police. One of my other selves said Bela was missing, dammit, and I wanted to know what had happened to him.

I stood in the doorway, silent as a wraith, pointed the flash into the room, and flicked it on. It met the startled gaze of one very large white dog who raised his head from his bed and said *whuf* in a loud and irritated manner. There was a sound from the bed. I swung the flash and met another surprised pair of eyes. These were blue and sleepy, in a pale little face under a wealth of corn-silk hair.

"Grace!" I said.

"Oh, hi, Jason. I wondered if you'd ever get home," she said sleepily. "I was so tired, I decided I'd lie down for a minute."

She had picked one of my T-shirts to do it in. It hit her at her knees, making her look like a little girl dressed up in some grown-up's clothes. She held out her arms like a little child, still half asleep, and I sat on the bed and gathered her up, while Bela subsided back into his huge basket, deciding everything was all right.

"How'd you get in?" I whispered.

"Through the dog door." She giggled. "I talked to Bela first, so he'd know who it was. He was on one side whuffing, and I was on the other side explaining. He let me in, though."

"Oh, Grace," I said, inadequately, holding her tightly.

"I'm so glad you got home," she murmured.

"Why?" I asked, expecting some tender revelation, like separation had made the heart grow fonder.

"I'm awfully hungry," she said.

So much for tender revelations. Grace did that to me all the time. In a mood of half-amused, half-annoyed affection, I changed into something more comfortable. Grace retained the T-shirt. We went into the kitchen and I made her a six-egg omelet and about half a pound of fried bacon, which she ate without pause. There were some English muffins in the freezer. She finished up with five muffin halves, liberally doused with ginger marmalade, and most of a quart of milk.

"You're sure that's enough," I said sarcastically, noting the way the knit fabric clung to her breasts. Grace is small but shapely. At least that's the word I use to myself when I'm trying to control my breathing.

"I haven't been eating very well," she confided. "Mostly stuff at coffee shops. They never give you enough."

I had never known Grace to have enough anywhere. Her appetite was a matter of constant amazement to me. Now, however, it seemed to be momentarily satisfied, for she sat back with a pleased little sigh and demanded to be told everything about the murder and the clue I'd found and everything.

"I don't want to think about Ron all weekend," she said. "I just want to be with you."

"Fair enough," I told her, mentally sorting out the Fred Foret case for her perusal while fighting the urge to drag her into the bedroom. After the meal she had just eaten, however, she was entitled to a little digestion time. Actually, the time stretched to two pots of coffee before everything was told with all the ramifications and bits and pieces.

"I worked on the Steinwale case," she said, surprising me. "I was one of the first people on the scene—that is, after they found out she was dead. She wasn't just slumped over. Her arm was sort of crooked into the arm of the bench." She illustrated, bending her left arm and thrusting the elbow up and back. "Those benches, the metal arms come down from the back, making a kind of triangle. Her elbow was shoved into the triangle, holding her up."

"Did you think at the time the body had been arranged that way?"

She shook her head. "I didn't think so at the time, no. There was no reason to think so. She could have been arranged, but she could have been sitting that way, too. If she had been sitting that way when she was shot, she might have just slumped forward without falling, the way we found her."

"How about the magazine in her lap? Did you think that had been put there?"

She furrowed her brow, remembering. "It wasn't a slick magazine," she said at last. "Or maybe it was, but it had a brown paper cover. Like a mailing cover. Like she'd grabbed it out of the mail and brought it along. I can't remember what the magazine was, so I couldn't have felt it was important. It'll be in the property room, down at the station. The case was never closed."

We talked about that for a while, trying different scenarios, without getting anyplace. Finally, we ran out of things to say about the case.

"That's all very nice," she said. "Sounds like you've been busy. Now, what's bothering you?"

"I haven't a clue yet," I said. "Nothing fits together."

"I don't mean about your puzzle," she said. "I mean about you."

I had to think about that. What about me?

"Did you get another one of those letters offering to sell you information about yourself?" she asked. "Last time you got one, you had those same lines in your forehead."

Suddenly, surprisingly, for no reason at all, I had tears in my eyes.

"Shush, shush," she was saying. "Dammit, Jason. Who's doing this?"

"Some con man," I said. "Somebody who knows a little about me and thinks he can get money out of me."

"You know, we could handle this. The police, I mean. We could set a trap for the person, find out who, without risking your money. I'm pretty sure it would be called extortion, you know."

I did know. I'd thought of that. "Grace, if we did that, suppose we did that. Suppose the person really does know something. Something I'd just as soon not know."

"Like your daddy was a horse thief?"

"Like he was something worse than that. Or my mother was. Or the reason for my abandonment was. . . ."

"None of that has anything to do with you!"

"That's what Jacob always says. I believe it. Intellectually. Privately, emotionally, I don't want to deal with the reality. I particularly don't want to deal with a reality which may end up in the papers, a 'story,' something for the curious to titillate themselves with. *Local Merchant's Lurid History Revealed.* I had enough ghastly headlines when Agatha disappeared. There were enough when they found her body. I don't want any more."

She didn't protest. She nodded. She understood. "Well then,

you'll just have to wait until you know what you want to do. Eventually, he'll get tired of writing letters and try something else. Or he'll give up."

And if he gave up, I'd never know.

Grace took me by the hand. We left the dishes where they were. Fifteen minutes later, I'd forgotten all about it and didn't care who I was or where I was or anything about the day-to-day world at all.

I called Eugenia and Mark early and told them not to bother to come in, to take Saturday morning off. Eugenia told me she'd planned to do just that, and Mark wanted to get together to talk about the puzzle. I told him Monday would be soon enough.

Grace and I talked about finding Sally Streeter. I'd already done the easy things, like looking in the phone book and calling Information. She didn't have a phone under that name, listed or unlisted. Since she'd moved only recently, she wouldn't be in any city directory. Public Service might have a listing, but that would require subterfuge. I went over the notes I'd jotted down just after my visit to the apartment house where she'd lived.

"Bingo," I told Grace. "And church bake sales. The manager of the place she used to live said Sally was into bingo and bake sales."

She gave me a questioning look. "Bingo?"

"Once an addict, always an addict," I pontificated. "You can help find her. Tomorrow maybe."

Not Saturday, however. We spent the day in totally mindless and pleasurable doing-nothing. We soaked in my sybaritic tub. We drank wine. After a rushed trip to the deli, we ate enormously. At least, she did. We took a drive in the mountains, ending up at a favorite restaurant. In between, we went to bed together whenever we felt like it. Grace, being very solicitous of my feelings, did not tell me she didn't love me. Perhaps, I told myself, she had forgotten that. Sunday morning we parked outside the apartment house where Sally had once lived. We had a thermos of coffee in the front seat, Bela and Critter in the back. About ten-thirty, the Campbell-kid apartment manager came out of the place, bright brass hair frizzed like a pot scrubber, and walked down to the corner. Ten minutes later a station wagon pulled up and she got in. We followed the station wagon to the Church of the Living Gospel. Signs on the lawn of the Catholic church across the street advertised Wednesday night bingo.

The Campbell kid, an elderly couple, and a younger couple got out of the station wagon and went into the church. There was a remote chance that Sally might show up at the Church of the Living Gospel. If so, she'd probably come out with the Campbell kid. Dog, cat, Grace, and I went to a pancake house for a second breakfast (hamburger patties for animals, omelet for me, giant pancakes for Grace) and were back outside the church when it let out at noon. The Campbell kid came out with the same crowd she'd gone in with. No Streeter.

The four of us went to the park, got into a volleyball game, made friends, got home about four. Bela had scored the winning point by jumping at the ball and hitting it with his head. He still looked a little puzzled by the unaccustomed adulation. My leg hurt like hell. Which meant the exercise had probably been good for it.

The phone book listed the Church of the Living Gospel as a "charismatic" congregation. I couldn't find a "charismatic" church listed on the far west side of town. I turned my attention to the Catholic churches. There were half a dozen of those out toward Golden. I made a red mark beside each one that was located in a likely area. Tomorrow morning would be time enough to call.

"You going to drive me to the airport?" Grace asked from the living-room doorway. She was dressed, ready to travel. I hadn't even thought to ask her how long she was staying.

I swallowed my disappointment and asked, "When does your plane leave?"

"About an hour," she said. "I can get a cab if you're busy."

I wasn't that busy. I took her, and kissed her goodbye, and dropped her off. When I got back to the house, it seemed very, very empty.

When Mark came in on Monday, I gave him the phone book and pointed out the red check marks. "Call these churches and ask if they have bingo. Ask if, by any chance, your friend Sally Streeter has been playing bingo there for the last six or eight months. If they don't know, find out when bingo is and make a note."

I'd had another thought. While Mark was busy with the Catholic churches, I called the Church of the Living Gospel and asked the woman who answered if she knew of a charismatic church out toward Golden. She didn't know, but the minister, Mr. McCall, might know. She told me I might catch him around noon, and I said I'd call back.

I didn't have to call back. Mark came into my office about ten-thirty, grinning up both sides of his face.

"Bingo?" I asked him.

"Bingo. She plays at Our Lady of Peace. Tuesday nights. A recent but very faithful player, according to the church secretary who runs the games with her mother-in-law."

We spent some time considering the likely feelings of middle-aged women who have been "taken advantage of," before agreeing on an approach for the following night. Back to business.

"How's the Duchesne job coming?" I asked Mark.

"Duchesne, Duchesne," he murmured. "Why does that sound familiar?"

"Mark!" I said warningly, suddenly having visions of Gladys with a meat ax, coming after me, her daughter and the new in-laws close behind.

"It's fine," he said. "Paint's finished. Carpet's going in today.

Curtains will be ready Wednesday. So far the only thing missing is a shower curtain and new towels for the bathroom.
Someone said they'd take care of that." His tone was unmistakably impudent.

"I don't remember anyone saying that."

"I'm sure someone did."

"Well, since I can't remember, you'd better take care of it."

"Foul, Jason. Foul."

I pretended not to hear him.

On Tuesday night we played bingo. At least Mark did, while
I circulated asking questions until someone pointed Sally
Streeter out to me. She was at the end of a long table playing
eight or nine cards at once, the mark, so I hear, of a professional bingoer. Once I had her located, Mark and I settled into
the game. We spent eleven-fifty and won a toaster-oven. Sally
won a fifty-dollar pot. When she left, we approached her in the
brightly lighted hall with fifty people around, hats in hands, so
to speak, where she could not possibly feel threatened.

"Mrs. Streeter," I said. "My name in Lynx, Jason Lynx. This
is my associate, Mark MacMillan. May we please have a moment of your time?"

She looked around, doubtfully, taking assurance from the
crowd. "What do you want?" she asked ungraciously, her
hands tightening on her purse, which she held up in front of
her like a barrier to protect herself from us both. Sally was
what Jacob would have called zaftig: light-haired, rosy-
cheeked, definitely plump.

"Mr. Fred Foret was a dreadful man," Mark said. We'd
agreed in advance he would say something like that. "Everyone knows he was a dreadful man. We're looking into something Mr. Foret did, and someone told us you had known him
slightly."

She turned bright brick red and we both looked away, pretending to be interested in someone else. When we looked back, she had herself under control.

"We understand he used to talk to you," I said. "It's terribly important that we learn everything we can about him. If now isn't convenient . . . ?"

"It's just," she fumbled with her purse, looking around again. "This is very public."

"There's a pancake house down the street," Mark suggested. We'd located this and two other possible meeting places before we'd come to the church. "It's open now. We could have coffee, or tea. . . ."

"Tea," she said. "I'd like a cup of tea. I really would."

"We'll meet you there," I suggested. We'd decided it would be less threatening for us not to suggest driving her. She agreed. She went out. We followed, not too closely. She drove directly to the pancake house, as though she'd been there before. We met her inside. When we were seated and had ordered coffee and pie for us, tea and a muffin for her, we sat quietly, letting her look us over.

When I looked at her I thought of the faint smell of floor wax, lavender, hot ironing, and baked chicken. Though she was a few years older, she was Beaver Cleaver's mother, except around the eyes. They looked vulnerable, as though there was something in her house she couldn't get clean and she was afraid someone would notice.

"He wasn't a nice man," she blurted. "I thought he was. Last fall, he was very sweet to me for a while, and I thought he was a nice person, but he wasn't."

"We know," Mark replied, taking a bite of lemon pie. "He was a louse."

"He was a bastard," she said, surprising us both. "A real died-in-the-wool bastard. That's what my father used to say about someone like him. When I saw in the paper he was dead, I was glad!" She trembled an unsuccessful laugh. "That's awful. That's just awful, but I was glad."

"What can you tell us about him?" I asked.

"I don't know what you want to know," she said, sipping her tea, tears at the corners of her eyes. "I was very lonely, and I thought he was all right. Only it turned out he wasn't. And I waved my little gun at him and made a fool of myself." She gulped, suddenly aware of what she'd said. "I didn't shoot him! I couldn't shoot anything! But I didn't care when somebody else did."

"Have the police questioned you?" Mark asked.

She shook her head, tears forming in her eyes, ready to spill over. I recalled the trail we had followed to get to her: from Marge to the guy in Boulder, to the apartment house manager, to bingo, to here. If Marge hadn't mentioned the man in Boulder to the police, likely they wouldn't have found out about Sally. Marge hadn't known about her.

Since she was very close to weeping, I tried to change the subject a little. "Did he talk about himself?"

"All the time." She tried the laugh again, at herself. "Honestly, Fred never talked about anything else."

"Well, just try to remember some of the things he said about himself and mention them. We'll try to figure out which ones are important."

"Those things he got into," she said. "Est?"

"We already know about that."

"The peace-marching thing with the children."

"We know about that."

She thought. "He used to go into his ex-wife's apartment all the time."

"Go into?"

"Sneak into. He took a key from his daughter's purse and had a copy made. He used to go over there when nobody was home and sneak in."

Bingo. Ross's suspicions had been correct. Still, it seemed an odd habit to confess to an acquaintance. "Did he tell you why he did that?"

"To find out what she was up to. Lycia. His wife. He told me she wasn't good for the children and he had to keep an eye on her for their sake."

"They're scarcely children," Mark said. "In their twenties."

She looked shocked. "The way he talked, I thought they were young teenagers. He said they were still young and impressionable, particularly his daughter. He said his ex-wife gave his daughter too much freedom, that she ought to have more direction, more sense of purpose. That she'd be happier if she were kept away from undesirable people and didn't have so many decisions to make."

"Undesirable people?"

"Some man she was seeing. He told me he was going to break it up. That the man's family was too much for Shannon. That Shannon wouldn't be able to cope with their level of sophistication."

"Sophistication," I repeated. So the breakup of Shannon and young Ancini had been planned. "Anything else?"

"He said his ex-wife was trying to be a writer and she was no good at it, but maybe she'd pay him not to tell anybody. Then he laughed."

I could make no sense out of that. "A writer?"

"He said she was writing a book or something. Something like that."

"When was that?"

"Oh, a long time ago. I really don't remember."

"Did Fred ever mention Melody Steinwale?" I asked. "The information we have suggests that he used to meet her in the park and talk to her there."

"If that's the woman who married the artist, he used to talk about her a lot," she admitted. "That was before . . . well, when we were just friends, you might say. Acquaintances. I used to see them together, and I asked if she was a relative, and he said no, she was just a friend, that she needed someone to guide her." She looked both angry and embarrassed. "I think he wanted her to be more than that. I saw the way he looked at her. I heard his voice when he talked about her. He was trying to get into her bed." Her face was red, and the words came out raggedly. "But she was too . . . too smart for him."

We gave her time to get herself together.

Mark said, "Is that all you can think of?"

She nodded, then stopped. "Except . . ."

"Except?"

"He said once he'd told the girl in the park she should get some back for herself."

"What do you think he meant?"

"I'm not sure. He used to say things like that all the time. He said everybody needed to find ways to get theirs, more or less, and it was up to each person to make things come out even. He used to smile when he said that, kind of show his teeth. I told him it made him look like a wolf, but he just laughed. He said sometimes a little blackmail was a good thing, only he called it 'calling in the IOUs,' or something like that."

Beyond that, she had nothing else to tell us. I asked for the bill and we walked Sally out to her car. She got in, started to shut the door, then stopped. "It seems very odd to me now," she said. "Talking about blackmail and getting even and all that kind of thing. And him talking about that girl all the time. Looking back, I guess he was telling me over and over he wasn't a nice person. But when I was with Fred, he never made it sound like . . . anything unethical. He made it sound as though he was doing what was logical and right, what everybody did, or doing it for somebody else. . . ."

"Or as though if you objected it was because you were stupid," I suggested. I had noticed that tendency on Fred's part.

She nodded, tears at the corners of her eyes once more. "Yes. As though anybody with brains would agree with him. He wasn't a nice man," she said. "He hit me once when I disagreed with him. I guess that's why I didn't argue with him. I don't know why I even went on seeing him." She pulled slowly away from us, turning her head so we wouldn't see her cry.

We watched her drive off.

Loneliness, I thought again. The things it makes us do!

"She reminds me of my mother," said Mark. "Somehow you don't think of people that age getting sexually involved, getting sick and embarrassed over it."

Mark's mother wasn't that much older than I am. Not that much older than Lycia Foret. I didn't comment.

5

My phone rang Sunday morning about eight, just as the spe-cies-assorted three of us were about to have breakfast and then go out for a little exercise. It was Marge Beebe, sounding mys-teriously aggrieved.

"I've found something among Frederick's things," she said. "Something you ought to see."

"I was about to feed us and take the dog and cat to the park," I complained. "Can it wait till tomorrow, Marge?"

"You ought to see it, Jason. Really. I don't know . . . I can't imagine. . . . I need you to come see it, really." Her voice shrilled away in something approaching barely controlled panic.

I grumbled, but I got out the car. The animals didn't mind as much as I did, but then they didn't have to drive. Being Sun-day, however, there was far less traffic than usual, so it only took half an hour or so.

Marge didn't even supply me with coffee before plunking down a nine-by-twelve brown envelope and a large square cardboard box in front of me. Then she went to the other side of the room and sat down, staring at me as though I was sud-denly contagious.

"What is this?" I asked, indicating the box. It had been sealed all the way around with tape, but the tape had been cut.

"Open it," she said. "Just open it."

I opened it. It was packed with money, new hundred-dollar bills in neat wrappers. I counted one bundle and multiplied in my head.

"There's over half a million dollars here," I said in astonishment.

"I know," she whispered. "I know. It was in the bottom of a footlocker, from the storage room in the basement of Fred's apartment. I was going through his things, and there it was. With the other thing. Open it. Read it. I don't want to talk about it. I just don't know. You'll have to read it."

So I read it. It was handwritten, several pages, and it seemed to be an outline for a mystery story, not a very original one. I'd seen the plot at least twice before, once in a movie and once on TV, involving A and B, each of whom has a person he wants to kill, but doesn't want to be caught. A offers to kill B's victim, and vice versa, at a time when, as the logical suspects, each will have an alibi. I couldn't see why this had occasioned Marge such distress.

"Whose handwriting is this?" I asked when I'd read part of the first page.

Marge tried to answer, but it took two tries before it came out. "Lycia's," she squeaked.

My mouth went suddenly dry. I tried to speak a couple of times, finally managing, "Something Fred kept when she left Washington?"

"Read all of it," she said in the same somber squeak.

Halfway down the second page was a date, as though she'd stopped writing a letter and then continued at a later date. The whole thing had that quality, like a memo or letter to someone else. The date was in June, two years ago. Therefore, this was not something Lycia had left behind in Washington when she left Fred. This was something she had written, at least in its current form, only fairly recently. "How did Fred get it?" I asked, knowing damned well how he had. This was undoubtedly one of the "personal things" Lycia had found missing before she changed the locks.

"Read it all," said Marge.

So I read it all, not liking it particularly. Not liking it at all, as a matter of fact. The Lycia who fascinated and enthralled me simply would not have thought this way, though any real human being undoubtedly might have. The outline of the plot was fleshed out with a good many examples of why the victims needed killing. When I'd finished, I leaned back and gave Marge a somber look of my own. "The way this reads, there's an older woman with a destructive daughter-in-law, and a younger woman with a destructive ex-husband, and they agree to kill for each other, right? You figure this for Harriet Steinwale and Lycia?"

She nodded, silent, watching me as though I'd just crawled out of the earth carrying something dreadful. Her eyes were huge.

"Come on, Marge. You don't think that either of those women . . ."

"What am I supposed to think?" she shouted at me. "It's all there, all planned out. How the older woman will be out of the country when her daughter-in-law dies. Harriet was out of the country! And all that money! Where did Fred get all that money?"

"I don't know where Fred got the money, Marge. Where Fred got all the money may have nothing at all to do with this other thing. And this other thing may have nothing to do with reality."

"I don't care what it has to do with. Right there, in Lycia's handwriting, there's a plan to kill Fred."

"Among other variances from fact, it says that the younger woman would be at an afternoon medical meeting when her ex-husband is killed," I said. "Fred wasn't killed in the afternoon, it was morning, and Lycia was home, with her family."

"Lycia wasn't supposed to be the one who did it anyhow. And maybe they changed the plan."

"Maybe they didn't do it at all." I couldn't imagine the woman I had sat across the table from on Friday night killing anyone. She had cared too deeply about life and the meaning of it. She had cared too much about the saving of it to take it. She was . . . I would have sworn she was that most priceless commodity (Proverbs), a good woman. The Lycia I had met simply could not have killed another woman, however silly and destructive the victim was.

"I want you to find out," Marge said, tears running down her face. "I can't see Lycia or the family again, not any of them, not until I know."

I went over to her and patted her on the shoulder. "Come on, Marge. I don't think this is anything. At worst, a way of working out frustration on Lycia's part by a little daydreaming. At best, an attempt to get a little variety, write something. Lots of people are closet writers, and lots of writers take out their own frustrations on their characters."

"Lycia hated Fred. Ross hated him."

"Marge, they disliked him. They had good reason. He was a real pain, particularly where your niece was concerned. Lots of us have people we dislike. We fantasize killing them or maybe we even joke about killing them. Hell, I've done it myself! That doesn't mean we actually do it."

"Poor Shannon," she sobbed. "He was so . . . so overbearing with her. That's why Lycia left him, you know. She never said a word to me, but I think maybe he used to abuse her. Poor Shannon . . ." Her face flowed with tears.

"I will look into this," I said. "I promise you I will, Marge."

"I want you to take the papers and that box," she cried. "I'm leaving. I told Silas this morning, before he left for work, I'm going to Arizona to see my daughter. I'm going to stay a while. This has all been . . . it's been too much." The tears were flowing freely now, and I patted for a few minutes more before

I asked her if by any chance there had been a gun among Fred's things in the storage locker. She said no. I'd been wondering where Sally's gun had ended up, ever since she'd said Fred had taken it away from her.

After a few more pats and a few more snuffles, I ran for it. I took the package and the manuscript with me. Even though I didn't believe it . . . Well. I wasn't sure. She called to me as I left. "Silas will know where to reach me. You let me know if you find anything out, will you?"

I nodded, saying that I would. It wasn't a promise. I didn't feel like making any promises, and once again I was glad I hadn't taken any money for whatever it was I was doing.

The money could go in the old safe in the basement, along with Marty O'Toole's handgun. I hadn't given Marge a receipt, but I would send her one as soon as I knew definitely how much cash was in the box. She'd have to decide what to do with it, eventually; there was nothing I could do about it but take it off her hands temporarily. There might be nothing I could do about the manuscript either. I considered whether I could approach Lycia about it, or Harriet Steinwale. Who else would know anything about it? It wasn't precisely the kind of thing one talked about to the family, or the kind of thing the family would talk about with outsiders.

When we got home, Bela and Critter were ravenous. Most unlike herself, Marge hadn't even offered them a drink of water. I fed them, then set about fixing my own breakfast with the manuscript on the kitchen table, where it could be perused again in the hope that some kind of sense would emerge.

I went over the handwritten pages again while I ate toasted bagels and jam, hoping it said something else. It persisted in saying the same thing I had read initially.

"Suppose," it started out. "Suppose two women were very good friends, and each of them had someone she wanted dead." Then it went on to describe the daughter-in-law who was driving a son mad with her debts and her flirtations, and the ex-husband who was driving a daughter crazy with his violence, omniscience, and efforts at control, just as he had done when she was a child. Finally it talked about the two women each killing the other's bête noire, and the alibis each would have. One of the women was a doctor. . . .

I chewed my bagel, not tasting it, trying to find holes in this unexpected and unacceptable revelation. Unfortunately, I didn't doubt that Fred had stolen this manuscript from his ex-wife's apartment.' Marge said the writing was Lycia's, and I really didn't doubt that either. The only real question was whether the manuscript was an actual plan or only a bit of catharsis. If the thing was actually a *plan* and not merely a bit of wool gathering—if it *was* a plan, and if I set my prejudices concerning Lycia aside, then I had to accept that Lycia Foret might have killed Melody Steinwale as her part of a deadly bargain with Harriet. In which case, Harriet had killed Fred.

But if Lycia had killed Melody after Fred stole the manuscript, wouldn't Fred have assumed he was the next victim? There was all that business Sally Streeter had brought out. All that "getting even" and suggestions of blackmail. The presence of the manuscript and the money together . . . well, it certainly suggested blackmail. I wondered if Lycia could have come up with half a million. One doctor might have trouble, but two surgeons might be able to raise that much. Suppose Fred had stolen this manuscript, then blackmailed both Lycia and Ross after Melody's death. "Pay me, or I'll give this to the police."

Would they have paid?

If the manuscript had been written only as a catharsis, Lycia would probably have told Fred to give it to the police and the hell with him. Which implied that if she had paid, she had also committed murder. And how had Fred tried to protect himself? If he had thought he was to be the next victim, wouldn't he have done something? Left the usual sealed letter with his attorneys? Or, more likely, wouldn't he have demanded blackmail from both Lycia and Harriet—Harriet had far more money than Lycia did—threatening them both with exposure?

As I sat there staring at the manuscript, I thought that in a way the fact that Fred had it might actually serve to exonerate Harriet. If she knew Fred had it, would she have dared kill him without recovering it first? Perhaps she had tried, but had been unable to find it. Even Marge had found it only long after the fact.

My eyes went glazed. I was totally preoccupied. Bela had become bored with his food and decided to steal an egg bagel from the back of the kitchen counter. Kuvasz dogs are tall and long and they can reach. He did it with a certain amount of decorum, actually, without knocking anything over, while I looked right through him, seeing him do it but thinking of Fred and Lycia and the whole ugly tangle. Once Bela had the bagel impaled on his front teeth, he tried to decide whether it was a rubber ball or something edible by dropping it and watching it bounce, then picking it up again and trying to chew it. The bagel fought back. Bela put a paw on it and pulled. Critter was crouched under the kitchen table, staring at this exhibition and growling. Suddenly aware of all this, I said to Critter, "That's right, Critter. Tell him off. What's with this crazy dog?"

The words had an eerie resonance to them, that flash which is almost déjà vu, a remembrance of the thing itself, and I repeated the phrase to myself, testing for weird. "What's with this . . . with this dog?"

Then the connection was there, the question I'd asked Mark once before but had not pursued. The morning that Melody was killed, she'd been walking her dog. What had happened to Melody's dog?

Dogs don't just disappear, not usually. Ambler said that Melody had had a fat collie. If she had a fat collie in tow when she was murdered in the park, one might expect the fat collie to set up one hell of a racket. Or maybe just run away, leash trailing.

Either would have attracted attention, and since people might well have recognized the dog as belonging to Melody, they'd have noticed her "sitting" on the bench, they'd have said something. "Hey, miss, your dog's running away." In fact, she hadn't been found for some time. Therefore, maybe there had been no fat collie in tow at the time. Or? Or someone took the dog. Someone the dog would go with?

I thought of the shelties I had seen in Lycia's place, all curled up in their baskets under the window, leashes hanging on the back of the door. If Lycia had murdered Melody, she could simply have taken the dog by its leash and led it away.

It was a tantalizing idea, one I didn't know what to do with. It wasn't proof of anything. Or was it? Apologizing to both animals, I left them at home and went for a walk, not quite sure where I was headed until I ended up there, or right across the street at least, slouching in a doorway like a spy, staring at the Louvre apartments.

A man came out with two poodles; the same two I'd encountered before. They tugged him into the plantings and let fly while he pretended not to notice what they were doing. Through the plate glass of the lobby I could see Lycia Foret talking to someone while her shelties sat politely at her feet. She came out in a moment, the shelties tugging her down the sidewalk at a rapid walk. She passed the poodle owner with a nod and a pointed look at the defilement taking place among the plantings and zoomed off toward the park. Belatedly, the poodle owner steamed away in her wake. Not even considering what I was doing, I followed them. I didn't know what I wanted. I didn't know what I was after. The park was on the way home, in any case.

When we got there, Lycia was a long block ahead. The poodle owner found the first bench inside the greenery, gave a furtive look around, and slipped the leashes on both dogs. Evidently this was the usual thing. They zipped off into the shrubbery, snuffling and making treble conversation with one another while he sat back on the bench, wiping his very red forehead and settling his plump person into a slouch.

Lycia was too far ahead to catch up to. Nothing brilliant presented itself to mind, so I sat down on the bench and re-marked, "They'll wear you out, won't they?"

"I am not a dog lover," he said sadly. "They are not mine. I am merely stuck with them."

"That's too bad," I offered. "Dogs take a lot of work if you do it right."

"I don't want to do it at all," he snapped. Then he sat up straight and scowled, as though at himself. "Excuse me. I shouldn't talk this way. The dogs belong to my mother, and when she went into the hospital, she made me promise not to put them in a kennel because they're her babies. So I promised. I'm sure they're perfectly nice animals and a lot of company, but all they do is interrupt my train of thought by whining to go out."

"I see," I said. "You . . . ah, need to concentrate."

He agreed with this, without giving any indication why con-centration was necessary. We sat in uncompanionable silence, watching the dogs chase one another. Finally, he said, "I'm working on the ice-cube series."

"Ah?" I said.

"I'm an inventor," he offered by way of clarification.

"Ah!" I said again.

"The spider in the ice cube was mine. That sold very well. When we were finished with it, it looked remarkably real. Off center, you know, so as not to look purposefully planted. We tried all kinds. The long-legged ones work better. . . ."

"Spider?"

"In an ice cube. For putting in drinks. Joke."

"Ah."

"That's what I invent. Joke products. I've tried to use these animals for inspiration, but all the jokes to do with dogs have already been taken. . . ."

"I see," I said. "You mean like the plastic . . ."

"Yes. That's always been a good seller."

"As a joke?"

"In the salad at parties, or on someone's bed. You know."

I disclaimed any direct experience with faux dog excrement in the salad or on the bed. "My name's Jason Lynx," I offered. "I have a shop over on Hyde Street."

"Willie Stevenson," he said, offering me a limp hand. "The spider sold so well that they want me to come up with some other things to put in ice cubes. Not real cubes, of course. Plastic ones. I've been thinking about fish. . . ."

"Small fish," I suggested sympathetically.

"Minnows," he agreed. "Little silvery ones. Somehow that doesn't have the proper . . . oh, I don't know, impact."

I couldn't think of any comment to make about that. He pursed his lips and glowered. I presumed this was his concentration expression and did not interrupt him. We sat, he thinking of horrors to inflict upon the innocent, I thinking of my own horrors if it turned out Lycia was guilty.

After a time Lycia came back, jogging gently along behind the shelties. She saw me, waved and said hello, but didn't stop. Willie Stevenson rose to his feet and called the poodles. They came to his call, albeit reluctantly. Someone had trained them well.

"You really should walk them more often," I said. "You know, they can't hold it forever."

"I know." He gave me a guilty look. "I usually take them out whenever I hear Mrs. Foret go out. I live right across the hall, so whenever I hear her talking to the dogs, in the hall, you know, I take the poodles out. She's kind of my reminder."

"Sometimes, maybe you don't hear her," I suggested, remembering the morning I had first gone into the Louvre, the morning the poodle had almost peed on my leg.

"When the girl goes, I don't hear her," he agreed. "The Foret girl never talks to the dogs in the hall." He regarded the two pups without either interest or malice. "I'm really not a dog person. I'm not a cat person either. I'm just not interested in animals."

Except spiders, I thought. And minnows. "Well, we'll hope you won't have to look after them too much longer."

He nodded solemnly without responding, and went in the direction Lycia had gone, leaving me to follow. I thought that in one sense it was a pity the poodles weren't his dogs. If they had been with him last fall, he might have been following Lycia on the October day when Melody had died.

Mark hinted for a progress report several times during the next few days, but I put him off. I had a seven-point-buck dilemma draped over the fender of my car, and no idea how to skin it or butcher it. On the one side, I had this passionate belief that Lycia couldn't kill anyone. But, just but, if she had, I wasn't at all sure I wanted to do anything about it. On the other hand, such evidence as we had indicated that she had at least thought about doing so and had probably been blackmailed because of it.

If Fred actually had blackmailed her. If that's where the money had come from. And where else?

I'd spent a lot of futile time trying to think where I might get more information. There were only a few sources who might tell me anything more. Sally Streeter maybe. If Fred had said a little more to her than she'd so far been willing to tell us. Greg Steinwale maybe. If Melody had said something to him, and he'd been paying enough attention to remember. Shannon Foret maybe. If Melody had confided in her, which didn't seem really likely, but there had been that strange, teasing relationship the art instructor had referred to. Though, how would one ask Shannon personal questions without sending her into hysterics?

Or I could get Marge's number from Silas, call her, and tell her I was bowing out.

Or I could lose the manuscript. I considered that for a while.

William Sandiman, my old mentor at the Smithsonian, was often fond of saying, "When in doubt, do nothing." I took off my memory hat to Sandiman and resolved to do nothing at all for a while. I told myself maybe I'd get an idea in the middle of the night. Maybe it would all come to me in a blaze of celestial fire. Besides, I had a legitimate excuse for stalling for a day or two: I had another project in hand, one dealing with Nellie Arpels and Willamae Belling. I had written their names in my notebook, with a message to myself beneath: "Since you have no aged mother of your own to cosset, take these lonely old ladies to lunch."

"A worthy project," I said aloud, trying to convince myself it was an adequate excuse to quit fumbling with the Steinwale-Foret puzzle.

"Were you talking to me?" asked Mark from his office.

"No." I gave him what I confidently hoped was an angelic smile. "I was telling myself to go out and do a good deed."

"I didn't know you were a Boy Scout," he mumbled. "If you really want to do a good deed, find a shower curtain for Gladys. I can't find anything the right color."

"White," I said. "Buy a white one and take it over to that friend of yours who paints T-shirts."

"Belly-boy?"

"If that's his name."

"His name is Horatio Bell Hutchins III. And he only paints things that are either erotic or scurrilous."

"Ask him to make an exception," I suggested. "As *his* good deed for the day."

Mark's lips curled in a magnificent sneer. "He claims to be a decorator of ephemera."

"Tell him shower curtains are at least as ephemeral as T-shirts." They were, too. When they get soap-scummy, four people out of five throw them away and buy new ones rather than try to clean them. At least so my acquaintance down at the Bath Shoppe had once alleged as he looked fondly over rainbow acres of shower curtains and stroked his cash register. "Besides, they offer a wider scope. How much can you paint on a T-shirt?"

"Belly gets quite a lot on. One of the priests over at Blessed Sacrament wanted the Sistine Chapel ceiling on one."

"All of it?"

"I think it was just the creation of Adam. Or Eve. One of them. No, it was Adam, because Belly painted him with an erection and the priest refused to pay him."

"If he can do Michelangelo, he can do Gladys Duchesne's shower curtain. Have him do the same kinds of flowers as are on the wallpaper. Flowers are the sexual organs of plants, and he can be as erotic as he likes with them."

I was trying hard, but even this silliness hadn't made me forget for one instant that I was suspecting Lycia Foret of murder. And Harriet, of course, though it seemed to be Lycia I chiefly regretted. All the nonsense did was delay the issue, making it less immediate. As would my good deed, which had assumed major-project dimensions.

Definition of *project:* Any job which requires more than one phone call to complete.

Definition of *major project:* Any job which requires more than one phone call and the cooperation of another person.

Taking Nellie to lunch wouldn't be easy. She had been out of her second-floor bedroom in the house across the alley only once in recent years. I figured one strong man could carry her down while I went ahead with the chair, if Janice Fetterling, Nellie's daughter, would agree. I could hire a hospital worker to do that. We'd go by Ambu-Cab, if Janice would go along to take care of any personal or sanitary matters that might come up. I had already checked with a few restaurants to find one that was what is euphemistically called "handicap accessible." This can mean that while they have a toilet large enough for a wheelchair, the tables are set so close together that no wheelchair can reach the toilets. Anyhow, I'd done the homework, and had decided on a new place on Seventeenth Avenue, which, though it looked exactly like the restaurant that had been there before, had the advantage of good reviews on the food and table spacing adequate to guarantee mobility for Nellie.

I'd also invited Willamae Belling, begging her to come as a favor to me. I'd told her I needed her along to make conversation with Nellie—as though Nellie had ever had any trouble conversing with anyone who happened by. Since the expedition was to be the following day, I had only today to buy each of the ladies a gift to make the occasion festive, one for Nellie for being herself, one for Willamae for being such a nice client, and something special for Janice for being helpful and coming along. I went out to do so, leaving Mark to struggle with the shower curtain.

Also, after the shopping trip I had another appointment with the plastic surgeon, and the least said about that, the better. That night I took my pain pills and slept on my stomach.

The fated day arrived. Janice and Nellie and I arrived at the restaurant to find Willamae already ensconced. I introduced the ladies. Nellie took one look at her and shrieked, "Willa-*mae* Foster! Is that you?" And we were off to the races.

I don't know why Janice and I were along. We agreed that the weather had been nice. That Denver certainly was bigger than when we were children. That we wished it was more the way it used to be. That the restaurant was nicely decorated though a little noisy. That the food was very good. Meantime, Willamae Belling née Foster and Nellie Arpels née Wyler were reliving old times seventy years ago, around the time of World War I.

It turned out that Willa-*mae* Foster (pronounced with the accent on the *mae* rather than the more gentil *Will*- amae I had assumed) had moved away when she married. When she returned, some years later, she had no idea her old school friend had stayed in town or what her name was. So, suddenly, here they were, and I smiled and nodded and said yes, ma'am, it really was amazing, and thanked whatever gods might be that they had been friends back then, not enemies.

Remember Calvin Boome?" Willamae asked. "Did you ever see his books? Remember Louise Storm?"

"Stormy," mourned Nellie. "She died real young. Only forty."

"Drank herself to death," said Willamae. "She was so fun."

"Remember Jackson Wetherbee and that Cosson girl?"

Both of them dissolved in giggles.

"Remember Cora Frame?" Nellie said. "Wasn't that awful?"

Willamae got a prissy expression and shook her head. "Did you believe she didn't know?"

"Oh, I don't think she knew," Nellie said. Then, catching my half smile of dazed incomprehension: "Cora was a girl we knew. She was adopted, only she never knew it. People didn't used to tell their adopted children, you know, Jason. Anyhow, she fell in love and married this man, and he was adopted, too, and after they were married and she was expecting a baby, somebody told him he was adopted and it turned out they were full brother and sister. Willamae and me, we knew her. She was in school with us."

"I just always thought something should have told her he was her brother," Willamae asserted. "She should have known."

"They didn't look anything alike," Nellie objected. "They didn't, Willamae. He was dark and she was light. She was a little bit of a thing and he was stocky. I don't know why you think she would have known. Animals don't know, and if anybody ought to, they should."

"What happened to them?" Janice asked around a mouthful of quiche.

"It was annulled," said Willamae with a grimace.

"And the baby?"

Nellie shook her head. "Nobody ever knew what happened to the baby. Cora left. Just went right away. Maybe she had it and gave it up." She chewed reflectively. "It's a wise child knows its own father, Willamae. I was saying that to Jason just the other day."

We had a good lunch. Afterward, Willamae came back to Nellie's with us and visited a while, and when she left she said she'd be over to visit again real soon.

Janice made a hmphy noise at me as I was leaving. "If Mama starts having visitors, I'll have to clean house more," she said.

"Do you care?" I asked her.

"Not if it'll make Mama happy," she said with a kind of half smile. She was wearing some of the perfume I'd given her.

The next day was Friday. We plunged into work. I got a pile of invoices figured, talked to Myron, made a pest of myself over the Duchesne job, finally had Eugenia tell me to go back to my office and leave her alone.

Mark came in as I sat staring at the wall.

"What's the matter?"

I grumped something.

"Something's the matter, Jason. You don't usually go all over itchy like this unless something is."

"I don't think Lycia Foret killed Melody Steinwale," I said. "I don't care how many outlines she wrote." So then by way of explanation I had to show him the paper and tell him about the money.

"I wish Grace was here," he said. "She could go ask questions."

I pondered this. Pondered whether I wanted Grace there, asking questions about Lycia Foret. I decided, on balance, I did.

I'd mentioned my strange attraction to Lycia. Now Mark asked, "What is it with the woman, Jason? Is she beautiful or what?"

I couldn't answer that. I had no idea or what. She wasn't that beautiful. And she was older than I by some years. And she was spoken for. And I was inexplicably drawn to her. I threw up my hands.

"I think you'd better really dig into this," Mark said with a serious look. "If you really like her and think she's innocent, then you'd better get busy and prove it. Otherwise, Marge Beebe will come back and decide to turn all the stuff over to the police, and maybe it will be too late."

"I have no idea where to go next," I confessed.

"Well, usually when you don't have any idea where to go next, you sort of mull around through the mud until something jumps into the water and goes plop," he said.

Which was a good enough description of the way I conduct myself.

So I made a list of all the mulling around I might do, and that took a good part of the day. At four o'clock, Mark came in, very pale, and said, "Jason, we're in trouble."

I looked up, wondering who was suing us for what this time.

"Belly-boy left town."

"So?"

"He had the shower curtain. I told him I'd pick it up this afternoon, but when I got down there, he'd left town. Some relative of his died. The place is locked up."

I found myself thinking that Belly-boy's relative might not be the only one who died. If Gladys Duchesne didn't get her guest rooms finished on time . . .

"What time are Gladys's in-laws arriving?"

"Seven. Tonight."

"Where does your friend Belly live?"

He told me. Luckily, not one of the better parts of town. I got out the lock picks and we went, with Mark muttering at my side. Words and phrases like "You don't really mean to . . . You wouldn't really . . . What if we get caught . . . ?"

Jacob taught me to pick locks. One needs to in this business.

People lock their desks or their dressers or whatever, and then they move away or die and somebody sells the furniture. It doesn't do an antique dealer's reputation any good to provide the vicarage with a seven-drawer highboy full of unsuspected pornography or provide a little girl's desk fully equipped with lurid love letters. Therefore, one picks locks. I had found a few interesting things in my time, and a few I wish I hadn't.

Belly's place was an apartment in the near downtown north or largely ethnic side of town. Mark kept watch while I fiddled. I almost had it when the door across the hall opened and a brass trumpet of a voice demanded to know what we were doing.

Without a moment's hesitation, Mark said, "Belly told me to feed his cat while he's at the funeral," Mark drawled. "But the key he gave me doesn't work. So I called the locksmith."

"Oh," said the voice. The door slammed, and I got the one I was working on open. The shower curtain was spread across Belly's worktable, a symphony of coral blossoms, each, if one cared to look closely, very reminiscent of certain aspects of human female anatomy.

"Oh, Lord," said Mark.

"She'll never notice," I told him.

"The in-laws will!"

"They'll be far too well bred to comment."

I folded the curtain into its box and the two of us went scurrying away with it, like two white rabbits, muttering and looking at our watches. We let ourselves into the Duchesne house. I could hear voices in the back of the house, Gladys's high one and someone else. We slipped upstairs like thieves, and entered the redone guest suite. The wallpaper on the fireplace wall was an all-over coral and lavender floral on cream. The colors were picked up in the love seats and in the curtains. The carpet was cream, and so was the bedcover. The rattan chairs had been sprayed lavender, with coral and white striped cushions. There were two large lamps with creamy shades next to the bed, and I tried them to be sure they worked and had large enough bulbs. We had used the tables from our shop. There were tissues in the drawers, along with a few readable books. We hung the shower curtain, straightened the towels, sneaked back down the stairs, and left the keys on the hall table. Gladys should be happy. Her brother the banker should be happy. He shouldn't call my loan before I was ready to repay it. I crossed my fingers and prayed.

The thought of the half million in the safe in the basement fled across my mind. I told the thought to begone, a little shocked that I'd been tempted. Jacob had taught me not to be a thief, and it was the first time I'd considered stealing in years.

Thinking of the loan, I made a mental note to call Myron and ask him how he was coming with our sale. Then Mark went off to his place and I went home in a sober mood to feed animals and refer to the list on my desk. Beginning tomorrow, if Myron gave me bad news, I was going to start scrounging for cash money. If Myron gave me good news, I was going to stir mud. I needed Grace to help me stir mud. And for other reasons. I called her.

"Jason," said a weary little voice. "What time is it?"

"About suppertime," I told her. "What are you doing asleep?"

"We got Ron out of jail. So he brought a bunch of his rowdy friends over here to celebrate and I didn't get to sleep all night."

"You got him out? Great!"

"It was a plea bargain. We didn't even need the lawyer. He'll be in again inside a year, Jason. He doesn't have any sense. He talks this serious line about staying out of trouble, but he can't say no to anything."

"Are you coming home?"

"Tomorrow," she said. "My plane gets there at six in the evening."

A feeling of pure pleasure welled up from somewhere, and I stopped worrying about Lycia Foret.

I met her at the airport, took her home, helped her unpack. She looked worn out, and I suggested she catch a night's sleep and I'd see her the next day. She shook her head, looking sad and lonely, eyes squinched half shut.

"He hasn't learned anything, huh?" I asked. "You really think he'll just get into trouble again?"

"I really do," she said, crying. I gathered her up and we sat on the couch, her snuffling and me rocking her. "What's worst is, I decided there was nothing I could do. I could keep running out there all the time, but it wouldn't do any good. He just hasn't any *sense*, Jason!"

I rocked and murmured nothing much.

She said the same thing three or four times, in different words, then there was quiet. I looked down to find her fast asleep. The only thing that would help brother Ron, so far as I could see, was if somebody hired him a keeper. He had that self-conscious naïveté Grace had often described as common among some youngsters, the kind that says, "Oh, yes, I know there's tigers out there, but they won't bite *me*." And they never believe the tigers will either, until they look down and find themselves disemboweled and the beast readying for the final blow. It always comes as a surprise. The girls who end up with a pimp, amazed that any such thing could have happened. The boys who end up in jail, sentenced to life, not knowing quite how.

I laid Grace on her bed, covered her with a blanket, and went out to get some food. I figured she'd wake up and be hungry, and there wasn't anything to eat in the house. While I was at it, I stopped by the shop and picked up Critter. He'd be company for Grace. When he got home, he explored every inch of the apartment, being sure all the pieces were there. His inspection included a few deep, diagnostic sniffs of the sleeping woman on the bed. Then he settled down on the couch and began to purr, as though some unhappy suspicion had been allayed. He had not been abandoned after all, merely sent on leave.

She woke up about ten to sit on the couch stroking Critter while I fed her supermarket burritos with cheese and green chiles and corn chips and guacamole and fruit salad and cookies and told her the latest about the case. Told her more, perhaps, than I'd intended. When I'd told her about it before, I hadn't dwelt upon Lycia.

"You say you think you recognize this Lycia woman?" she asked.

"Not exactly," I said, unsure of what I'd said. "It's a funny feeling. . . ."

"Maybe you *do* recognize her," Grace said firmly. "The thing you've got to remember, Jason, is you were three years old when you were left at the Home. Kids that age can remember a lot, but not in words. They're really just starting to talk well then. So they remember faces and smells and sounds. This Lycia may look a lot like someone you remember, your mom or some other person who took care of you."

I felt the back of my neck, feeling the spiky scabby little knots of hair growing there in the old scar tissue. "I didn't think anyone had taken care of me."

"Somebody did," she averred. "Even though you got hurt when you were real little, before you got hurt somebody took care of you."

I wasn't persuaded, though it was possible. If Lycia resembled someone I had known, perhaps loved, as a child, it could explain my unwillingness to believe she had done anything bad, my desire to find any other explanation.

"Who are you going to talk to next?" Grace wanted to know.

I told her my three sources. Streeter. Greg. And lovely little Shannon. "I haven't any idea how to approach Shannon," I confessed. "She's like a butterfly. I'm afraid if I come too close I'll cripple her."

"Let me do that," Grace suggested. "She's less likely to fly to pieces if some woman talks to her, particularly someone not a lot older than she is. Besides, I've got a legitimate reason. The case is still open, so I can take some of my own time to go back and look at Melody's murder again."

"Shannon's taking some classes," I suggested. "You'd probably do better if you find her somewhere away from the family. Sometimes she walks the shelties, though I think she stays away from the park."

"Leave it to me," she said with a yawn. "Suddenly I'm so sleepy again."

I took the hint. When I left, she was curled up on the bed with Critter across her feet, the two of them making a corporate noise somewhere between a snore and a purr.

Since I was leaving Shannon to Grace—who would get to it as soon as she could—I decided to try Streeter again. She'd given us her number when we had talked to her at the Pancake House, so I called her the following morning and asked if she'd mind having lunch with me. She was doubtful, a little hesitant, but I told her we'd come up with some questions maybe she could help us with. I'd jotted down some notes. There was the money, of course. Plus the manuscript Lycia had written. Plus his relationship with Melody Steinwale. That's what I really wanted to talk about.

Despite her hesitation, Sally Streeter seemed slightly more relaxed than the last time we'd talked with her. "I've decided to forgive and forget," she said with a rueful smile. "I was spending too much time hating him. So I just decided to put it down to experience and forget it."

"Not quite yet," I begged her. "There are three things we really need to know more about."

"Three?"

"Fred's sister found a lot of money, cash, that Fred had hidden. We haven't a clue as to where it came from. . . ."

Her face stayed blank, but a wave of red washed over it. So. She knew something about that.

"Then there's that book you told us about, the one he said his wife was writing. And last there's his relationship with the young woman you saw him with, Melody Steinwale."

She fiddled with her food, thinking. "Honestly," she said, "I don't know anything about the book except what I told you."

"Which means you do know something about the other two things," I said softly. "Come on, Sal."

She fiddled a bit more, gave me a quick look out of the sides of her eyes, then told me, almost in a whisper, without looking at me.

"It was a little while before . . . before I got really involved with him and then moved. I was in his apartment. I used to take him things to eat, and sometimes he'd offer me some coffee or a drink and we'd talk. I'd talk about my husband, and he'd talk about himself. So this time I was there, having a drink, and the phone rang, and he answered it and said her name. 'Melody?' Like that."

"You overheard the conversation," I suggested.

"I didn't eavesdrop!" she exclaimed. "I didn't."

"I didn't think you did. You were sitting in the living room, and Fred was on the phone right around the corner in the hall, right? You couldn't help but hear." I hadn't seen Fred's apartment, but I'd seen one in the same building and there was a phone alcove with a built-in seat and table in the hall. It was a pretty good bet all the apartments were very much alike.

"I couldn't help but hear," she agreed.

"And what did he say?"

"He didn't say anything at first. Then he said, 'Besides having influence in high places, my sweet, I have enough to make life interesting, as I've told you before.' Then he didn't say anything, then he said, 'I have it. What I do with it is my business.' "

She took a mouthful, without seeming to taste it, washed it down with iced tea, then went back to playing with her food.

"Sally?"

"Then he said, 'That's pure supposition on your part.' And 'You'd have a hard time proving that.' And, finally, 'You little witch, try it and you'll be sorry.' Then he hung up."

"Was that all?"

"That was all, except he was furious. I could tell from the way he spoke. Those might not be the exact words he used, but pretty close. As soon as he hung up, I went into the kitchen with my glass, pretending I hadn't heard him, because he was really angry, and when he got angry, he was mean. When he came in the kitchen, he had red patches up on his cheekbones and he was breathing funny. He told me I should leave because he had to go out, very harshly, just like that. Like 'Get out, Sally, get out of my way.' "

"When was this, Sally?"

"Oh, when was it? I don't know. It was three or four days before I took my gun back and waved it at him. . . ."

"Took your gun *back?*"

"He . . . he took it that same day. That day he had the phone conversation."

"Sally!"

She bridled. "Well, he did! He told me he had to go, so I left. Then, about an hour after that, he showed up at my apartment and asked me if I still had the little gun my husband gave me, and when I said yes, he said he'd take it someplace for me and have it cleaned and oiled."

"And you gave it to him."

"I don't know about those things. Don't you have them cleaned and oiled, like a car? I thought he was being kind, because he was sorry he'd been so abrupt."

Honestly! Some women! "You gave him your gun."

"Yes. And he brought it back to me a few days later, and that's when . . . when he stayed at my place."

"And you ended up waving it at him. . . ."

"Because it was right there, in the box he'd brought it back in, on the coffee table. Usually it would have been at the back of the closet shelf, and I couldn't have waved it at anybody, but it was right there that time. But he took it away from me."

"And he never gave it back."

"No. I don't know what happened to it."

"Do you happen to know what kind of gun it was?"

"A little one," she said doubtfully. "It held six bullets. A twenty-two? Does that sound right?"

I cut and chewed and ruminated. After a time, I asked, "Sally, what did you think Fred's conversation with Melody meant?"

She flushed brick red. "I think he was talking about sex. About having enough of it to make life interesting even though he was a lot older than her."

"How about the 'influence in high places'?"

"Oh, he was always saying that. He meant people he'd met in Washington or on the peace walks. I tried to tell him once they didn't even remember his name. You think the Prime Minister of England remembered the name of this guy trailing along after these kids with these candles? She might have been smiling a nice political smile, but she was thinking about the kids probably spilling candle wax on her carpets, believe me. When I told him that, Fred got real angry. That's the time he hit me. After that, I never disagreed with him."

"And the rest of the conversation with Melody?"

"I told you he wanted to go to bed with her. I just know he did. He'd probably been propositioning her. So she said something nasty to him, like the thing he said to me. About his not being up to her standard or something." She heaved a breath that was like a dry sob, and I reached across the table to pat her hand.

"Come on, Sally. He was a bastard. So you think she said something snide, do you?"

"I think she did. Something about his being too old or something. Then he said she was assuming, she couldn't prove it, and she said something even worse, and he called her a witch. Or maybe it was a bitch, I don't know."

"When you knew he was angry at her, and then when he took your gun, and then when you read in the papers about her being shot, did you connect it up?"

She turned away from me, tears starting in her eyes. "Oh . . . oh, of course I did. I'm not stupid. Of course I did. But then I talked myself out of it. I told myself nobody would shoot somebody else just because that person didn't want to go to bed with them. That's not enough reason to kill somebody!"

I didn't really think so either. I made a few notes in my pocket notebook, and asked, "What about the money, Sally?"

"I saw it once. A whole box of it. He didn't know I saw. I went over with some pie, and knocked, and he didn't answer, but the door was open, so I just went in. And he was in the living room, bent over the coffee table, stuffing all this money in a box. . . ."

"You didn't tell him you saw it?"

"I went back out, to my own place, and I never said a word. I'll tell you the truth, Mr. Lynx. It scared me, there was so much of it. What went through my head was drugs. The only time I've ever seen that much money was on TV, when they were doing drug deals, you know? And then, later, when I had a chance to think, I knew how silly that was. Whatever Fred was doing, it wasn't drugs. But it was his business, and he got nasty when people interfered with his business, so I never said anything."

"When did you see the money?" I asked.

She shook her head. "I can't remember. Last summer, I think. It could have been before. I was his neighbor for almost two years."

I thought about it. If Fred had been blackmailing Lycia, it had to be after Melody had died. But Sally hadn't seen the money after Melody had died, because she'd broken with Fred right after that happened. Was the money Sally had seen some other money? Had he made a career of blackmailing people?

We finished our pie and our coffee and I took Sally back to her apartment building lobby, where she was greeted with squeals of delight by three equally plump ladies who wanted a fourth for bridge. I left her in their generous hands, hoping I wouldn't have to bother her again.

The conversation she had overheard did not fit in with anything else I knew about the Steinwale-Foret puzzle. It had to be connected somehow. I ran over the sequence in my mind. Fred had met Melody at a birthday party given for his daughter Shannon, had built on the acquaintance with Melody, and had propositioned Melody. That much was understandable. But the rest of it? That business about "You'd have a hard time proving that." Somehow that didn't sound like a sexual challenge.

Suppose Melody had found out that Fred was blackmailing someone. Not Lycia, someone else. Somehow, Melody puts two and two together and says to Fred, "You don't have enough money to interest me, Fred."

And he says, "Aside from friends in high places, I have enough to make life interesting."

And she says, "Better be careful how you spend it, Fred."

And he says, "I've got it. How I use it is my business."

And she says, "I know where you got the money, Fred. You got it illegally."

And he says, "You're assuming that."

And she says, "You got it by blackmail."

And he says, "You'd have a hard time proving that."

And she says, "I could give some information to the police."

And he says, "You try that and you'll regret it, you little witch." Or words to that effect. At which point, Fred borrows the gun from his neighbor lady, kills Melody, then cleans and oils the gun, pretends he's had it at a gun shop when he returns it to his neighbor. Then he goes to bed with the neighbor lady. . . . Why? To establish an alibi? With some vague idea of getting her on his side in case anyone ever got suspicious?

Though Sally had talked herself out of believing her gun killed Melody, I wasn't at all sure it hadn't. Fred hadn't returned it. With Sally mad at him, perhaps he had had second thoughts about the wisdom of giving her a gun that could link him to murder.

How could I prove that's what had happened?

It only made sense if Melody knew about the blackmail! If Lycia knew Fred blackmailed people, she could have told Ross and Shannon could have overheard. Or Lycia might have told Harriet and Melody might have overheard that conversation, or Greg might have overheard, in which case he might have told his wife. Unless Fred, full of braggadocio, had told her about it himself.

No good to ask Ross or Lycia. No good to ask Harriet. Greg was so centered on his art, he probably wouldn't remember. Shannon was probably our best bet.

Grace would have to find a way to ask her if she had ever heard Fred Foret's name associated with blackmail.

It was only then that I remembered Greg's remark at his birthday dinner about sticky fingers. Melody had told Greg that Fred had sticky fingers. Greg had mentioned it; then Ross had interjected a comment, and I'd never asked him what he meant. I made a note. When I talk to Greg, ask him again what he had meant by sticky fingers.

Grace picked up a pizza and brought it to my place that night. We raided the wine cellar for something Italian and she stuffed herself with over one-half of a very large double-cheese hold-nothing pizza while I had two small pieces and Bela got the last ones. I'm sure some animal-rights person probably would hold me culpable for feeding Bela pepperoni sausage, olives, and anchovies, but he'd have been crushed to have been left out.

Afterward, Grace allowed as how she felt like spending the night with me. I asked her if my lascivious comments or my playing kneesies with her during supper had influenced her in any way. She said she hadn't noticed. I inquired whether my breathing heavily at her all evening had caught her attention, and she disclaimed any knowledge of such breathing. She said she just felt friendly. As a matter of fact, she felt extremely friendly for some little time. When she had finished feeling friendly, I gasped for air, washed my face in cold water, and then came back to bed to accept her head on my shoulder and put my arms around her silky bare skin. After feeling friendly (as well as before, but, thank God, not during) Grace usually feels either hungry or talkative. We talked about what Sally Streeter had had to say.

"You think he killed Melody?" Grace wanted to know.

"Only if he had a reason. It could have been because she spurned him, though I find that a little remote. A sexual refusal, even one accompanied by some raillery, wouldn't have been enough reason, not even for Fred. He'd have hit her for that, not shot her."

"But if she knew something incriminating and threatened to go to the police?"

"It's all assumption, Grace. In order to establish a motive, we have to prove that there was blackmail and that Melody knew about it."

"I'll talk to Shannon tomorrow," she sighed, turning over and pressing her warm bottom against me.

"Be careful."

"It's all right, Jason. I've met trembly little girls before. Sometimes they're only that trembly when the family is around."

6

I called Trish the next morning, told her I was looking into Fred's death for Marge, and also told her there seemed to be some connection between Fred's death and Melody's. I didn't go into the actual connections, most of which were rather theoretical, but I did mention the way the two bodies had been similarly arranged and the fact that the two victims had known each other and had talked occasionally in the park.

"Do you think Greg would talk to me about Melody?" I asked her.

Long silence.

"Jason, he's just getting over . . ." Another long silence. A sigh. "It might be therapeutic."

"Is he still grieving over her?"

"No. It's not grieving. I don't know what it is."

"You'd be welcome to sit in. . . ."

"No. No. Maybe talking about it would be good for him. I'll make a lunch date for you, how's that?"

I told her that would be fine, anytime, even today. She called back in about ten minutes, saying today. I said I'd pick him up at the studio about one, then spent twenty minutes trying to remember a restaurant with enough privacy so that our conversation wouldn't be remarked upon. There was a little French place on East Colfax that was usually half empty by one-thirty, which was probably as early as we'd get around to conversation. I made a reservation.

I was at my desk by eight, in time to receive a call from Gladys Duchesne. She said the putative in-laws loved the guest rooms. So comfortable. So colorful. Such an original shower-curtain design. The Mifflins wanted to know where they could get one like it. Such a pity the Mifflin son and the Duchesne daughter had had a big fight over the weekend and there wouldn't be a wedding after all.

I told Mark and we both broke up laughing, though Eugenia didn't find it in the least funny.

"All that work!" she fumed. "That impossible deadline with virtually no profit, and there isn't to be a wedding!"

Mark and I decided later she'd been hoping for an invitation.

Myron called, returning my call. Yes, the deal looked like it was going through on the furniture. I sighed a deep sigh, realizing for the first time just how worried I'd actually been. It looked like Fred's mystery money was safe, and I wouldn't have to fight temptation.

When I picked Greg up, I noted that Trish had managed to get him into a clean shirt and tie and jacket, though his eyes seemed still focused on something in the studio. By the time we'd driven across town, he'd come to a little, and he approached the restaurant and the menu fully conscious. He ordered lamb. So did I, telling them to please cook it pink, not raw. Steak, as in tartare, I can take raw; fish, as in sashimi, I can take raw; but not lamb.

"You had some questions about Melody?" he asked as he buttered a roll and took a big bite out of it, spraying crumbs in all directions and surprising me considerably. I'd thought I'd have to sneak up on the subject.

"I need to know more about what she was like," I said. "You probably knew her better than anyone."

He shook his head, as though disagreeing. "I knew her," he admitted. "I think."

"What was she like?"

He got a faraway look. "She could be angelic," he said. "Like a sylph. Like a pet bird. She could be funny. She could make me laugh. She could do sweet things that made me feel loved and cared for. And then she could turn around and be someone else. Sometimes I wanted never to see her again. Sometimes I wanted to lock her up to keep her out of trouble. She was always getting into trouble. . . ."

I waited. He was gone somewhere. I needed to bring him back. "What kind of trouble?" I prompted.

"With men. She flirted. All the time. With everybody. She was seductive. She seemed . . . oh, I don't know. Edible. Like cotton candy. Sweet, and luscious, and . . . insubstantial. Inconsequential. As though you could have her and it wouldn't matter. It wouldn't lead to anything. . . . And then she'd be hurt."

I waited again. He sighed, accepted his soup, and began to eat it hungrily. I didn't prompt him again. After a time, he said, "When she got hurt, she'd begin spending money. Or she'd start saying we had to have a house of our own. Or something. Whenever her feelings got hurt, she'd start accumulating things. Shoes. Jackets. Even putting deposits on furniture for the house we didn't have. . . ."

"I understand your mother offered you a house."

"Yes. A modest house. Mom was right. Wherever we lived should have been within our means to maintain. Melody didn't want that. She wanted . . . I don't know what she wanted. Whatever she had, it was never enough."

"Did she ever mention Fred Foret?"

"He was one of her conquests, that's all. She always told me about them. As though to tell me that other men found her attractive. She knew I loved her, but I couldn't always give her the things she wanted, so then she'd tell me . . . about other men liking her. Or she'd wear something Rich had given her. It was almost as though she thought, if I loved her enough, if somebody loved her enough, some miracle would happen and she'd get whatever it was she wanted."

"She equated not getting what she wanted with not being loved enough."

He nodded slowly. "That's right. But no amount was ever enough. I went to Mom time after time, for this, for that, always for Melody. Eventually Mom said no, no more. In the hospital, the doctor told me that Mom was right. No matter how much Melody was loved, it could never be enough, because she was trying to make up for not loving herself, and she didn't love herself because of the way she was raised. It made sense. I could accept it. Maybe if she'd lived, we'd have . . ."

He fell silent. Our meals came, and we ate them, with me feeling like the worst kind of rat for dragging him through this again. He had obviously suffered enough.

Still, one must persevere. "Greg, you said Melody had said something to you about Fred Foret's having 'sticky fingers.' Can you remember what that was about?"

He put down his fork and stared over my shoulder, that abstracted, concentrated look back on his face. "Not really. It's just something she said about him." He focused on my face then, as though he really saw me. "Jason, sometimes I tried not to listen. Can you understand that? It hurt too much to listen. I just smiled and kind of made noises in my throat and didn't listen to her. She was telling me this man, this Fred Foret, who's connected with people my mother knows and likes, has propositioned her and wants her to go to bed with him, and she's making quite a song and dance out of it. . . . More than usual, I mean. As though it was more important than all the other times. And I didn't want to listen. I didn't want to."

"I don't suppose anyone else would know what was going on there," I said, more saddened by his tone than by the lack of information.

"Rich might know," he said.

I cleared my throat. "I thought she'd left Rich long before she met Fred."

He looked at me, a clear, limpid gaze with pain at the bottom of it. "She never left Rich," he said. "She always went back to Rich, now and then. She always had some new present he'd given her. Especially when I couldn't afford to give her anything much. Last Christmas, we were broke, and we agreed not to give each other presents. At Christmas dinner, Mom complimented Melody on her dress and she said Rich had given it to her." He grinned, a brief, humorless grin. "Needless to say, Mom wasn't pleased."

"Did she ever say anything to you about blackmail?"

"Blackmail? No. You mean someone blackmailing her?" He sounded agitated at this.

"No, no. Someone else being blackmailed."

He shook his head at me, then went back to his meal. When he had finished, he put his utensils beside one another, lining them up with finicky care. "It's a funny thing. When I was married to Melody, I thought she made the sun rise and set. Only, when she'd been gone for a while, I realized how tired she made me. I was always tired around Melody, and worried, and apprehensive. Sometimes she could make me feel ecstatic, you know, but she seldom made me feel good. . . .

"Trish makes me feel good. She takes charge of details, lets me get on with my work. If I yell at her about something, she says, 'You're hungry. You're probably tired. After you eat and sleep, we'll talk about it.' She's strong. She's calm. She knows I care for her. She doesn't ask me to prove it twenty times a day. . . ." He took a sip of water. "I love her. And yet . . . yet sometimes . . . sometimes I miss Melody so much I could cry."

There was such yearning in his voice, I could hardly bear it. There didn't seem to be a lot to say after that. I dropped him back at the studio, hoping, whatever else he might say to Trish,

he would not say to her what he had said to me. Honesty has to
stop somewhere.

Grace had called and left a message saying she had talked to
Shannon Foret. I called her back, and she answered in her
"official policeperson" voice, saying she would get in touch
with me later. That meant someone was at her desk, or, considering how long she'd been gone, several persons.

Lucinda Hooper called. John had sent pictures of his new
highboy to some dealer on the Coast, asking for an appraisal. It
had come back ten thousand higher than he'd paid for it. She
sounded awed.

I bit my lip and kept my voice calm. "That's a New York
price, Mrs. Hooper. He might not get that for it here." And if
the bastard didn't trust me, to hell with him.

"I understand," she bubbled, "but he's very excited. Anyhow, his birthday is next week, and I want you to pick something out."

I asked her how much, and she said some little thing in the
ten-thousand range. I went downstairs to see what I had in the
fifteens. Screw them.

"You have a Chippendale fire screen," said Eugenia. "It has
an impeccable history and is in immaculate condition."

She was right. The thing had been around so long I'd almost
forgotten it. It was in the basement, so I went down to fetch it.
Eighteenth-century fire screens shouldn't be confused with
modern metal fire screens. The purpose was quite different.
Antique fire screens were not meant to be put near the fire;
they were meant to stand well away from the fire and throw
shade upon a person. They often came in Ma and Pa pairs, and
they have, typically, a gracefully carved tripod leg with some
turned ornamentation to lend weight, and then a tall, slender
pole. Fastened to the pole with a brass adjusting screw is a
square vertical screen covered with needlepoint or, sometimes,
printed cotton. The screen can be raised or lowered as needed

to screen the face or hands from too much heat. The one I had was mahogany with the screen worked in an all-over needle-point design of formalized roses and leaves. It stood about five feet tall, and the screen measured a few inches less than two feet square. Because they look a little bit like folding tables, some of them have been converted into tables, or vice versa. Converted tables are worth far less. This one was and had always been a fire screen, and the needlework was original and in good condition.

Chippendale and Hepplewhite-style fire screens are rare and expensive. Good American ones are worth more than most English or European ones, because there are fewer of them. The one I had had been in the same family for two centuries, had moved from Connecticut to St. Louis in the 1800s, and from there to Kansas City at the turn of the century, and then to Denver. It had only been sold when the last surviving family member had died. The needlepoint was quite faded, as it would be, and the stand showed wear on the feet and on the adjusting pole, as it should. Dealers call this wear "patina," a combination of tiny scratches and abrasions resulting from use. One never, never "refinishes" to get rid of patina, though a quick rub with furniture polish is acceptable. Eugenia gave it the cleanup while I vacuumed the needlepoint screen, and we set it aside to show Lucinda Hooper.

"Of course, you're going to ask twice what it's worth," Eugenia said sarcastically.

"Tell her fifteen thousand," I said. "Which is what it would sell for on the Coast. And a letter from me establishing its provenance." Provenance is important when antiques are regarded as investments. Later purchasers may want to know who originally owned it and where the dealer got it.

"It was tagged at ten," she complained.

"It's now tagged at fifteen." I smiled sweetly. "That'll give you bargaining room." Actually, I'd paid almost seven for it at auction. We also polished up an Empire pedestal-base card ta-

ble and a little Queen Anne country tea table. Myron had paid
eight thou for the one and six for the other, at a winter auction
in the middle of a blizzard with nobody there but him and, as
he put it, three other lazy dealers. The Queen Anne had had a
loose leg, but the pieces were all there and after I'd repaired it,
the only thing newer than 1740 was the glue. Once the selection was complete and I'd tagged the tables at fourteen and
thirteen thou, respectively, I went back upstairs and left Eugenia to deal with Mrs. Hooper. Any of the items would be a
reasonable buy and would hold their value very well, or there
were other things in the showrooms that might appeal.

Grace called me back about suppertime. I invited her over,
and she showed up breathless, with a tape recorder in one
hand and a sheaf of papers in the other.

"I recorded her," she said. "I had it hidden in my purse."

"Is that legal?"

"This was unofficial," she explained. "On my own time."

"What's all the paper?"

"The file on the two killings. Nothing there of any help,
Jason. I just thought you might want to see them."

"Is that legal?"

She grinned at me and wrinkled her nose. It wasn't legal.
Or, rather, it wasn't in accordance with regulations, put it that
way. While she threw together a vast and eclectic salad in my
kitchen, I skimmed the files. She was right. There was nothing
there of any help and almost nothing I didn't already know
except the time of death for Melody. From the stomach contents, coffee and a roll, consumed, according to Harriet
Steinwale's cook, at six-thirty in the morning, Melody had died
about seven. When we sat down to our salads, Grace put the
recorder on the table and turned it on. After the usual hiss of
running tape, I heard her voice.

Grace: I'm Detective Willis, Miss Foret. I'm interviewing
people who knew Melody Steinwale, just to see if we can learn
a little more about her.

Shannon (hesitantly): I didn't know her all that well.

Grace: Your art instructor says the two of you were fairly close.

Shannon: No. That was her. She was close. She fastened herself onto me. (The voice was petulant, almost childish.)

Grace: Can you tell me about that?

Shannon (sighing): Mother gave me a party for my twenty-first birthday. Harriet Steinwale came down to wish me happy birthday, because Harriet is Mom's close friend, and Harriet brought her son, Greg, and his wife. Even though she lived right upstairs, I'd never really met Harriet's daughter-in-law before.

Grace: Who else was there?

Grace tapped the off switch and said, "This kid was really uptight, so whenever she got too nervous, I asked her something easy, okay?"

I told her it was okay with me. She got up from the table, fetched a loaf of whole-grain bread and a cube of butter, buttered three large pieces to go with her salad, sat back down, and turned the recorder back on.

Shannon: There was our family, and Ross, and Harriet and Greg and Melody. And my father. He just showed up. And some of my friends from school, about six of them. And Keith's date. Not Stephanie, the girl he knew before. Julie somebody.

Grace: And that's the first time you'd ever met Melody.

Shannon: Yes. I'd seen her before, like in the elevator, but not really met her.

Grace: But she "fastened onto you"?

Shannon: She did. At the party she found out I was taking an art class that summer, and later she showed up at the same class. Everyplace I went, she'd show up. Always asking me to have coffee or go out for a beer. I don't even like beer. She wouldn't listen when I said no.

Grace: The art instructor says she stuck to you fairly tightly.

Shannon: I couldn't get rid of her. I told her to leave me
alone, I didn't like it, but she wouldn't.

The recorded voice had risen in both pitch and tempo.
Grace was getting some leftover ham out of the refrigerator.

Grace: Did she ever talk about her husband?

Shannon (surprised): No. Why would she? I didn't want to
hear about her husband.

Grace: Did she ever talk about any member of your family?
(Pause.) How about your father?

Silence.

Grace: She did talk about your father.

Shannon: I didn't want to hear it. I didn't want to hear any
of it. She was at me all the time about it. About how he wanted
her to go to bed with him. I didn't care! She asked me if I
thought old men like that ought to go after young girls not
much older than their daughters. She was always asking me
things like that. Always wanting to talk about sex. I just didn't
care! It wasn't my business. I told her to stop, but she just
laughed.

Grace: So Melody told you that your father had attempted or
was attempting to seduce her.

Shannon (angrily): I don't think that's the word. Seduce. He
just wanted to do it to her, that's all. There wasn't any seduce.
Both of them, that's all they wanted to talk about. I don't want
to discuss it. It doesn't have anything to do with anything!

Grace tapped off the recorder again, finished building her
ham sandwich, and refilled her salad bowl. Beneath our feet,
Bela sighed. We weren't eating anything he especially liked.

"Where did you conduct this interview?" I asked.

"In her apartment. After everyone else had gone off to
work."

"What do you make of it?"

"I don't know." Grace chewed some lettuce, rabbitlike. "She
was very upset. There's only one more question on the recorder. I asked her if she'd heard anyone in her family mention

the word 'blackmail.' She said no. The way she relaxed immediately when we got off the subject of Melody and Fred Foret makes me believe she was telling the truth. The word 'blackmail' didn't bother her at all."

I rubbed my head. "Greg Steinwale suggested I talk to Rich Beacon," I said. "Evidently, Melody never really severed that relationship."

"You think Melody might have told him something?"

"He's about the only source we've got left," I complained.

Grace, now building a second ham sandwich, nodded in sympathy. "Something weird here, isn't there, Jason? All the time I was talking to this girl, I had the feeling she knew something she wasn't telling me. Not the blackmail. Something else. If I'd just known the right question to ask . . ."

"I've got a question for you. How many sandwiches are you going to eat, on top of half a loaf of bread on top of three helpings of salad?" I wondered in amazement.

"I'm hungry," she said, sighing. "I'm always hungry." There was mustard on her lips.

It was one of the things I found most endearing about her, once I got over the initial surprise. Grace weighed around a hundred eighteen or twenty, dripping wet, but she ate like two starving stevedores. It took very little to make her happy. Just lots and lots of food. I leaned across the table and kissed her in the middle of the mustard. She looked both surprised and gratified.

Rich Beacon was not the kind of person I could simply drop in on. I could not get past his secretary at his office. At his home, I could not get past either of two adamantly polite-voiced servants. I thought about it the next day, thinking up different approaches and discarding each of them as unworkable. Beacon played golf, but I didn't. I didn't belong to any of the clubs he belonged to. We were both symphony supporters, but he was out of my league. Finally, I decided to ask Neal

Ambler if he would make an introduction. Ambler knew Rich, and he more or less knew me. More importantly, he had cared about Melody enough to want her murderer found.

Ambler was out of town for a few days, so that whole matter had to go on hold. I went to see Nellie, who announced proudly that Willamae had been to see her three times. I dropped in on Jacob, who was in a fretful mood. Grace had to work late three nights running. Mark had received a final Dear John letter and wedding invitation from his friend Rudy, so he was about as gloomy as anyone could be and still survive.

"The bride's someone he's known for years," Mark said. "A girl whose older brother he went to school with. Her parents know his parents."

"Catholic girls' college?" I wanted to know.

Mark nodded. "She's thirty. He sent me a picture. She has more hair on her upper lip than I do. I'll bet she's a virgin."

"Rudy tell her about himself?"

Mark shook his head.

"Well, you could always go to the wedding, and when the priest asks if there is any reason these two should not be joined together . . ."

"I don't think they do that at Catholic weddings," said Mark. "I don't think I could do that even if they did."

"Well, visualize it anyhow," I suggested. "As catharsis." Everyone else was having one. Why not Mark?

Ambler got back in town the next day. I explained what I needed to talk to Rich Beacon about.

"You're kidding!" he said. "You mean, she went on seeing old Rich after she was married?" There was something in his voice very like pain.

I said so her husband had told me.

He sneered. "What's the matter with that kid? No guts?"

"I think he told himself he was being understanding, Neal. I gathered he tried to convince himself that Beacon was a father figure to her and she needed to keep his friendship."

"Father figure, hell. Money figure, more likely. Or good stud. He was still giving her things?"

"According to Greg, yes."

"I'll be damned."

"Can you get me an introduction?"

"Tell you what. Rich and some of us play a little poker at the Petroleum Club every Friday. That's tomorrow night. I'll take you as my guest, and you can see if he'll talk about it."

"I'd rather just . . ."

"Draw poker. Table stakes. We generally have about five hundred to a thousand in the pot. Bring money." And he hung up on me. He had sounded rather hostile.

At this point I must digress once more to say something about the Home.

"Homes" for neglected or abandoned children, as a class of charitable endeavors, do not by and large have much money. Even when state-supported, they are likely to have budgets which vary only from modest to slim. The Home in which I was reared was no exception to this rule. This means that the employees of such places, by and large, are either extremely dedicated or virtually unemployable. Only these two classes of people will accept the starvation wages offered.

Some of the people I remembered at the Home had been of the former type. May their halos always shine in heaven. Some of them had been of the latter type, including Mrs. Opinsky and Mr. Josiah Basil, the janitor. Mr. Josiah Basil, when I knew him, was a man in his seventies. He had spent his better years gambling through the length and breadth of these United States and several Latin American countries. Though he professed to know all about roulette and blackjack and what he called chemmy, mostly what he knew about was poker. He knew straight poker and he knew crooked poker, draw and stud and six other kinds, and he taught me and Jerry Riggles and Prense Brown and a couple of older guys all of them. Old Josiah used to deal hands face up around the table and then

cover them up and make us list all the cards that were showing. Then he'd bet a couple of rounds and make us list all the
cards that were probably being held if nobody was bluffing.
Josiah had memorized the odds on every possible draw of the
cards, and he taught them to us as though they had been multi-
plication tables. Then, just in case that hadn't sunk in, he
taught us to cheat.

Thus, when Neal Ambler hung up on me after making his
little offer, I was not panicked. Yes, I could play draw poker
with the big boys and probably limit my losses to what I could
. . . well, if not afford to lose, at least compensate for losing. I
hadn't had any practice lately, but it isn't the kind of knowledge you forget, and there was always Fred's money in the
basement.

This is by way of explaining why I didn't call Ambler back
and tell him to forget it. Hubris, I guess. Or stupidity.

I was introduced to the group the following night. There
were five of them. I made the sixth. Ambler, Beacon—call the
others Charles, Davis, and Evans. All about the same age, well
fed, well massaged, sleek, hair newly trimmed, eight-hundred-
dollar suits and handmade shoes. Something a little desperate
about Davis maybe: a little overeager to see his cards. Beacon
himself was the epitome of well-greased money. Big. Extremely well tailored, barbered, and manicured. Black hair just
turning gray at the temples. A beefy, handsome face with a
wide, recurved Greek-statue mouth. Michelangelo's David at
fifty. Not unlike the others, really, all of them relaxed and easy
or damned good actors.

Beacon said, "Neal here tells me you're looking into
Melody's murder." This was while the other four were getting
drinks and generally getting settled.

"I am, yes," I said.

"Anybody paying you to do that?"

"No," I said, shaking my head. "I'm not a professional at
that. I don't take money."

"Some kind of interior decorator, are you?"

Well, well. The man had done some digging. "No," I said. "Basically I'm a dealer in antiques. I do decor as a sideline to that, but I prefer to do it only for clients who have bought antiques and want an authentically period look. My education is in art and history, not in design."

"What do those things cost?" he asked. "Antiques."

I didn't believe for a moment he was as naïve as that question indicated. "Some antiques are priceless. Many of those are in museums. Some are cheap. Many of those are in junk shops. Some antiques range in value from a few hundred to a hundred thousand dollars, and I have stock across that range."

I didn't tell him the bank had a mortgage on most of it. He probably knew it without my telling him. He probably ate bank vice presidents for lunch.

"Is that right?" He gave me a patronizing smile, pointed out a seat for me to occupy, and we settled down to play cards.

They began chatting about oil in the manner of men who spend a lot of time together, light, joshing conversation which betrayed an intimate knowledge of one another's pasts. Charles joshed Ambler about an exploration deal that had fallen through. Ambler teased Beacon about some wells they'd drilled in the early sixties. "Those Magdalena wells were so dry, every mornin' we had to start over 'cause they'd blown away durin' the night." My only excuse for being so slow to catch on was that I was thinking about what questions I wanted to ask Beacon rather than concentrating on what was really happening. I had three pat hands in a row, either in the initial deal or after I'd taken cards. I'd taken one little pot and lost the next two. It wasn't until I got the fourth pat hand that I realized what was happening. The fellas were having fun with the new boy. The only way they could have set this up was for every dealer to have an identical used, carefully stacked deck. I hadn't seen anyone switching decks, but then I hadn't been looking. They'd done it so smoothly I knew the sweethearts had played this little game with novices before.

We anted up and the dealer asked for cards. I kept one pair from my full house and asked for three. There was a slight, a very slight pause in the flow of the game. If I got three cards, the deck would be out of synch, and none of their hands would work either. Then we could play some honest poker. That is, if there wasn't any fancy finger work going on.

I watched the dealer pointedly enough to be almost insulting. Evans. He fumbled with the cards, but he dealt them off the top. I thanked him in a pleasant voice, my companions went around asking for ones and twos, and we settled down. I ended up with a full house again, if you can believe it. What I had received in the draw were the three nines Charles had been expecting. He was to my left and had taken two and three cards, alternately, each hand. My full house took that pot, and I was even.

Next hand was a nice little straight. I took two cards off the top of it and asked for two. I got a pair of the threes my neighbor'd been expecting, which went nicely with the three of clubs I'd held on to. Pure chance. That was the way they'd stacked them. Three of a kind was enough for the next pot, too. After that, I didn't notice any more chicanery, though the smoke got pretty thick after a while. After an hour or so, when I was a few hundred ahead, we broke for drinks and refreshments, and Beacon took me over to a table by the window where we could look down on the city.

"What did you want to know?" He was amused, if anything.

"I want to know anything Melody said to you about Fred Foret."

He stared into his glass. "To tell you the truth, son, I didn't pay a hell of a lot of attention to anything Melody said. She talked a lot, that little gal did, and most of what she had to say was like chickens clucking."

"Anything you can remember."

"One little thing did catch my attention. She talked about turning him over to the FBI to get even with him. Seems like he was putting the moves on her pretty hard, and she kind of resented it."

"I didn't know the FBI had jurisdiction over seductions."

"Don't ask me, son. I'm tellin' you what the lady said."

"You went on seeing her after she was married?"

"Put that the other way, son. She went on seeing me. She'd call me up every now and then, and we'd have a little supper together. I'd give her some little present I'd sent my secretary to pick out, and we'd have a few drinks and a little snuggle for old times' sake. You know."

The man's complacency angered me. "Her husband thought she regarded you as a father figure."

He reddened, I thought at first with anger, but then he bellowed with laughter. "Damn, if she thought I was her daddy, she sure oughtn't to've done what we done. And her looking like she enjoyed it, too." He went on laughing, gradually mellowing. "Oh, son, she was an all right little girl so far's little girls go. Had cute little ways. Real sweet in bed. It was nice havin' her around makin' Ambler's eyes bug out. He was always crazy about her. I played fair with her. Had her teeth straightened out. Sent her to the best place to have her hair done. Sent her to school. Gave her charge accounts at good stores. Bought her lots of clothes, lots of shoes. Got her funny foot fixed. . . ."

Something clanged. "Funny foot?" I asked. •

"She had this little old web between her toes. I got a doctor to fix that for her so she could wear those barefoot shoes the girls wear. Little old Melody, she did all right."

I didn't answer him. As soon as I could, I excused myself and left (still ahead by about fifty dollars, which wasn't enough to make anyone at that table mad), thinking all the time of what Nellie had said.

It had been right there in front of me and I hadn't seen it.

When I got home, it was late, but I called Silas anyhow and got Marge's number. I woke her up and asked the question I should have asked her long ago.

"Marge, what was Fred's full name?"

She sighed, trying to wake up. "Fred?" she asked vaguely, as though she'd never known him. "Oh, Fred. Frederick Charles Maudlin Foret," she said. "Maudlin was my mother's family name."

I thanked her and hung up.

Rick Maudlin. Nellie was right. It was a wise child that knew her own father.

I had a pan of homemade lasagna in the freezer. Along about ten in the morning I stuck it in the oven, and it was ready to eat by the time Grace showed up at half past noon. Mark joined us while I made my revelations and we "reviewed the problem." We agreed that it was a toss-up between Lycia and Fred as Melody's killer; if Lycia had done it, then probably Harriet killed Fred. If Fred killed Melody, then who killed Fred? Sally? Marty O'Toole? Simmons, for some reason unknown? Ross?

"Fred didn't know she was his daughter," Mark marveled. "How could he not have known?"

"Why would he have?" Grace asked in a practical voice, taking a third helping of lasagna. She had her napkin tied around her neck and it was well covered with cryptic messages written in stringy cheese, punctuated with tomato sauce. "He'd probably forgotten about ever being married to that woman. What was he, nineteen? Twenty?"

"But wouldn't he be the least bit suspicious when Melody talked about hunting for her father?"

"She wouldn't have said a word about that to Fred," Grace opined. "Not a word. The first time she saw him at that party, she heard about the webbed toe or saw it, and right then she figured him for her father. He knew her as Greg Steinwale's wife. If she didn't tell him where she was from—or if she told him a fib about it—why would he suspect?"

"Jason says the art instructor told him Melody said she and Shannon looked alike," Mark went on doubtfully.

"That was her little joke," Grace said. "They didn't look alike. If they had looked alike, Fred might have realized, but they didn't look alike, so Fred hadn't a clue. Also, I think Melody was punishing Shannon for being Fred's daughter."

Mark looked puzzled.

"Fred simply abandoned Melody. He and Lycia were divorced, but he still presumably acted like a father toward Shannon. Melody probably resented that. So she played this nasty game. . . ."

"A vengeance game," I said. "Rich Beacon says she mentioned the FBI in connection with Fred. That and getting even." There was still something wrong in the FBI reference, but whatever it was eluded me. My notebook had a list of things I'd thought of, and I referred to it, deciding what to do next. "I've got a few loose ends I can work on. Melody's dog, for one."

"What about me?" Mark asked in his depressed voice.

"You can find out whether Ross and Lycia have borrowed money lately. Or, since they might have had a half million to give to Fred, find out whether they've cashed in any stocks or bonds or sold any real estate. I need to know the same thing about Harriet Steinwale. . . ."

"There are some brokers I know. . . ." His voice drifted off.

I figured Mark knew people he could ask questions I couldn't get answers to.

"How about me?" asked Grace.

"You can find out if Marty O'Toole has ever been charged with violence of any kind. Has he ever assaulted anyone? Or threatened anyone with a gun?"

If something didn't break, I would fire some bullets from that gun in the basement and give them to Grace to check against the bullets they'd taken out of Fred, but I didn't want to pull O'Toole in that deeply just yet. Poor guy. He'd already had quite a lambasting.

I kept the business about the collie dog for myself. When Grace had left and Mark had gone back to work, Bela and I went out for a quick walk to stir our blood and our brains. When they were sufficiently stirred, we sat in the middle of the park and let the muck settle. There had been something useful in my visit to Lycia's apartment, if I could just remember what it was. It lingered in my head, just out of reach.

I shut my eyes and visualized arriving, the half-open door, Lycia in a robe welcoming Marge. The living room. Sunlight, plants, a lot of color. We went through into the kitchen. It was a small room. Crowded. The shelties were in their baskets under the window. The door was a swinging door. When Ross got up from the table, I moved back to give him room.

The dogs' leashes had been hanging on the back of the kitchen door just where I hang Bela's. Plus . . .

Plus half a dozen framed certificates from community organizations. The Lighthouse. There were several from the Lighthouse.

What else? One from a child abuse prevention group. One from an animal rescue organization. Not a name I recognized.

"Come on, Bela dog." I nudged him out of a happy dream of freely chasing squirrels, and we ran home, with me ignoring the aching leg almost the whole way. I thought I would recognize the name of the organization if I saw it.

As I did immediately on looking at the list in the phone book. Ani-pals.

The phone rang and rang before someone answered. "Hi there," I said to the breathless voice. "I hope I didn't catch you at a busy time? I'm calling for Dr. Lycia Foret, actually. She brought an old collie in there last October. It was a Thursday, I think the eighteenth. She'd like to know what happened to the dog. Do your records tell you that?"

There was a frantic burbling at the other end.

"No, no. She has no complaint at all. She's just curious, and she asked me to find out for her. . . ."

The voice retreated. There were paper noises. Eventually the voice returned.

"Put down the following week," I said. "Yes, well, she really didn't expect it would have been adopted. Thank you very much."

Damn. Damn, double damn. Dr. Lycia Foret had delivered an old collie dog to Ani-pals on Thursday morning, the eighteenth of October. Melody Steinwale had died while walking her dog on Thursday morning, the eighteenth of October. The following week, since no one had adopted it, the dog was "put to sleep."

And the person I least wanted to prove anything against had become my foremost suspect.

After struggling with myself for most of two nights, I decided to talk to Lycia Foret. I called her, told her I was looking into Fred's death for Marge, and asked if I could come over.

She told me no. Shannon was home, and she didn't want Shannon upset. Some policewoman had recently upset Shannon, and Lycia didn't want that to happen again. She would come to me.

I made a fresh pot of coffee, got out the good china, put on a pot to boil, in case she preferred tea, and was hunting for Agatha's linen napkins when she arrived. My preparations had breathed much of romance and very little of interviewing a murder suspect. I felt silly and a little undignified.

She, however, was charm itself. She complimented me on the shop, on the various pieces in the hall as I escorted her upstairs, on the office itself. She spoke knowledgeably of the Rococo Revival side chair by my desk, a chair much like one her grandmother had had in her sewing room.

"Grandma's had lions' heads on the back," she said. "I like

the grapes better. I never liked leaning back on those lions. I was always afraid they'd bite me."

"Where was that?" I asked, smiling despite myself.

"In St. Louis," she replied, returning my smile. "Where I grew up. Mostly. Until I came out here when I was twenty to go to school."

"That's when you married Fred."

She nodded, no longer smiling. "It seems so ridiculous now, Jason. May I call you Jason? It seems ridiculous now that we attached so much importance to sex then. I don't know if you can conceive of how important it was to be a virgin when one married. One was brave, clean, reverent, and a virgin when married. . . ."

I tried to look encouraging, wondering what the hell she was talking about. She saw my confusion.

"You wonder what I'm going on and on about, don't you? Ten years later it was all different. The sexual revolution had happened, and it was all different. You grew up in a different time. But for me, for young women in my group, virginity was important. So a lot of us married too early and quite unwisely. We couldn't maintain virginity over the long haul, so we got married, and then we found we couldn't handle marriage either. That's what I'm trying to tell you. I didn't know Fred at all when we were married. I didn't know any man, really. My father was long gone. My older sister, who'd raised me, was . . . Well, she wasn't there to give me any good advice. So I married this man and had two babies, and things were so busy I didn't notice that I really didn't like him very much. And we went to Washington, and I liked him even less. And when Shannon was seven, we left him and came home, Shannon and Keith and I. I didn't divorce him, I just left him. It was only when he came back here five years later that I divorced him."

"Amiably?"

She belied her hectic words with her tranquil smile. "Oh, in the end it was amiable, yes. I would have preferred that Fred stay in Washington, but he said he needed a change. I think he may have burned his bridges in Washington. Something he said implied that he left just in time. In time for what, I don't know. I know he enjoyed teaching at the university. Shannon told me he had many plans for his retirement. He always had these enthusiasms, est, UFOs, one thing or another. He was always looking for final answers. Lately he was working on world peace again, I understand. I haven't seen him half a dozen times in the—what is it?—nine or ten years since."

"But he saw Shannon," I said. "That was the trouble, wasn't it?"

She looked down at her hands. They lay quietly in her lap, but she stared at them, as though they were snakes, writhing. Perhaps they wanted to writhe, but she kept them quiet. "Yes," she said, almost in a whisper. "He did see Shannon."

"At dinner the other night," I commented, "Ross had something to say about it."

"Ross would." She smiled. "Oh, yes. Ross would."

"And then there's this," I said, laying the manuscript on the desk in front of her. "Marge found it. Among Fred's things."

Her eyes fastened on the manuscript. "I rather thought she might find it somewhere. I even thought of looking for it after he died, but decided against it. I hoped he'd lost it, but then, Fred wouldn't have done that."

She tore her eyes away and got up then, only her haste betraying any agitation at all. She strode to the window, looked out at the building next door, through the office window into the neighboring offices where, I knew, several pale persons bustled about all day like gnomes, shifting paper.

"Lycia," I said. "I'm not an enemy. I'm not the police. I'm not . . . I'm not official."

"What does that mean?"

"Just that. If you can explain it away, do. If you can't, tell me to go to hell. I'm not going to give this thing to anyone."

"But Marge might."

I gritted my teeth. "I don't know."

She sat down again, sighing. The sigh made me remember my manners. "Lycia, would you like some coffee? Some tea?"

"Jason, I would like a drink. Scotch? I'd even settle for gin in a pinch."

I think my mouth dropped open. Maybe not. Why did I think she wouldn't drink? I went to the kitchen, got her a scotch on the rocks, sat down behind the desk, and waited while she gulped half the drink without ever losing that tranquil look. She set the glass down, took the manuscript in her hands, and flipped through it.

"I wrote this to save my sanity," she said. "Well, Harriet and I both did. We shared drafts back and forth. We had coffee and cried together. Then we decided we weren't killer types—I guess I decided that—and we said hell, let's figure out something else. Of course, that was before Greg went in the hospital. Before Fred broke up Shannon's engagement. . . ."

"Are you saying you intended to kill but changed your mind?"

"I'm saying we'd never actually intended to kill anyone. We just fantasized the idea. It was fun, kind of. Like wiping out our problems with a big eraser. But it wouldn't have worked, we knew that."

"Can you give me any information as to who killed your exhusband?" I asked.

She gave me a thoughtful look. "I honestly can't," she said. "Though I could name a dozen who, like me, probably were glad he died."

"You don't think Harriet . . ."

She laughed. "We decided, I told you. We said we weren't the type. I remember the conversation. We were having lunch at that restaurant on top of the bookstore after a board meeting for the Lighthouse. One of the other members had been his usual obstructive self, and I looked at Harriet and said, 'Let's blow him away, bam!' And we broke up. And I said I couldn't, ever, and she said she knew that."

"But you bought a gun."

"I did. Yes. Some time ago. Before I realized who was going through the apartment. I got rid of it, though, long since. Buying it was one of those silly things one does when one is frightened."

"But Ross has a gun."

She was silent for a moment, thinking. "He did have one when he moved in with me, but his was stolen. Things being stolen is why we changed the locks."

"Fred made a remark to one of his acquaintances about your writing a book, and about your paying him not to tell anyone."

She laughed. "That sounds like Fred. Yes. He told me he'd 'gained possession' of that paper you have there. 'Gained possession' sounds better than 'stole,' which is what he did. He asked me what it was worth to me to get it back, and I told him nothing."

"Nothing?"

"Nothing. I didn't want it back. I don't know why I kept it at all. Fred knew I hadn't killed Melody. He knew I couldn't kill anyone. He just thought I might feel the manuscript was incriminating enough that I'd pay him for it. I told Fred to do what he liked with it, that telling tales out of school often went both ways, and we left it at that."

"Would he have tried to get money from Harriet Steinwale?"

She laughed in honest amusement. "After Fred and I talked it over, I don't think he'd have asked for money from anyone again."

"You had something on him?"

"We're not discussing that, Jason. You wanted to know about a plot for a story that Harriet and I wrote and I've told you about that."

So she had had something on him. I looked over her shoulder, avoiding her eyes. "Can you tell me one thing?" I indicated the paper. "Did Ross know about all this?"

She shook her head. "Ross knew Fred had been sneaking around in our apartment, yes. As soon as I figured it out, I told him. He knew Fred took things, yes. Ross didn't know about the story Harriet and I had written, no. Ross didn't know Fred had taken it and tried to sell it back to me. Ross gets very angry, and I didn't want him any angrier at Fred than he already was."

"I'm afraid there's something else," I said.

"Having met you, I was sure there would be." She smiled, a tightly controlled smile. "What is it?"

"The collie. Melody's collie."

Her expression didn't change, but her color did. It drained away. The rueful smile remained, but in an ivory face. Then a faint flush came back. "Oh," she said. "Well, you'll have to talk to my neighbor about that."

"Your neighbor?"

"Mr. Stevenson. From across the hall. He saw it all. He'll tell you about it, I'm sure." She stood up, drank the last few drops, rattling the ice with her tongue. "I haven't killed anyone, Jason. Ross hasn't killed anyone. We didn't. We don't. It's not our kind of thing. Even Fred, insensitive as he was, knew that."

She turned, stooped as though dizzy, but it was only to stroke the carved grapes on the back of the chair, the acorns and leaves, the twining vines. In a moment she walked out and away. I sat there, looking after her, wondering why I felt so bereft. After a minute, Mark came in and I told him what she had said.

"Stevenson? Who's he?"

I explained about the inventor of sickening ice cubes, the jokester with the poodles.

"Are you going to go see him?"

I was, of course. I had to.

The following morning I was waiting outside the Louvre,

trying to look inconspicuous. I saw Shannon come out with the shelties, but she turned to walk toward town. Stevenson had said he sometimes didn't hear her, but evidently this morning he had, for he and the poodles emerged about five minutes later. I trailed them to the park, no downtown walk for Willie, and sat myself beside him on his usual bench.

"Did you solve your minnow problem?" I asked.

He turned, took a minute to remember who I was, then nodded, the corners of his mouth turning up, ever so slightly. "Oh, yes. Yes, indeed. The problem was, we were thinking of whole fish, don't you know? No shock value in that, is there? Heh, heh." His laugh was like his mouth, tightly managed.

"So what did you do?"

"Half a fish," he crowed triumphantly. "All raggedy, as though it had been bitten in half. Like half a worm in an apple."

I considered this for a moment. "Perfect," I pronounced. "True genius."

"That's what the sales manager said." He nodded, agreeing with me. "He said exactly the same thing."

We enjoyed his triumph in silence for a moment or two.

"I wonder if you could help me with something," I asked him. "I'm investigating a case that took place here in the park, and Mrs. Foret says you were probably a witness."

"Me? Oh, no. I haven't witnessed anything at all. Not since that accident on the freeway three years ago. . . ."

"This wasn't that kind of thing. Mrs. Foret said you would know about the collie. . . ."

"Collie? Dog?"

"Last October? Mrs. Foret and the collie?"

"Oh! The lost dog!"

I nodded. "Could you tell me about that?"

"Well, I was here, where I usually am, and the dogs were over there in the bushes. I was reading a letter from my sister, one I'd just got, and this strange dog ran up to me. Kind of a fat, old dog. I thought maybe I'd seen it before, you know, but I wasn't sure. And it barked. It barked at me, and it wouldn't stop. I didn't know what to do. So I looked down the sidewalk, and Mrs. Foret was coming into the park. So I yelled to her, about this dog. And she came over and took it for me."

"She was coming into the park."

"From the apartment house. She came down into the lobby while I was getting my mail, and then she came along behind."

Behind him? "What time was this?"

"Early. Very early. Before eight. Not long after seven."

"Then what happened?"

"Well, she took the dog, and she said for me to come along, we'd look for the owner. So I got Mother's dogs, and we went around the park. And she asked people if the dog belonged to them, people on benches, you know. People are so rude. One lady didn't even answer. She was probably drunk."

I could guess which lady. "Over on the far side of the park," I suggested. "Sitting on a bench, with a magazine."

"Yes. Only she wasn't sitting. She was sort of slumped over, and the magazine was on the bench. Mrs. Foret helped her sit up and gave her her magazine. Maybe the woman was deaf. Mother used to say we have to make allowances for people. Maybe she was deaf and didn't hear."

"Did Mrs. Foret shake her or anything?"

"No. Of course not. She just helped her sit up, and put the magazine on her lap, and then she told me we probably couldn't find the owner, so she'd take the dog to a shelter."

So Lycia had found Melody already dead. According to the police report, dead for a very short time. Why had she straightened up the body and propped the magazine in its lap? I knew an answer to that. When she found Melody dead, she was immediately reminded of the manuscript Fred had offered to sell her. So she had gone quietly away. I didn't blame her. Stevenson was looking at me curiously, wondering what this was all about. I changed the subject.

"You had the dogs last fall, then? Your mother's been ill a long time."

He shook his head. "Oh, you thought she was still in the hospital? No, she was ill a long time, but she died. That's why I have to keep them, you see. I promised. They're very young dogs. I imagine they'll live years and years yet." He sounded hopeless about it.

The pups deserved better than that. "You promised your mother you wouldn't put them in a kennel. Did you promise her you wouldn't find them a good home? Somewhere where they could run and play? With someone who likes dogs?"

He looked up, hope dawning on his face. "How would I do that?"

"Let me see what I can do," I suggested.

He beamed at me. "That would be wonderful. I never thought of that. I wonder why I never thought of that. I should have, because I'm not an animal person. I'm really not. It always surprises me when people are, like Mrs. Foret, just taking that strange dog by the leash and taking it away, and it just went with her, just like that. It didn't even whine, except when she was with that drunk woman."

Yes, that had surprised me, too. I toyed briefly with the idea that Lycia might have been making her second trip of the morning when she took the collie, but I could think of no reason why, if she had already shot Melody, she should have returned.

"Will you call me? Will you let me know? Can I help you?" Willie Stevenson wanted to know.

I smiled and told him no, I'd get in touch with him, that I had a particular person in mind who might like to have the dogs. He went away with protestations of delight, leaving me to sit there on the bench, glad of what he'd told me, and yet more confused than ever.

I was back with Fred as first suspect in Melody's death, except that if Lycia had told me the truth about there being no blackmail, the only feasible motive was wiped out.

And as far as Fred's death went? If I believed Lycia, I hadn't a clue.

7

Believing Lycia seemed to be the only thing to do. By noon that day, Mark reported back to me that he had found out who handled Lycia and Ross's financial affairs and, since he knew the man rather well, had "dropped in on him." Mark had invented a story about an extravagant investment venture in partnership with Lycia and Ross, and his broker friend had told him frankly that the couple didn't have the resources to do what Mark proposed.

"He didn't come right out and tell me, that wouldn't have been ethical, but he gave me enough to put two and two together. From what he said, I know they've been putting what extra cash they have into annuity programs and some rather modest investment schemes. My friend commented that doctors make good money, but that living takes most of it. The one interesting thing he let slip was that Lycia has cut back her contribution to her annuity program lately. The broker has no idea why, except that she told him she was strapped for cash, but there haven't been any stock sales or borrowing against annuities or anything like that. What she's diverted from her annuities can't amount to more than a few thousand. In any case, the important thing is that neither Lycia nor Ross could have come up with half a million. They just don't have it and never have had."

"She's strapped for cash? How much is a few thousand? And when is lately?"

"I got the impression we're talking about maybe eighteen hundred or two thou a month, Jason, for the last six or eight months. Moreover, it hasn't changed since Fred died. She's still starving her annuity plan."

An interesting little fact which took us nowhere. A few thousand a month, only recently, did not add up to half a million dollars.

"How about Harriet Steinwale?"

Mark shook his head. "Her affairs are out of my reach, Jason. She could come up with half a million easy, that much I do know."

"I don't think it's likely that she did," I said. "Why would she pay? The thing wasn't in her handwriting. I don't think she'd have paid Fred to suppress it, particularly after Lycia told him to do what he wanted with it."

"If Lycia's telling the truth."

It came down to that, always. In my judgment, she'd been telling the truth. I typed a short letter to Marge Beebe, telling her there was a witness to the fact that Lycia had arrived in the park after Melody was dead. Since Lycia had not killed Melody, it was extremely unlikely that Harriet had killed Fred. I told Marge the manuscript had been merely a way of letting off steam, not a plan for murder. I said the money she had found had not come from Lycia or Ross, that though Fred had tried to hit Lycia up for money, she had refused to give him anything and my research indicated that Lycia was telling the truth about that. I didn't mention that the money might have come from Harriet Steinwale. Maybe Marge wouldn't think of that.

Marge would believe Lycia was innocent just as I did, because she wanted to. She had never really liked thinking her ex-sister-in-law was guilty of anything.

Being well and truly stalled, I got out a pad and pencil and

made a list. Making lists is often unproductive, though sometimes seeing a name in writing jostles a brain cell into making
a connection.

Who did I have for Fred's murder?

Marty O'Toole. All other avenues having failed, it was time
to fire Marty's gun and give the bullets to Grace.

Sally Streeter. She said Fred took her gun away with him,
but maybe he actually hadn't. Or maybe she'd bought a new
one. Perhaps I could find out exactly what kind it had been.
Talk to Sally again.

Lycia or Ross. Who both had reasons to hate Fred for what
he was doing to Shannon, but who also had an ironclad alibi
along with the rest of the family. Of course, Marge had told me
that. I could check it out myself.

Some X person who had known Fred before, on one of his
peace marches, in Washington, at the university. Ask Simmons
if Fred had mentioned any enemies. Hell, ask everybody.
Check into Simmons himself, just in case.

Then there was Ancel Ancini, Shannon's fiancé. He certainly had reasons to hate Fred, and we hadn't even considered
him seriously.

And Harriet. Couldn't leave her out.

Who did we have for Melody's murder?

Fred himself. He was the most likely candidate. Except that
there seemed to be no motive if the blackmail idea was merely
a will-o'-the-wisp.

There was Neal Ambler. He'd been half in love with her.
Maybe she'd driven him to murder, somehow. Maybe he'd
bought her paintings from her, then had an appraisal of them
and had been infuriated. No. The man I'd talked to still
thought she was a great artist. The man I'd talked to was besot-
ted.

Then there was Harriet again, because of what Melody had
done to Greg. Except that Harriet was out of the country
when Melody died.

And Greg. Except that he was in the hospital. Of course, I hadn't personally checked either Greg's alibi or his mother's. I made a note to ask Grace to bring the police reports back again. The police had undoubtedly checked, and they had the facilities to do it better than I did.

I wondered if I should add Nina Hough to the list. Melody had been ruining the gallery business, and maybe Nina had felt strongly about that. She didn't seem the type to shoot anyone, but then, who did in this crazy bunch?

Rich Beacon. He was the shooter type. I remembered his hands, wide, hard, hairy on the backs. Not someone to let anyone get the better of him. But what motive? Had Melody known something about him and tried to use it as leverage? I put his name down. The man was tough and mean and well protected. If he'd killed her, I'd probably never find out about it. If she'd known something about him, it would have to have been something serious. Something his lawyers couldn't quite take care of. Murder. Rape. I toyed with the rape idea for a while, but it didn't seem to jell. Melody seemingly had been quite willing to continue her relationship with Beacon, even though he was old enough to be her . . .

Wait. Could I possibly be wrong about Fred?

What had Ambler said at that poker game? Something about a well he and Rich Beacon had been partners on. The Magdalena well. He'd drawled it out. Mag-dah-lay-nah. And Beacon had told him he didn't even remember how to pronounce it. Something.

I called him.

"Well, well, the big winner," he said.

"Fifty-two dollars is not big," I contradicted him.

"If you include me, and you, and Rich, you were the big winner," he said. "Charles walked off with the table. What do you want to know now?"

"The other night, you mentioned a well you and Rich drilled in Texas. The Magdalena well?"

"That's right. Right near Magdalena Creek in south-central Texas, which is why we named it that. Nice, juicy girl's name. For all the good it did."

"Dry hole, hmm?"

"Drier than a spinster's twat. Why?"

"Why was Rich saying you didn't know how to pronounce it?"

Ambler laughed. "Rich, when he was nineteen, twenty, he went to school in England, where his daddy was something big with the U.S. government. He went to Oxford, to what I'd call Magdalen College, only over there they pronounce it 'Maudlin.' He was always calling that dry well the Maudlin well on Maudlin Creek and snootin' around in boots and a white shirt talking the King's English. He only did it to make us crazy, not that we weren't crazy enough."

"Neal, did he ever talk about that well around Melody?"

"Shoot, Jason, he talked about anything that crossed his mind around Melody."

I hung up and thought about that. Surely not. According to Ambler, Beacon had spent a few thousand dollars hunting for Melody's father. He knew the story. Surely he couldn't have actually been . . .

Or had he only pretended to look?

Damn. Rich from Maudlin could have called himself Rick Maudlin. But had he? And wouldn't the same idea have occurred to Melody? Had she threatened to expose him as an incestuous old man? Had he killed her? What would he have been when she was living with him? In his mid-forties?

It was extremely farfetched, indicating exactly how frustrated I was. No, I was not wrong about Fred and Rich had been out of town when Melody died. It had to be Fred. It was his name. It was his style.

I threw up my hands and went out to lunch with Nina Hough. She had invited me to an opening at the gallery that afternoon, and I had invited her to lunch first. I needed a break from the whole stupid business. I couldn't remember a puzzle which had been so annoying.

Why?

Because the more I found out about the two victims, the less I really wanted to catch whoever had done it. I had promised Marge I would look into the matter. I hadn't promised her I would do anything about it. In fact, I told myself that today might be a good day to give the whole thing up.

I had decided to do just that, but when I got back that afternoon I found Mark and Grace waiting for me all shiny-eyed and bushy-tailed.

"Mark had an idea!" bubbled Grace.

"About money," crowed Mark. "Fred's money. Did you look at the series numbers?"

"Did I look at what?"

"Honestly, Jason. The things you don't know. Every time they change the money, like every time we get a new Treasurer of the U.S. or a new Secretary of the Treasury, they start a new series of money. It says so, right on the bills. Series 1969, or series 1974, or series 1981. If you look at Fred's money, you can maybe tell how old it is."

I think I gaped. It had never occurred to me. Since there was nothing else to occupy our attention at the moment, they came downstairs with me while I opened the safe and put the cardboard box on the old pool table I haven't been able to get rid of. When I opened the box, Grace gasped. Mark, as one might suppose, did not seem impressed.

We each took a stack of money and started looking for the series dates. I found lots of sixties and lots of seventies. Then a few fifties. A lone bill from the forties. We shuffled and muttered our way through a good dozen bundles before I said, "There aren't any eighties."

"There's nothing after 1977," Mark said. "Carter's administration."

I put the bundle I'd been fumbling with back into the box. "Do we need to look at all of it?"

"Not if it's all like this," Mark said. "Though some bundles might have later dates."

I groaned, and we looked at all of it. Nothing later than 1977.

I think I groaned again. Even though I had believed Lycia Foret, even though Sally's observation had seemed to clinch it, I hadn't been certain. This made it certain. "This isn't blackmail money at all," I said. "But it does explain why Melody threatened him with the FBI."

Mark gave me a puzzled look.

"If this money was accumulated before 1977, it was done while Fred was in Washington! Fred was working for the Department of Defense, and he was in charge of research contracts. This money had to come from kickbacks! When he was with the DOD he must have taken cash bribes for grant awards. When I talked to Lycia, I couldn't help thinking she had something on him to make him so docile about the divorce. He'd probably started doing it years ago. I wondered how he could afford to fly all over Europe on that world-peace stuff, and he's been doing it for years. That should have told me the money antedated recent events. He must have bragged to Melody about having money he'd made in Washington. He probably hinted and winked and told her how sly he'd been. She told Greg he had sticky fingers. That's what she meant. She assumed he'd gotten the money illegally, and she threatened him."

"How do you know that?" Grace wondered.

"Because of the phone conversation Sally Streeter overheard. Sally thought Fred and Melody were talking about sex. I thought they were discussing blackmail money. They were actually referring to bribery money dating from Fred's years in Washington. Remember, Melody said something to him about not being rich enough to interest her. So he said, 'In addition to having friends in high places, I have enough to make life interesting,' meaning money. Then she twitted him about where he got it and what he did with it, and he said he had it and what he did with it was his business.

"She said he got it illegally. He said she was assuming that. She said he was a thief, and he said she'd have a hard time proving it. She said she wouldn't try to prove it, she'd tell the FBI and let them prove it. And he told her she'd better not try it or she'd be sorry."

"Then he borrowed Sally's gun and shot her?"

"I think it very likely."

"Then who killed Fred?"

I shook my head, mentally adding a couple of names to my list. Ambler, in revenge, because he knew Fred had killed Melody. Greg, also for revenge, because he'd found out Fred killed Melody. And how had either of them found out?

I had no idea.

"This just gets worse and worse," Grace said. "Why did you think these two killings were connected in the first place?"

"Both the bodies had been kind of 'arranged,' " I said. "It made me think maybe the same person. But that turned out not to mean anything. . . ." I hadn't told them about Lycia's finding the body, and I didn't intend to. Somehow, I couldn't bear anyone else knowing anything bad about Lycia.

"No, it obviously didn't," she fretted. "Jason, I'm tired of this one. We're not getting anywhere."

I agreed with her, soberly, then told both of them we needed a vacation from it all. Grace said okay, she was going to catch up on her paperwork and paint her bathroom. She didn't look at me when she said it, so I knew she was going through another one of her "Jason and I are just friends" arguments with herself. Mark said he was going to take the weekend to meet some new people. I crossed my fingers for both of them, and for me.

A few days went by. My leg was better, so Bela and I were taking longer walks. We stayed longer in the park, meeting more people, many of whom wanted to know what had happened to my pet tiger. Grace had promised me a kitten, next time her cousin in Cheyenne's female cat had one of Critter's litters. I was looking forward to that. Bela missed Critter. He'd enjoy a kitten. Pets need pets, too.

As do old ladies. I called Willamae Belling and told her a sad story about two poodles condemned to live the rest of their lives with a man who didn't like them. She almost cried.

So it was with purpose in mind that I went searching for Willie Stevenson. He was on his usual bench, concentrating deeply. I hated to interrupt him.

When he heard about Willamae's offer for the dogs, however, he almost grinned. Almost. "When?" he asked. "Oh, how soon?"

I told him I'd pick up the dogs that afternoon and transport them, a sack of kibble, their dishes and impedimenta, to Willamae's house. That they would love her. That they would have a fenced yard. That they would think they were back with Willie's mother again. That she needed them because she was a lonely old lady. The man was almost delirious with joy.

"It'll be so nice to walk without them again," he said. "To just walk, you know, at my own speed. Stop when I want to. Go when I want to."

I admitted that was always a nice feeling.

He must have thought he had sounded ungracious, for he was quick to explain himself. "Even people who like animals feel that way," he assured me. "Even Mrs. Foret. She sometimes walks without the dogs."

I smiled and nodded and said yes, I sometimes walked without Bela, trying to think of the last time I'd done so. Rarely. Very rarely.

"That day she rescued the lost dog, she didn't have her dogs," he bubbled at me. "That was a lucky thing, wasn't it? She might not have been able to manage three of them."

I smiled and nodded again and told him I would see him that afternoon around two.

I was halfway home before I realized what he had told me.

I didn't tell either Mark or Grace that I was going to Harriet Steinwale's, any more than I had told them about Lycia finding Melody's body. After settling the poodles in at Willamae's, I called Mrs. Steinwale and asked if I could drop in that evening. I told her I thought I knew who might have killed her daughter-in-law, I half expected her to tell me to go to the police with it, but she made no objection to my visit.

It was raining slightly when I arrived about eight thirty. She took my wet coat and offered me a drink. I accepted. We went into the huge living room. There was one table lamp on, in the far corner. She made the drinks at a bar-closet in that corner, then we sat across from one another in the dim room, looking out over the lights of the city. It was barely dusk, but the lights were beginning to come on—lights of traffic, lights reflecting along the wet streets, lights in the buildings, a sequined pattern, shifting and glittering as darkness came.

"When my husband was alive," she said, "we used to love to sit here in the evenings, watching the lights. In the country, we always looked at water. In the city, we looked at lights. Rainy lights are best."

"Have you been widowed long?"

"Twenty years. Too long."

"This is a big place," I said, looking about me. It was big, but elegant, with a well-used charm. "Did you live here with your husband?"

"When Max and I first lived here, we had three children, and Max's father was living with us. It didn't seem large then. I've been in this building almost forty years. We own part of it, of course. The rent is reasonable." She smiled to herself. Private joke.

"I didn't know Greg had siblings."

"He doesn't now. Our daughters died very young."

No wonder she was so passionately devoted to Greg. He was all she had left.

She was watching me intently. "You didn't come here to talk about my family, did you?"

"I came to ask about Melody, actually."

"I didn't know her at all well. Even though she lived here we had very little contact."

"I think I know who killed her, Mrs. Steinwale. Would you tell me, please, whether she ever said anything to you about Fred Foret and Shannon."

"You know about that?" Whatever she had expected me to say or ask, it had not been that. I had upset her badly.

Not knowing what "that" was, I equivocated. "I know something about it, yes. Ross mentioned . . ."

"Ross shouldn't. Not to strangers." She looked down at her hands, square capable hands, neatly disposed in her lap. When she spoke it was so softly I had to strain to hear her. "Yes. Melody had found out about that. She seemed to think it would shock me or hurt me to learn of it. It did hurt, of course, though not in the way she thought. I'd already heard about it long ago from Lycia."

"What exactly did Melody say?"

"She told me about Fred Foret's attempted incest with Shannon when she was only seven years old. She didn't say 'attempted,' of course. I already knew from Lycia that it was more than a mere attempt, though Lycia always refers to it as 'attempted' around Shannon."

I took a swallow of scotch to wash out the bitter taste in my mouth. "Shannon remembers this?"

"Of course she remembers. She was seven, almost eight years old. Lycia found out about it almost immediately, packed up the children, and left. It was Shannon's abuse that spurred her to go to medical school, to work for the Lighthouse, to prevent other girls from suffering the damage Fred had done to her daughter. I'm surprised that Ross talked about this."

"He alluded to it," I murmured. "Not in any great detail."

She sighed, unaware she had told me something I didn't know.

"Lycia divorced Fred because of this incident," I said.

She nodded. "When Fred came back to Denver, he actually expected to be with his family again. Lycia told him she would make the matter public if he made any attempt to fight her divorce or gain custody of the children. According to Lycia, he told his sister a pack of lies, but he was reasonably sensible about it. Then."

"How did Melody find out about this?"

"From Shannon. After that party in June, a year ago, evidently Melody tried to strike up a friendship with Shannon. She actively pursued the child, harassed her. Shannon told Lycia about Melody's almost persecuting her, and Lycia told me. Evidently Shannon tried to fight her off, tried to make Melody leave her alone, but Melody persisted. Melody twitted her for being a virgin, and Shannon broke down and screamed out how her father had attacked her when she was a tiny child. Even that didn't stop Melody. She went on plaguing the child. . . ."

Like a crow, picking at a bloody wound, I thought. Like a carrion crow.

Harriet murmured, "Lycia came to me for help. I said I'd talk to Melody. Greg was in the hospital. Melody and I were here alone in the apartment for a while, before I left for Mexico. Sometimes she ate with me rather than eat alone. At the dinner table I challenged her with her behavior toward Shannon. She laughed at me. She said there was no reason Shannon should be allowed to be happy. She repeated to me what Shannon had told her about her father, and seemed disappointed when I said I already knew. She said she didn't give a damn about Shannon. She dragged Fred's name into the conversation

by saying that Shannon wasn't the only one Fred had tried to
have sex with, that he'd tried with her as well, that he'd told
her he knew 'what little girls liked.' Melody said Fred bragged
to her that he had accumulated a small fortune when he
worked for the Department of Defense. She believed he had
taken bribes for awarding contracts. It poured out of her, all
about Shannon, all about Fred, like acid, bubbling out of her,
uncontrollably. She seemed to need to tell me, as though I
cared. And she said she would harass both him and Shannon
all she liked. I don't know why she hated them so."

I knew. "Melody came here to Denver looking for her father, Harriet. A father who had abandoned her when she was
an infant. At Shannon's birthday party, Melody learned that
Fred, Shannon's father, was also her father."

The color left her face as though dusk had entered the room.
She went gray, suddenly haggard. "He . . . he was what?"

"Fred was married when he was very young to a woman in
Baltimore. She died shortly after her baby girl was born. Fred
left the daughter in the care of an elderly aunt, gave her a false
name, and never came back. Subsequently he married Lycia
without ever telling her he had been married before. The child
in Baltimore was Melody. She came here to Denver to find her
father. His name was supposed to be Rick Maudlin. Fred
Foret's full name was Frederick Charles Maudlin Foret. He
never used his full name. Lycia knew it, of course, but she
never knew Melody was searching for a father by that name.
Marge knew it, but she knew nothing about Melody. Even
though Melody lived here in this apartment with you for
years, Lycia and the others seemingly never really met her
until the birthday party."

Her voice was harsh as she answered. "Melody was never
interested in meeting my friends. She had friends of her own.
The rooms she and Greg shared had their own entrance. They
ate out a lot. Though they shared this apartment, we seldom
encountered one another. That was as much my wish as theirs.

I didn't like her. I tried, but I couldn't. I saw what she was doing to my son." She wiped her eyes. "Poor child. No wonder she was so pitiably destructive. . . ."

I looked away, stared out the tall windows at the lights of the city. "You must admit that it's odd, living here in the same building, that Shannon and Melody had never met."

"They met for the first time at that party, and it was a fluke that Greg and Melody were there at all. We had some legal things to go over that afternoon, Greg and I, and the lawyer was late. Greg was fretting about being away from the studio. Melody was sulking because he wasn't paying attention to her. I said, 'Let's drop in down at the pool and wish Shannon a happy birthday.' It was an impulse. It's the only reason we were there at all. . . ."

I nodded my understanding. "It was at the party Melody discovered that Fred had a webbed toe. Melody had had one, too. Someone had told her such anomalies run in families. Shannon had had similar webs, and probably said so at the party. From that moment on, Melody knew Fred Foret was her father. She didn't tell him who she was. When he tried to seduce her, she refused him but she told Shannon all about it. She wanted to hurt his other family, don't you think? Hurt him, hurt his other daughter?"

Harriet rubbed her hands over her face, as though trying to rub something away. "I suppose. Yes. That would have been like her. She always wanted to hurt me, because I was Greg's other family. She couldn't bear to share him."

"You used the word 'persecuting,' and what Melody did to Shannon was that. Melody followed Shannon, bothered her, probed for areas of discomfort, then insisted on talking about them. She pushed Shannon. She brought up the incest, again and again, and insisted on dwelling on it. She drove Shannon out of her mind."

Harriet rubbed her face again, lifted her glasses back, over her head, rubbed her eyes, then put the glasses back on, adjusting the band that held them. She looked old and tired.

"Who killed Melody, Mrs. Steinwale?"

"Why, I suppose Fred did, Mr. Lynx. No doubt Melody threatened to expose him for what he was, and he killed her."

"I think he intended to, Mrs. Steinwale. I don't think he actually did."

She stared at me through her huge-lensed glasses, like an owl. "If not he, then who, Mr. Lynx? You think you know. You obviously came here to tell me."

I did know. In a way Lycia had told me, Lycia who had told me nothing but the truth. "It was Shannon, wasn't it? For some reason, Lycia was worried and went after her. What was it? Did Lycia find a gun missing?"

"I don't know what you mean," Harriet whispered.

"Lycia went to the park looking for Shannon. When she saw Melody's dog running loose, she knew something had happened. She took the dog and went looking for Melody, putting on a show for Willie Stevenson by asking other people as well. Then, when she found Melody, already dead, she propped the body up on the bench, took the dog, and left the park. That's inexplicable, Harriet. Simply inexplicable, unless she was protecting someone. She wouldn't have protected Fred."

"Children," she murmured. "Families. There's nothing so important."

I waited, but she said nothing more. After a moment, I went on. "I suppose, after a while, she found Shannon and took her home. Or Shannon simply came home. Later that day, Lycia took the collie to the shelter. I don't know which happened first, but I'm sure both things happened."

"Why would she have done that?" She wasn't really curious. She knew the answer.

"Taken the collie to the shelter? To give the family time. So there would be no questions asked. Greg was in the hospital. You had your own part of the apartment. If the dog was gone, no one would ask about it. No one asked about it even after Melody was found."

She said nothing. I found her passivity irritating.

"Don't you think Shannon needs help?"

The words burst from her. "She's getting help. Good Lord, Mr. Lynx, Lycia is paying out thousands every month for help for Shannon! Do you believe putting the child through a trial and locking her in a hospital would help her more? She's been under psychiatric care since the day Melody died, just as she was for years after her father did what he did. She would have been all right if Fred had let her alone, but once he came back here, once she was no longer a child, he started in on her again. Between her father and Melody, they were destroying her. Such an unkind, evil man, Fred. And Melody! Such an angry, hating girl!"

"Couldn't Lycia protect her from him?"

Harriet made an impatient movement. "Psychiatrists! Her therapist wanted her to deal with her father. Learn to handle him, put him in his place. Her therapist kept telling her to be strong, set Fred aside, put him out of her life, but she seemingly wasn't able to do that. He was like an evil genie, sitting on her shoulder, warping her. She needed to grow up, to have friends, to have a lover or a husband. She needed Fred to go away and let her grow up, to stop trying to control her!"

She was glaring at me. I glared back, taking in the huge round spectacles she was wearing, the low sensible shoes, the shapeless dress in an elegant fabric. Not a young woman. And yet a woman capable of much.

She turned away from me, speaking firmly. "You mustn't think such things, Mr. Lynx. Your imagination is running riot. Fred killed Melody. I'm sure of it. Let me freshen your drink." She took the glass from me and turned toward the bar, turning on another lamp as she passed it. In the glow of the bulb I saw the band of woven elastic that held her glasses.

"You're not wearing your contacts tonight," I commented.

"An infection," she said, putting ice in my glass. "I get them every now and then and have to do without my contacts. I hate glasses. I have funny bumps behind my ears and glasses won't stay on unless I use an elastic. Then if I use the elastic, they make blisters, so I have to put something under them. . . ."

"I found a shred of that elastic," I told her. "On the tree where Fred died. It took me some time to figure out what it was. There was a tuft of fiber from a sweatband, too."

Silence. Rigidity. "Do you think I shot him?"

"What am I supposed to think?"

A long silence. Finally, a sigh. "Yes. I shot him." It was only a whisper.

"Lycia said you weren't the type, either of you. Not the killing type."

"She isn't. Perhaps I found that I was."

"Where did you get the gun you shot him with?"

Silence. She was thinking. "It was Ross's. Lycia didn't know he kept it, but he had it hidden in his bedside table. One day when I was down there, I took it."

"What did you do with it?"

She turned and looked at me again, stirring the drink. Then she handed it to me, calmly. "I disposed of it," she said, running her fingers through her gray hair. "It and the sweatband and the clothes I was wearing. Somewhere they won't ever be found."

"Why did you arrange the body that way? How did you know how Fred usually looked?"

She shrugged. "I'd seen him there. I walk in the park, too, occasionally. I don't walk a dog, but I do walk, and whenever he saw me, he always wanted to talk."

Yes. Fred had always wanted to talk. "Did you get the idea from that fantasy you and Lycia had created?"

She stared at me, then smiled, a remote, almost fatalistic smile. "Perhaps. Yes. Fred couldn't or wouldn't understand that he was destroying his own child. Lycia told him. Ross told him. He only smiled, and said they were wrong, that Shannon needed him, needed his 'protection.' He was opaque to understanding, don't you know? He was so completely egocentric, she was only a mannequin for him to manipulate for his own gratification. He could not see what he was doing. He was killing her. I couldn't let that happen."

"Because you and Lycia had planned it?"

She thought for a moment, reasoning it out. "No. Because I love Lycia. Because I couldn't watch her suffer. Because she's my friend. Because Shannon is still a child, and sometimes children need more protection than the law can give them."

Silence. I didn't know what else to say.

Harriet mused. "It's strange that one can know all the causative factors that go to make someone like Melody, or Fred. One can know and sympathize. And one can still hate them for what they are. Were. I can be desperately sorry for them and still be glad they are gone."

They were gone. Melody and Fred both. No one really grieved for Fred, but I remembered Greg's voice as he yearned for Melody.

Harriet stood at the window, musing. "With them gone, maybe Shannon can forget. I hope Greg can forget. Shannon will go on seeing her doctor, and gradually, she'll grow up and get well. Greg and Trish will have a healthy life together. When you get to be my age, you long for family to go on into the future. I had three children. Both my daughters died very young. I have only Greg now, and Trish, and little Frosty, and maybe, I pray, another baby or two to come. I'm not worried about Greg anymore. Trish will take care of Greg."

"And all's well that ends well?" I asked. "Murder is to be allowed to go unpunished?" Even to my own ears, I sounded shocked.

She shook her head at me. "You know nothing about punishment, Mr. Lynx, if you think that. If you want to turn me in, go ahead. I warn you, I'll get a good lawyer. I won't admit a single thing. It will be your word against mine."

I stood and walked over to the window beside her. I didn't want to turn her in, though not for the reasons she supposed. "What do I tell Marge Beebe?" I asked. "She wants to know why her brother died."

"Tell her . . . tell her his sins came back to get him," she said. "Does it matter which sins?"

It didn't matter which sins. There were a dozen victims who could have killed Fred Foret. A dozen who probably wanted to. As long as Lycia hadn't done it, did Marge care who?

"That place you and Lycia work for," I said. "The Lighthouse. Does it need money?"

"Always."

When I'd talked to Marge last, she'd said she didn't want Fred's money. I had to do something with it. There was no way to return it. Fred had stolen much that couldn't be returned. Innocence. Joy. Youth.

I made up my mind, finally. "I don't think anyone else needs to know what I told you about Melody being Fred's daughter." Marge didn't need to know. Nor Lycia.

She agreed, with a nod.

I said, "Thank you for the drink. I don't imagine we'll be seeing each other again soon."

She cocked her head, waiting.

"Will you tell Lycia and Ross . . . tell Lycia I enjoyed knowing her."

"You won't be seeing them either?" Was it hope in her voice? Or something deeper and more sardonic than that?

"I think they would find that more comfortable."

Harriet would tell them I knew . . . what I knew. My knowing would make them wary and defensive. Harriet might tell them she didn't think I intended to do anything about it, but they would doubt that. Any effort at friendship on my part would be suspect. They needed to let memories die as well.

I got up, found my raincoat by the door, slipped it on. "I hope Greg and Trish will be very happy."

"Trish has a talent for happiness," she said. "She creates it where there is none."

From the way she said it, I could tell she knew. She knew her son still longed for the woman who had almost driven him mad. Ah. Well. As they say.

Grace and Mark seemingly had no trouble accepting Fred as Melody's killer. I told them Harriet Steinwale had confirmed Melody's assumption that the money had been taken as kickbacks when Fred worked for the DOD. I had told Marge Beebe that Fred killed Melody, and why. My conscience didn't hurt me over this. Fred might have done it. He had intended to do so, even if he hadn't done it. And if he hadn't done it, the only reason was that she was already dead. If we could find two guns and identify them as having belonged to Lycia and Fred, we would know for sure. I didn't think they would ever be found.

Grace and Mark still wanted to know, of course, who had killed Fred.

"I don't think we'll ever be sure," I said. "I told Marge about Fred's having stolen the money while he was at the DOD and about Melody's attempt to blackmail him or turn him in or whatever she had in mind. I think Marge understands what must have happened. The name of the actual killer—someone out of his own past or someone avenging Melody. . . . I don't think Marge feels she needs to know exactly who."

"And the money?" Grace wanted to know.

"The money has been sent to a charity," I said. "Anonymously, by a bonded messenger who stayed while it was opened in front of witnesses." Remembering a previous charity rip-off I'd been acquainted with, I'd had sense enough to assure all that cash couldn't be made away with. "Marge said she didn't want any questions from the IRS." The Lighthouse would benefit, which was the only really good thing about this whole matter.

"I wish I could close the police file," said Grace wistfully. "But I can't do that without dragging in a lot of people, and the lieutenant would want to know why. I'd need the Beacon guy. And he'd have some high-powered lawyer. I'd have to question Harriet Steinwale, and so would she." She gave me a long, level look.

"Let it go," I suggested. Grace served the law, but she didn't mind serving justice, occasionally. In this case, we'd already achieved as close to justice as we were going to get. She made a face, but she let it go. Mark gave me a look, much like one of Eugenia's looks. He thought I knew something I wouldn't tell them. Well, I did. And I wouldn't. After a few days of hints which I pretended not to notice, he forgot about it.

Grace was another matter. Her seeming acquiescence had been only temporary. A week or so later we were lying at opposite ends of my oversized bathtub, two glasses of chilled champagne sitting on the tile and a selection of carefully selected nibbles on a platter within reach. I'd rationed Grace to one every five minutes so I could have some. It had been an intermittently slothful Sunday, and we'd enjoyed every minute of it.

Out of the steamy blue she said, "You didn't tell me everything, did you? About Fred and Melody."

I thought about lying and discarded the notion. Even though Grace kept insisting we were only friends, I had no intention of giving her ammunition for her belief that Agatha and I had had a relationship which Grace and I could never have.

"No," I admitted. "I didn't tell you everything."

"Is it because I'm a cop?" she wanted to know, sounding more than a little hurt.

I considered that for a while. It was and it wasn't. "I thought you might think you should do something," I said. "I didn't want to put you in that position."

"Don't you think you ought to let me make up my own mind?" she asked. "This isn't some kind of aristocracy, is it? Or some sexist relationship where the educated male gets to make all the decisions?"

Being male or educated had had nothing to do with it, but try to convince Grace of that. So I slumped down until the warm water bathed all the sore tufty bits of hair growing on my scars and told her everything I thought. When I was finished, she ate a few more bits and pieces very slowly and thoughtfully, and finally told me I couldn't prove any of it and she couldn't prove any of it, and she didn't think she'd do anything about it. Later we went back to bed and made love. There was something new between us, or from her to me. Something almost like trust.

A time came, some months later, when memory was jogged forcibly and her decision and mine reared its guilty head. I was sitting at my desk on another Sunday, this a lonely late-fall one, staring at another one of those newspaper cutout messages (the fifth), which had been delivered in its plain brown envelope with the morning paper. My would-be informant was getting impatient with my unwillingness either to be informed or to pay for the privilege. "Last offer," this one said. Mr. Anonymous didn't know it, but it was getting harder and harder to ignore the invitation. I was getting to the point where I wanted to know. Jacob's sweet words notwithstanding, I really wanted to know. Or perhaps it would be better to say that I was reconciled to knowing. There were so many things I thought I recognized, so many people, like Lycia, I thought I knew. It would be good to know for sure. Or not, for sure. And put it behind me.

I thought I'd talk it over with Grace. If it was an attempt at extortion, I wasn't going to let the perpetrator get away. I put the thing in the bottom drawer with the others before spreading out the Sunday paper. The section that fell out on top was the one chronicling the things people get up to when they aren't attending to business: the so-called society pages. Two pictures filled the upper corners of the page, and I knew the people in both. From the left-hand picture Trish smiled out at me like a princess, Greg's bony features close beside, off on their honeymoon to New York, where there would be a prestigious gallery showing of Grale's new paintings. I crossed my fingers and said a nonsectarian prayer. She looked radiant. I couldn't tell how he felt.

The right-hand picture was of Shannon and the Ancini scion, she in bridal white, he in tails and looking as though he'd worn such garments from birth. Her flowerlike face bloomed up at me as she clung to her handsome husband's arm. The photographer had caught another face behind the couple: Lycia, a little out of focus but with her mouth unmistakably curved in that familiar, tranquil, untroubled smile. An Etruscan smile. A smile that covered some mystery, some secret I needed to know now as much as when I had first met her.

I pulled my eyes away from her image and concentrated on the bride, noting once again that Shannon isn't a tall woman. In the news photo, the top of her head came to her husband's jawline, and I recalled him as being about my height.

Harriet Steinwale, on the other hand, is a very tall woman, over six feet. If Harriet Steinwale had left that bit of fuzzy fabric on the tree, it would have been slightly above my head instead of where I found it—below my chin. By itself, not proof positive.

Add to that, when I had brought Marge to the Louvre apartments the morning that Fred had died, Stevenson was just coming down with the dogs. He hadn't heard anyone go out from the Foret apartment, so he was late. And yet, when I got to Lycia's apartment, the shelties were comfortably curled up in their baskets, not nervously running to and fro as dogs do who need to go out. They'd been out. If Lycia had taken them,

Willie Stevenson would have heard her and gone earlier. He hadn't heard, so Shannon must have taken the dogs out that morning, very early. The key to the door had probably been left in the door, not in Lycia's jewel box, though Lycia would have ostentatiously taken it from the jewel box later, after waking Ross to witness that fact. Wednesday was his and Lycia's day off, Marge had told me. Ross knew he wasn't on call. He would have allowed himself to sleep soundly until he was awakened.

Had Fred asked Shannon to meet him in the park so he could tell her once again how much better off she was without Ancel Ancini? What an irony if he had. Infuriated by him, spurred on by her therapist's suggestions that she be forceful and independent, and remembering that a gun had solved a problem once before, Shannon had decided to rid herself of another incubus. She had used Lycia's gun to shoot Melody, but Ross, ignorant of that fact, had kept an additional weapon in the apartment. Had Lycia suggested to Ross that he get rid of his weapon? Had he promised he would but then changed his mind? When Harriet said he kept the gun in his dresser drawer, it might have been true. Wherever he had kept it, Shannon had found it.

After Shannon had killed Fred, she had gone home and told her mother what she'd done. Lycia had called Harriet. And while Keith and Lycia and Shannon—I didn't believe Ross knew anything about it or he would never have talked to me as he had—had agreed upon an alibi, Harriet had gone back to the park and removed whatever evidence there might have been. The gun, if it had been dropped. The footprints, if there had been any. Harriet had arranged the body to look natural, as Melody's body had been arranged and for the same reason: to give the family time—time to tell Shannon what to say, time to get Shannon calm. Almost calm enough to make a good show when first Marge and I and then the police showed up. Her hysterics then had been put down to grief, or shock.

Perhaps someone had come down the path while Harriet was there, behind the tree. Perhaps she had merely felt faint. For whatever reason, Harriet had leaned back against the rough-trunked giant, the side away from the path, where Shannon must also have hidden. The tree was a grizzled patriarch. Harriet hadn't seen the tiny tuft of white fiber from Shannon's sweatband. She hadn't realized she had left a shred of elastic from her glasses higher up on the tree, over a head higher. Pure coincidence.

Why had Harriet confessed? To lead me away from her friend's child? Like a ground-nesting bird, fluttering its wings, risking its life to lead the fox . . . the Lynx away.

As he had been led away. Looking at the bride's pictured face, I did not see any evidence of madness. It must have been there at least twice. It might still be there, hiding just behind those sparkling eyes. Obviously her young husband did not see it either. Perhaps he would always be faithful and kind and Shannon would always be happy and it would never reappear again. If so, my conscience would remain clear, Harriet would not regret her part in the puzzle, and Lycia could continue to wear that tranquil Etruscan smile. She had never actually lied to me. She had said Ross's gun was stolen, and it was—by Shannon. She had said she had gotten rid of her own gun long ago, and she had, when Shannon returned it after killing Melody. She had looked me in the eye and told me neither she nor Ross had killed anyone, and it was true. She had said she couldn't honestly tell me anything, and from her point of view, she couldn't. Not honestly. Each thing she had told me was individually true. I had heard the truth and had not seen what the truth was hiding: this girl in her white dress, smiling up at her new husband.

Something dark and evil whispered insidiously that it would not turn out well and I would have much to regret. I pretended not to hear it. Weddings are for hope. Weddings are for families.

Families. I thought grimly of the five ugly letters in the bottom drawer of my desk which offered me . . . what? A family of my own? Harriet had said nothing was more important than families. Grace had told me the same thing. And Nellie and Mark and almost everyone else I knew, in one connection or another.

I had to take it on faith.